"The baby... W
Joshua asked.

Adie raised her chin. "I am."

The flash in his eyes told her that he'd assumed she'd given birth out of wedlock. Adie resented being judged, but she counted it as the price of protecting little Stephen. If Mr. Blue chose to condemn her, so be it. She'd done nothing of which to be ashamed. With their gazes locked, she waited for the criticism that didn't come.

Instead he laced his fingers on top of his Bible. "Children are a gift, all of them."

"I think so, too."

"He sure can cry. How old is he?"

Adie didn't like the questions at all, but she took pride in her son. "He's three months old. I hope the crying doesn't disturb you."

"I don't care if it does." He sounded defiant.

She didn't understand. "Most men would be annoyed."

"Crying's better than silence...I know."

Books by Victoria Bylin

Love Inspired Historical

The Bounty Hunter's Bride
The Maverick Preacher

VICTORIA BYLIN

Victoria Bylin fell in love with God and her husband at the same time. It started with a ride on a big red motorcycle and a date to see a *Star Trek* movie. A recent graduate of UC Berkeley, Victoria had been seeking that elusive "something more" when Michael rode into her life. Neither knew it, but they were each reading the Bible.

Five months later, they got married and the blessings began. They have two sons and have lived in California and Virginia. Michael's career allowed Victoria to be both a stay-at-home mom and a writer. She's living a dream that started when she read her first book and thought, "I want to tell stories." For that gift, she will be forever grateful.

Feel free to drop Victoria an e-mail at VictoriaBylin@aol.com or visit her Web site www.victoriabylin.com.

The
Maverick
Preacher

VICTORIA BYLIN

Steeple
Hill®

Published by Steeple Hill Books™

STEEPLE HILL BOOKS

Steeple
Hill®

Recycling programs
for this product may
not exist in your area.

ISBN-13: 978-0-373-82805-0
ISBN-10:   0-373-82805-5

THE MAVERICK PREACHER

www.SteepleHill.com

Printed in U.S.A.

Be kind and compassionate to one another,
forgiving each other, just as God in Christ
forgave you.

—Ephesians 4:32

To my husband, Michael…
Your faith inspires me,
and your love sustains me.

Chapter One

Denver, Colorado
July 1875

If Adelaide Clarke had been asleep like a sensible woman, she wouldn't have heard the thump on her front porch. As moonlight streamed through her window, she stopped breathing to block out the smallest sound. Last week a shadowy figure had broken the same window with a rock. She had an enemy. Someone wanted to drive her out of Denver and the boardinghouse called Swan's Nest.

Trembling, Adie listened for another noise. None came.

The thump had sounded like a rotten tomato. The sooner she cleaned up the mess, the less damage it would do to the paint, but she worried about waking up her boarders. The women in her house would fill wash buckets and gather rags. They'd scrub the door with her, but all four of them would tremble with fear.

Whoever had caused the thump could be lurking in the dark, waiting to grab her. Adie had been grabbed before—not in Denver but back in Kansas. Shuddering, she closed her eyes. If she'd been on speaking terms with God, she'd have prayed until she dozed. Instead she counted backward from a hundred as her mother had taught her to do.

Before she reached ninety, she heard a low moan. The timbre of it triggered memories of gutters, bruised ribs and the morning she'd met Maggie Butler. Adie knew about moaning. So did the women in her house. Mary had arrived bruised and angry in the dead of night. Pearl, thin and sick with pregnancy, had appeared at dawn. Bessie and Caroline, sisters from Virginia, had arrived in Denver on a midday train. Bessie had served with Clara Barton in the War Between the States and suffered from nightmares. Caroline had seen her husband lynched.

If a woman needed shelter, Adie opened her door wide, just as Maggie Butler had once opened *her* door to Adie.

She slid out of bed and reached for her wrapper. As she slipped her arms through the sleeves, she looked at the baby in the cradle next to her bed. No matter how Stephen Hagan Clarke had come into the world, he belonged to Adie. Grateful he hadn't been colicky as usual, she touched his back to be sure he was breathing. He'd been born six weeks early and had struggled to survive. Maggie Butler, his natural mother, hadn't been so fortunate.

Comforted by the rise of his narrow chest, Adie hurried down the staircase, a sweeping curve that spoke to the house's early days of glory. She crossed the entryway, cracked open the front door and looked down at the porch, staying hidden as she took in a body shrouded in a black cloak. A full moon lit the sky, but the eaves cast a boxlike shadow around the tangle of cloth and limbs. Adie couldn't make out the details, but she felt certain the person was a woman in need. She had owned Swan's Nest for three months and word had spread that she rented only to females.

She dropped to a crouch. "Wake up, sweetie. You're safe now."

Her visitor groaned.

Startled by the low timbre, Adie touched the dark fabric covering the bend of a shoulder. Instead of the wool of a woman's cloak, she felt the coarse texture of a canvas duster. She pulled back as if she'd been scalded. In a way, she had— by Timothy Long and his indulgent parents, by the people of Liddy's Grove, by Reverend Honeycutt but not his wife. Adie hadn't given birth to Stephen, but she could have. Timothy Long had accosted her in the attic. If she hadn't fought him off and fled, he'd have done worse things than he had.

Moaning again, the man rolled to his side. Adie sniffed the air but didn't smell whiskey. If she had, she'd have thrown water in his face and ordered him off her porch. Before meeting Maggie, she'd supported herself by cleaning cafés and saloons, any place that would pay a few coins so she could eat. The smell of liquor had turned her stomach then, and it still did.

Adie worried that the man had been shot, but she didn't smell blood, only dirt and perspiration. Judging by his horse and the duster, he'd been on the road for a while and had come straight to Swan's Nest, not from a saloon in the heart of Denver. Maybe he was a drifter or even an outlaw on the run. Adie didn't rent to men and didn't want to start now, but her conscience wouldn't let her close the door.

Neither would her common sense. What if the stranger died? A dead body meant calling the sheriff. Calling the sheriff meant exposing Swan's Nest to scrutiny. A reporter would show up from the *Denver Star.* The next thing she knew, she'd be answering questions that came dangerously close to revealing the truth about her son and Maggie Butler. Calling for help, even the doctor, put Adie and her son at risk. She saw only one solution. The man had to wake up and leave. Using all her strength, she rolled him to his back. "Wake up!"

He didn't stir.

None too gently, she patted his cheek. Black whiskers scraped her palm, another sign of his maleness and time spent on the trail. She pulled back her hand. "Can you hear me?"

Nothing.

The circumstances called for drastic measures. She hurried to the kitchen, filled a glass with water, then opened the high cupboard where she kept smelling salts. She lifted a vial, picked up the glass and went back to the porch. If the ammonia carbonate didn't wake the man up, she'd splash his face with the water.

Dropping back to her knees, she tried the smelling salts first. They stank worse than rotten eggs.

Her visitor got a whiff and jerked his head to the side. His eyes popped wide, revealing dilated pupils and a sheen of confusion.

"Wake up!" she said again.

He looked at her with more hope than she'd ever seen on a human face. "Emily?"

"I'm not Emily," Adie replied. "Are you ill or shot?"

He groaned. "I'm not shot."

"Are you drunk?"

"Not a drop." His voice faded. "No laudanum, either."

Why had he added *that?* Thoughts of opium hadn't crossed Adie's mind. "Here," she said, holding out the water. "This might help."

He reached for it but couldn't raise his head. Setting aside her reluctance, she put her arm behind his shoulders and lifted. As he raised his hand to steady the cup, she felt muscles stretch across his back. His shoulder blades jutted against her wrist, reminding her again that he had a physical strength she lacked.

He drained the glass, then blew out a breath. "Thank you, miss."

She lowered his shoulders to the porch, then rocked back on her knees. "Who are you?"

"No one important."

Adie needed facts. "What's your name?"

"Joshua Blue." He grimaced. "God bless you for your kindness."

Adie's lips tightened. Considering how God had "blessed" her in the past, she wanted nothing to do with Him. "I'm not interested in God's blessing, Mr. Blue. I want you to leave."

"Blessings aside," he murmured, "thank you for the water."

Adie didn't want to be thanked. She wanted to be rid of him. "Can you stand?"

"I think so."

"Can you ride?" she asked hopefully.

He shook his head. "I came to rent a room."

"I don't rent to men."

"I'll pay double."

The money tempted her in a way nothing else could. Before meeting Maggie, Adie had been homeless. She valued a roof and a bed the way rich women valued silver and jewels. It had taken a miracle—and Maggie Butler—to make Swan's Nest Adie's home. She owned it. Or more correctly, she owned half of it. Franklin Dean, the new owner of Denver National Bank, held the promissory note Adie had signed with his father. The older man had viewed banking as a way to help hardworking people, but he'd died a month ago. His son lacked the same compassion, and Adie had clashed with him the instant they'd met. They'd done battle again when he'd tried to call on Pearl against the girl's will.

Adie's blood boiled at the thought of Dean, all slick and shiny in his black carriage. She'd managed to keep up with her mortgage but not as easily as she'd hoped when she'd signed the papers. Her guests paid what they could and she didn't ask for more. So far, she'd made ends meet. She'd also served broth and bread for supper when the pantry ran low. No one ever complained.

A few extra dollars would be welcome, but she had to be careful. Swan's Nest lay on the outskirts of Denver, several blocks from the saloons but close to the trails that led to Wyoming and places notorious for outlaws. Before she rented a room to Joshua Blue, she needed to know more about him. Double the money could mean double the trouble.

"Are you an outlaw?" she asked.

"No, ma'am."

Adie wrinkled her brow. Human beings lied all the time. Timothy Long had lied to her in the attic she'd called her room. Reverend Honeycutt had lied to the town. Maggie had been as close as a sister, but even she'd had secrets. Adie studied the man on her porch for signs of deception. In her experience, evil men bragged about their misdeeds. Joshua Blue had offered a humble denial. She took it as a good sign, but she still had to consider Stephen. He'd been born too soon and had almost died. She feared bringing sickness into the house.

"What about your health?" she asked. "If you're ill—"

His jaw tightened. "If I had the pox, I wouldn't be here."

"But you fainted."

He grunted. "Stupidity on my part."

"That's not much of an answer."

"It's honest."

Looking at his gaunt face, she wondered if he'd passed out from hunger and was too proud to admit it. She'd had that

problem herself. Sometimes she still did. If she skipped breakfast to save a few pennies, she got weak-kneed and had to
gobble bread and jam. How long had it been since Joshua Blue
had eaten a solid meal?

"All right," she said. "You can stay but only until you're
well."

"I'd be grateful."

"It'll cost you four dollars a week. Can you afford it?"

"That's more than fair."

"You'll get a bed and two meals a day, but your room
won't be as nice as some. It's small and behind the kitchen."

"Anything will do."

Maybe for him, but Adie took pride in her home. She'd
learned from Maggie that beauty lifted a woman's spirits.
The upstairs rooms all had pretty quilts and matching curtains
Adie had stitched herself. She picked flowers every day and
put them in the crystal vases that had come with the house.
She thought about brightening up Joshua Blue's room with a
bunch of daisies, then chided herself for being foolish. She
had no desire to make this man feel welcome.

"The room's not fancy," she said. "But it's cozy."

"Thank you, Miss—?"

She almost said "it's Mrs." but didn't. Necessary or not, she
hated that lie. "I'm Adie Clarke."

"The pleasure's mine, Miss Clarke."

For the first time, he spoke naturally. Adie heard a clipped
accent that reminded her of Maggie. Fear rippled down her
spine, but she pushed it back. Lots of people traveled west
from New England. When she walked down the Denver
streets, she heard accents of all kinds.

"Can you stand now?" she said to him.

"My horse—"

"I'll see to it after I see to you."

His eyes filled with gratitude. "I'll pay for feed and straw. Double whatever you charge."

Adie had forgotten about his offer to pay twice what she usually asked. She felt cheap about it, especially if he'd fainted from hunger. "There's no need to pay double."

"Take it," he said.

"It's not right."

"It's more than fair," he insisted. "I'm intruding on your privacy in the dead of night. Please…allow me this small dignity."

Adie saw no point in arguing. If Mr. Blue wanted to protect his pride with money, she'd oblige. "Let's get you into that room."

She stood and offered her hand. When he clasped her fingers, she felt strength inside his leather glove and wondered why he hadn't eaten. Grimacing, he pushed to a sitting position and put on his black hat. Using her for leverage, he rose to his full height and faced her. Adie's gaze landed on his chin, then dipped to the Adam's apple above the buttoned collar of his white shirt. She judged him to be six feet tall, rail thin and too proud to lean on her.

She let go of his hand and turned. "I'll show you to your room."

She stepped over the threshold, paused at a side table and lit a candle. As she held it up, Joshua Blue stepped into the room and took off his hat. The candle flickered with the rush of air. Light danced across his craggy features and revealed a straight nose that struck her as aristocratic. His dark hair curled around his temples and brushed his collar, reminding her of crows gleaning seed from her mother's wheat field. Everything about him was black or white except for his eyes. They were as blue as his name. In a vague way, his gaze reminded her of Maggie except her friend's eyes had been pure brown. Stephen's eyes hadn't found their color yet. Adie hoped they'd turn brown, a closer match to her hazel ones.

Blocking her worries, she led her new boarder down a corridor with green and pink floral wallpaper, through the kitchen and down a short hall that led to his room. As she opened the door, she raised the candle. The tiny space looked as barren as she feared. The room had a cot and a dresser, but mostly she used it to store odds and ends she donated to charity or tried to sell herself. Dust motes floated in the gold light, and a cobweb shimmered in the corner of the ceiling. Not even daisies would have lifted the gloom. A mouse scurried away from the glow.

Adie felt embarrassed. "I'll clean it out tomorrow."

"It's fine."

"It's dirty."

"Not as dirty as I am," he said dryly.

She stepped into the room, lifted a rag from the pile on a trunk and swatted the cobweb. It broke into pieces and fell on her face. The vague sensation sent her back to the attic in the Long house, where Timothy Long had threatened to smother her with a pillow if she cried out. The storeroom had the same smell as the attic, the same dust and collection of unwanted things.

Adie wanted to run from the room, but Joshua Blue was standing in the doorway with his hat in one hand and his eyes firmly on her face. He'd trapped her. Or more correctly, she'd trapped herself. What a fool she'd been. Thanks to Timothy Long she knew better.

Show no fear. Stay strong.

The voice in Adie's head belonged to Maggie. As always, it gave her strength. She coughed once to recover her composure, then looked straight at Mr. Blue. "Do you need anything else?"

He looked pinched. "Do you have another candle?"

His tone made her wonder if the dark bothered him as

much as it bothered her. She indicated the top of the dresser. "There's a lamp—"

"I see it."

He lit the match and wick, then adjusted the flame. Adie stepped to the door. As she turned to say good-night, Mr. Blue took off his hat and tried to stand taller. He looked weary to the bone and frail enough to pass out again.

She had no desire to fix him a meal, but he needed to eat. "Would you like a sandwich?"

His face turned pale. "No, thanks."

Adie wondered if he had a bad stomach. "Broth?"

He swallowed as if his mouth had started to water. She could see him thinking, weighing her inconvenience against his hunger. She took pity on him. "How about bread and butter? Maybe with strawberry jam?"

"No bread," he said. "But I'd be grateful for a glass of milk."

Adie knew all about bellyaches. In addition to a cow, she kept a goat for Stephen. "I have goat's milk. Would that—"

"Yes, please."

"It's in the kitchen."

Holding the candle, she led the way down the hall. She set the brass holder on the table, indicated a chair and opened the icebox where she had two pitchers. The prettiest one, blue crystal etched with cornflowers, held the cow's milk she served her boarders. The other was smaller and made of pewter. She set it on the counter, took a glass from the shelf and poured.

As the stranger lowered himself to the chair, she heard a stifled groan. She turned and saw him sitting straight, but he looked as pinched as Stephen with a bout of colic.

"Here," she said, handing him the milk.

He took it, sipped, then drank more deeply. As he lowered the glass, he closed his eyes and exhaled.

The contented silence reminded Adie of her son after a late-night feeding. She glanced at the clock. Soon Stephen would wake up hungry and she still had to put the horse in the carriage house. If she hurried, she'd be back before her son stirred. If he woke up early, Rose or Pearl would check on him.

"I have to see to your horse," Adie said to her guest. "Will you be all right?"

"I'm much better."

His voice rang with authority, as if he were used to speaking and being heard. Adie could scarcely believe she'd taken him for a meager drifter. With the candle flickering, he filled the kitchen with the shadows of a giant. He frightened her, yet he'd just guzzled milk like a baby. Confused by her thoughts, she set the pitcher on the table. "Help yourself."

He lifted it and poured. "Just so you know, Miss Clarke. I'm an honorable man. You have nothing to fear from me."

As he raised the glass from the table, his eyes found hers and lingered. Adie felt as if he were looking for her soul. He wouldn't find it. She'd left that part of her heart in Liddy's Grove. Ever since, she'd drawn lines and expected people to stay behind them.

"I have a few rules," she said.

"Whatever you say."

"Under no circumstances may you go upstairs."

"Of course."

"Dinner's at six o'clock. If you miss it, you can make yourself a sandwich."

"That's fair." His eyes twinkled. "Anything else?"

If she made the list long enough, maybe he'd leave. Adie searched her mind for male habits she recalled from her days as an orphan. She'd lived with six families in four years. She'd also cleaned saloons and cheap hotels. She knew about bad habits.

"No cursing, drinking or smoking," she said.

"That suits me fine."

"No shouting," she added. "I can't abide by it."

Joshua Blue looked amused. "I'll try."

"If you use a dish, wash it."

"All right."

"I don't want you sitting on the front porch. If word gets out I rented to you, other men will knock on the door."

"I'll keep to my room or the stable. How's that?"

"Fine." Except his courtesy annoyed her.

The man's eyes locked on to hers. "I know where I stand, Miss Clarke. You've opened your home and I won't betray that trust. I have urgent business. Once I see to it, I'll be on my way."

What business? Adie wanted to ask but sealed her lips. If she didn't ask questions, she wouldn't have to answer them. "Then we're agreed."

"We are." He lifted the glass of milk, sealing the deal with a mock toast, a gesture that looked strangely natural considering his appearance.

Adie headed for the front yard where he'd left his horse. In the moonlight she saw a gray mare waiting patiently. Glad to be dealing with another female, she led the horse to the carriage house. The hens twittered as she passed the chicken house. Several yards away she saw her milk cow at the fence marking a small pasture. The cow spent most of her time grazing on the sweet grass, but Adie kept the goat, a cranky thing named Buttons, inside the outbuilding. Her son depended on the nanny goat and she couldn't risk it getting loose.

When she reached the carriage house, she lit the lantern inside the door, then turned back to the mare and inspected the things strapped to the saddle. Her gaze went first to a rifle jutting from a plain leather scabbard. A canteen hung from the saddle horn and a set of saddlebags draped the horse's middle.

Adie felt ashamed of herself for what she was about to do, but a woman with a secret couldn't be too careful. Only her friends knew Stephen wasn't her natural born son. Somewhere he had a father, a man Maggie had loved and protected with her silence. Adie didn't know the whole story, but she'd loved her friend and had admired her.

She felt otherwise about Maggie's powerful family. Maggie had said little about them, but she'd once let it slip that her brother was a minister. Rather than shame him with an illegitimate child, she'd left home. Maggie never mentioned her family's wealth, but Adie had seen her fine things—silk chemises and embroidered camisoles, stockings without a stitch of darning, shoes with silver buttons. Adie had been in awe, but it was Maggie's education that made her envious. Her friend had spoken French, played the harp, knew mathematics and could recite dozens of poems.

Adie's assumption of Maggie's wealth had been confirmed the day she'd died. Bleeding and weak, she'd told Adie to remove a velvet bag from a drawer of her trunk and look inside. Adie had gasped at the glittering gems. Maggie's dying wish still echoed in her ears. She had begged Adie to take Stephen and raise him as her own; then she'd squeezed Adie's wrist with her bloodless fingers.

"Leave Topeka tonight. Break all ties with me."

"But why?"

"Don't let my brother near my son. He'll send Stephen to an orphanage."

Adie had stood alone as an undertaker buried Maggie in a run-down cemetery; then she'd taken the jewelry and backtracked to Kansas City where Maggie had sold a few pieces of jewelry before coming to Topeka. The sixty-mile train ride to the bustling city had given her two advantages. She'd gotten a better price for Maggie's jewelry, and the railroad left

Kansas City in four different directions. If Maggie's family found the jewelry, they wouldn't know where she'd gone. If by chance a detective, or Maggie's brother, traced her to Topeka, the man would reach a dead end.

Adie had sold only what she needed for a fresh start, then bought a ticket to Denver because of its size. She wanted to open a boardinghouse, a place for women like herself and Maggie. For two days she'd held Stephen on the crowded train, struggling to keep him fed until they'd arrived in a city full of gambling halls and saloons. Pretending to have Maggie's poise, she'd stayed at a hotel, visited the bank and explained her ambition to the elder Mr. Dean, who had shown her Swan's Nest. The mansion had reminded her of Maggie and she'd bought it, using what cash she had from the jewelry sale and signing a two-year promissory note for the balance.

She could have sold more jewelry and paid for the house in full, but she feared leaving a trail for a Pinkerton's detective. Nor did she want to squander Stephen's inheritance. The remaining jewels—a sapphire ring, a pearl necklace, a bracelet and some glittering brooches—were his legacy from his mother, a gift from the woman who'd given him life but had never held him.

As Adie led the mare into a stall, she felt the sting of tears. Maggie had died three months ago, but she still missed her friend. She also feared strangers, especially men. If Stephen's father tried to claim him, Adie would have to make a terrible choice. On the other hand, she had no qualms about hiding from Maggie's brother. Considering how he'd shunned his sister, he didn't deserve to know his nephew. In Adie's book, he didn't deserve to breathe.

She lifted the saddle off the mare, set it on the ground, then stripped off the scabbard, the canteen and the saddlebags. She set everything aside, filled a bucket with water and gave the horse a measure of hay. Satisfied, she closed the gate to the stall, stepped to the saddlebags and dropped to a crouch. She had no business going through Joshua Blue's things, but she had to be sure he had no ties to Maggie Butler.

With shaking fingers, she worked the buckle on the bulging leather bag.

Chapter Two

As soon as Adie Clarke left the kitchen, Josh drained the glass of milk and poured himself another. He'd been aiming for her boardinghouse when he'd left Kansas City, but he hadn't intended to faint on her doorstep. Before he'd left, he'd seen a doctor who'd told him what he already knew. He had a stomach ulcer, a bad one that could bleed and threaten his life. At the very least, it offered daily torture.

Josh didn't care. He had to find his sister. Ten months ago, Emily Blue had left their Boston mansion with a satchel, her jewelry and Josh's bitter words ringing in her ears. He'd never forgive himself for that night. He'd said unspeakable things, calling her a name that shouldn't be uttered and accusing her of being a Jezebel. He'd made hateful accusations, all the time wearing the collar that marked him as a minister.

The memory sent fresh acid into Josh's belly. He had to find Emily and her baby and make amends. Until he found them, he refused to rest.

Never mind the stomach ulcer. The Apostle Paul had written of a thorn in his flesh. It had kept him humble. The ulcer often humbled Josh, though not as profoundly as it had tonight. Fainting on Adie Clarke's porch hadn't been in the plan when he'd left Kansas City on the word of Wes Daniels, a gunslinger who'd frequented the saloon where Josh had been preaching on Sunday mornings. Wes had told him about a boardinghouse called Swan's Nest.

"It's for women in trouble," he'd said, winking at Josh. "Maybe your sister's there."

Josh had left the next morning. Halfway to Denver, his stomach had caught fire and he'd stopped eating. Pure and simple, he'd fainted on Adie Clarke's porch out of hunger.

As he raised the glass to his lips, he said a silent prayer for Emily and her child. Somewhere in the world he had a niece or nephew he'd never seen. A little girl with Emily's button nose…a boy with the Blue family chin. Josh was imagining a child with Emily's dark curls when he heard a baby cry. High pitched and needy, it cut through his soul. For all he knew, Emily was sleeping right above his head. The baby could be his niece or nephew.

He wanted to charge up the stairs, but his common sense and Miss Clarke's stern rules kept him in the kitchen. Closing his eyes, he prayed for the child and its mother. He knew how it felt to wake up with a bellyache.

Above his head, the ceiling creaked. He heard the pad of bare feet on the wooden planks and imagined a mother hurrying to her child. The footsteps faded, then stopped. An instant later, the baby's wail turned to a hopeful whimper. He imagined the mother taking the baby in her arms, sitting in a rocking chair as she nursed it back to sleep. He listened for the creak of the rockers, maybe the hint of a lullaby. Instead the baby shrieked in frustration. Footsteps scurried back down the hall while the baby's cry stayed in the same room, growing louder. The pacing stopped over Josh's head, paused, then went halfway down the hall. He heard a door open, then another pair of steps, muted now as if two women were trying to be quiet on floors that wouldn't allow it.

When the stairs squeaked, Josh shot to his feet. Adie Clarke knew she'd rented him a room, but the women coming down the stairs would see a drifter in black, maybe an outlaw. Common sense told him to leave the kitchen, but he stood frozen with the hope of seeing Emily.

"Don't move, or I'll shoot you dead." The female voice, shaking with sincerity, had come from the shadow in the hall.

He froze.

"Get your hands up!"

As he raised his arms, his duster pulled open. Josh believed in turning the other cheek, but he wore a Colt Peacemaker on his hip. He'd learned early in his travels that riding unarmed into an outlaw camp caused more of a stir than a cocked rifle. Carrying a weapon was his way of being a Greek to the Greeks. The Colt made him familiar to the rough men with whom he felt called to share the Good News. Unfortunately, the woman in the doorway wouldn't see the gun as a calling card. Josh felt the weapon pulling on his belt and winced. He'd lost weight. If he didn't hike up the belt soon, he'd lose his trousers.

"Who are you?" the woman demanded.

"I'm a new boarder."

"Liar," she said in a stony voice. "Adie doesn't rent to men."

"She took pity on me." Josh peered into the hallway. He couldn't see the woman, but candlelight glinted off the double barrel of a two-shot Derringer. The weapon shook, a sign of her nerves.

"Where's Adie?" she demanded.

"Tending my horse."

"Why aren't you tending it yourself?"

Pride kept Josh from admitting his weakness. Before he could correct the mistake, the woman hollered down the hallway.

"Pearl! Get Bessie and Caroline! We have an intruder." The gun stayed steady. "Find Adie *now.*"

With his hands in the air, Josh heard doors open and the tap of feet on the stairs. In Boston, he'd enjoyed the Women's Auxiliary meetings. The ladies had fawned over him and the compliments had gone to his head. The women of Swan's Nest wouldn't be so appreciative.

Pain stabbed past his sternum and around his ribs. If he'd been alone, he'd have fallen to his knees, clutched his middle and curled into a ball. With a gun trained on his chest, he didn't dare move. The pain hit again. His shoulders hunched as he cringed, causing his arms to drop as if he were going for his gun.

The woman fired.

The bullet slammed into Josh's shoulder. He took a step back, caught his boot on the chair and fell against a hutch filled with china. Plates crashed to the floor and so did Josh. He didn't want to die. He had to find Emily. He'd shamed himself as a man and a minister. He had to make up for his mistakes.

"Don't shoot," he said. "I mean no harm."

The woman kept the pistol trained on his head. "We'll see what Adie has to say."

Josh lay on the floor, clutching his belly and smelling sulfur and blood. He'd seen men die before. In Boston he'd prayed with elderly gentlemen fading in their own beds. In camps west of the Mississippi, he'd seen men die from gunshot wounds, infections and disease. Curled on the floor, he listened to his own breath for sucking air, a sign he'd been hit in the lung, but he heard only a rasp in his dry throat. His heart kept an even rhythm, another good sign.

Judging by the pain, he'd been hit high in the shoulder. Silently Josh thanked God the woman had owned a Derringer and not a Colt .45. He'd live as long as she didn't panic and shoot him in the head.

He heard footsteps in the kitchen and opened his eyes. Bare toes and the hems of robes filled his vision.

"You shot him!" said a new female voice.

"What happened?" demanded another.

Could one of the women be Emily? The voices hadn't matched hers—one sounded Southern and the other was too high pitched—but he'd seen four pairs of feet. Josh wanted to look but realized it would be fruitless. He'd become thin and ragged, but Emily would have recognized him. He closed his eyes in despair.

In a breath of silence, he heard the hopeful cooing of a baby and looked up. The fourth woman had an infant in her arms. The goat's milk, he realized, was for the child. Expecting to be fed, it had settled into its mother's arms but was growing impatient with the delay. The cooing turned to a complaint, then a wail that dwarfed everything in the room, including Josh's pain.

"The baby's hungry," he said.

"Quiet," ordered the woman with the gun.

Josh could barely breathe for the pain. "Please. Feed it."

No one moved.

He raised his voice. "I said feed the baby."

He flashed on the night he'd clashed with Emily. Three times he'd told her to leave, betraying her love as surely as Peter had betrayed his Lord. Like the fisherman, Josh felt lower than dirt.

The wailing grew worse. The woman with the gun called to one of the others. "Get the milk, Pearl. I'll keep watch."

Emily had loved their mother's pearls, a strand so long it reached to her waist. Was she using an alias to avoid him? Maybe she *hadn't* recognized him. He'd changed in the past year. Even more worrisome, maybe she'd seen him take a bullet and wished him dead.

Bare feet, slender and white, padded across the wood floor. Josh tried to call Emily's name, but his belly hurt and the words slurred to a groan. He watched the woman's feet as she retrieved the pitcher of goat's milk, filled a bottle and warmed it in a pan of water on the stove. The baby, smelling food, shrieked even louder. Wise or not, Josh raised his head. The baby's mother wore a yellow robe, his sister's favorite color, but she had white-blond hair. Emily's hair was dark and wavy like his. He hadn't found his sister after all, but neither was this woman the baby's mother. Her belly promised new life and promised it soon. Closing his eyes, Josh prayed for the mother and child, wishing he'd done the same for Emily instead of driving her away with his foolish pride.

Adie heard a gunshot, dropped the unopened saddlebag and ran for the house. Mary, a former saloon girl, kept a pistol in her nightstand and wouldn't hesitate to use it.

Had Joshua Blue betrayed Adie's trust? She didn't think so. The man could barely walk. It seemed more likely that Stephen had awoken early and Mr. Blue had lingered over the glass of milk. Whoever went for Stephen, probably Mary, had seen Adie's empty bed. Maybe she'd heard the thump on the door and jumped to ominous conclusions.

She ran up the back steps and flung open the door.

"Adie!" The cry came from Pearl. "We thought—"

"I know what you thought." She dropped to her knees at the man's side. "He's hurt. We'll have to call the doctor."

Stephen shrieked. He needed to be fed in the worst way, but Adie feared for the wounded man's life.

Groaning, he rolled to his back, revealing the bullet hole in his duster. When she opened his coat, she saw a red stain blooming on his white shirt. With each breath he took, the blood spread in a widening circle.

Looking at her face, he mumbled something unintelligible. She hunched forward. "I couldn't hear you."

"I said...feed the baby."

Joshua Blue was lying on her floor with a bullet in his shoulder, bleeding inside and out, and he was thinking of her son. What kind of man put a baby before his own life? Using the hem of her nightgown, Adie wiped his brow. "Be still. We'll get the doctor."

"No." His voice sounded stronger. "No doctors."

"But you need help."

Someone lit a lamp. As it flared to life, Mary stepped closer. Adie smelled the residue of gunpowder and looked up. "Maybe Caroline can go for Doc Nichols."

The man lifted his head. "I said *no.*"

His refusal made Adie wonder if he was on the run. It wouldn't have surprised her. Everyone at Swan's Nest had run from something, including herself.

Mary scowled down at her. "Who is he?"

"I rented him a room."

"But you don't rent to men. You promised—"

"This isn't the time," Adie said.

She looked past Mary and saw Pearl at the stove. With her back to the rest of the kitchen, she lifted the bottle out of the pot of water and whisked Stephen into the front room where she could feed him in peace. Adie looked at Caroline. "Where's Bessie?"

"She went to get her nursing kit."

Mary finally lowered the gun. "Maybe she can take out the bullet."

Adie studied the man on her floor. His color had come back and his breathing seemed steady. Maybe they could avoid Dr. Nichols after all. Bessie hurried into the kitchen and dropped down next to Adie. She looked at the wound, checked the man's back for an exit hole, then lowered him gently to the floor. "The bullet's still in you, sir. It'll have to come out."

"Can you do it?"

"I can try," Bessie said. "I'm a trained nurse, but it will hurt."

"Go ahead," he said.

Bessie looked at Adie. "Get that pint of whiskey."

Adie kept it with the smelling salts for medicinal purposes only. Before she could stand to fetch it, the stranger clutched her hand. "I don't want it."

Why would he deny himself a painkiller? Adie was about to argue with him when Bessie interrupted. "It's not for your belly, sir. It's to clean the wound."

He relaxed but didn't release Adie's hand. She felt awkward comforting him, but they were both aware of the coming pain. When Adie didn't move, Caroline went to the cupboard for the whiskey. She gave the bottle to Bessie, then lifted the instruments from the nursing bag, put them in the boiling water and set out clean rags for blotting the blood. Bessie had opened the two buttons on the man's shirt, but it wouldn't pull wide enough to reveal the wound. Using delicate scissors, the kind most women kept for embroidery, she cut the shirt and tugged it back from a small hole oozing blood.

Adie's stomach churned. The hole in Joshua Blue's shoulder wasn't much bigger than a man's finger, but it had the potential to kill him with infection. In his weakened condition, he might not be able to fight it. Adie squeezed his hand. She feared for his health. She also feared for herself and Stephen. She'd just opened the first saddlebag when she heard the gunshot. Later, when he'd fallen asleep, she'd search his things.

"Whiskey, please," Bessie said matter-of-factly.

Adie watched as Caroline splashed whiskey into her sister's palm. As Bessie rubbed her hands together, Caroline dampened a patch of cotton and gave it to her sister. Bessie looked at the man's face. "This is going to hurt, sir."

He closed his eyes. "Just do it."

Bessie took a probe from the instruments Caroline had put on a clean towel. As she inserted it into the wound, Joshua Blue arched up. Bessie pulled back.

"Adie, Caroline. You'll have to hold him down."

The two women moved into position. On their knees, they each held a shoulder. As Bessie went to work, Adie felt the man straining against her hands. She also sensed acceptance. The bullet had to come out.

"I found it," Bessie said.

She removed the probe and lifted a pair of forceps. After a glance at her patient, she inserted the instrument, pinched the bullet and pulled it out. Joshua Blue groaned with pain. Adie wondered which hurt more, his chest or his belly.

Bessie held the bullet up to the light and examined it. "It's in one piece. We're done except for stitching this gentleman up."

He let out a breath. "Thank you."

"You'll do fine as long as the wound doesn't fester. Of course you'll have to rest up for a while."

He grunted. "How long?"

Adie had been wondering the same thing.

"As long as it takes." Bessie took a stitch with a needle and black thread. "Judging by your appearance, you're half starved. You need a week in bed and a month in a rocking chair."

Adie cringed. "That's so long."

Bessie gave her a motherly look. "It's what the man needs, honey. We'll be all right."

Leave it to Bessie to calm the waters. Mary would pitch a fit. Pearl, conscious of her belly, would stop coming downstairs. Caroline judged no one. She'd befriend Mr. Blue without hesitation, posing a problem of a different kind. Adie watched as the nurse stitched up the wound, snipped the thread and wiped the incision with whiskey. She inspected her handiwork, then wiped the man's brow with a clean rag. "We need to get you to bed. Can you walk?"

"I think so."

With Adie on one side and Caroline on the other, he leveraged to his feet. He looked like a kicked-in chimney pipe, but he managed to move down the hall. Adie started to follow, but Bessie stopped her. "I'll see to him. Go hold Stephen. It'll make you feel better."

"Thanks, Bessie."

"By the way," said the older woman. "Who is this man?"

"I wish I knew." Adie told her briefly about finding him on the porch. "He was in pain even before Mary shot him."

"Maybe an ulcer," Bessie said. "I've got a small bottle of laudanum. I'll fetch it for him."

Adie thought of his earlier comment about the drug but said nothing. She wanted Joshua Blue to fall asleep so she could finish going through his saddlebags, but first she needed to check her son.

"Whatever you think," she said to Bessie. "The sooner he heals, the sooner he can leave."

"He needs time," the nurse said gently.

Adie sighed. She'd cook meals for Joshua Blue and nurse his wounds. She'd change his sheets and wash his clothes. But time to heal—what he needed most—was the one thing she didn't want to give. The sooner he left, the safer she and Stephen would be.

As Bessie went down the hall, Adie headed for the parlor where she heard Pearl humming a lullaby to Stephen. She rounded the corner and saw both Pearl and Mary on the divan. Pearl looked lost, but Mary had crossed her arms and was glowering. Adie had hoped to check Stephen and escape to the carriage house, but she couldn't leave without explaining to her friends.

"Who is he?" Mary demanded.

"I don't know," Adie said. "But I'm certain he means no harm."

Mary groaned. "You can't possibly know that."

Adie couldn't be sure, but he'd come to the door sick and weak. "Look at him. He's downright scrawny."

"He's also dressed like a gunfighter," Mary insisted. "I know his kind."

Adie felt naive next to Mary, but she couldn't stop worrying about the stranger. She didn't want to argue, but she needed to set Mary straight. "He fainted on the porch. What else could I do? Leave him there?"

"You could have gone for the sheriff."

To protect Stephen, Adie kept to herself as much as possible. If a Pinkerton's detective visited Denver, he'd go straight to the law and make inquiries. The less the sheriff knew about Adie and her home, the safer her son would be. She gave Mary an impatient look. "It wasn't necessary."

"You're too trusting," Mary insisted.

Pearl sighed. "I wish you hadn't shot him."

"He went for his gun!"

Adie worried, but only for an instant. A man intending harm didn't tell a woman to feed a hungry baby. "He has belly trouble," she said to Mary. "He probably bent over in pain."

Recognition flitted across Mary's face.

Pearl went back to crooning to Stephen, who'd fallen peacefully asleep. Adie envied him. She wouldn't sleep that well until Joshua Blue left Denver. "I have to see to his horse."

Mary pushed to her feet. "I'll help."

"No." Adie waved casually, but her stomach had jumped.

She wanted to go through his things by herself. "It's been a long night. You and Pearl should get some sleep."

"If you're sure—"

"I am." Adie forced a smile. "I'll see you both in the morning."

Before Mary could ask another question, Adie headed for the back door. As she turned the knob, Bessie came down the hall. "Mr. Blue wants to see you."

The saddlebags would have to wait but only for a bit. With rubbery knees, she thanked Bessie and went to see Joshua Blue.

Chapter Three

In spite of Josh's protests, the woman nursing him had left a bottle of laudanum on the nightstand. He knew all about the drug and the lies it told. He'd first used it in Boston. With the renown that came with his sermons, he'd gotten an ulcer. The doctor he'd seen, a stranger because he'd wanted to hide his weakness, had given him something to calm his stomach, but it had led to embarrassing bouts of belching, something a man in Josh's position couldn't allow. He'd gone to a second physician, then a third. The last one had given him laudanum. It had helped immediately.

Looking at the bottle, Josh knew it would help right now. If he filled the spoon the woman had left—he thought her name was Bessie—he'd be free of pain. He'd be numb to his guilt, too.

The laudanum tempted him.

The craving humbled him.

Reverend Joshua Benjamin Blue, the best young preacher in Boston, maybe in America, had become addicted to opium. Thanks to Wes Daniels, the biggest sinner on earth and Josh's only friend, he'd kicked the habit three months ago in a Kansas City boardinghouse.

Thoughts of Wes made Josh smile. He hadn't succeeded in saving the gunslinger's soul, but neither had Wes corrupted *him*. They'd had some lively debates in the past few months…a few quarrels, too. Wes had understood Josh's guilt, but he didn't share his worry. As long as Emily had jewelry to sell, Wes insisted she'd be sitting pretty. Josh hoped so. For months he'd been visiting pawnbrokers in search of pieces he'd recognize. He knew from Sarah Banks, Emily's best friend, that his sister had bought a train ticket to St. Louis. Sarah had given Josh a verbal beating, one he'd deserved.

"How dare you cast stones at your sister! I know you, Josh. You're as flawed as the rest us!"

She'd been right, of course. With Sarah's remarks in his ears, he'd traveled to St. Louis, where he'd spotted a familiar brooch in a jewelry store. Emily, he'd learned from the shop-keeper, had sold it and moved on. A clerk at the train station recalled her face and thought she'd gone to Kansas City. Josh's only hope of finding her lay in a trail of pawned jewelry and the Lord's mercy. If he could have moved, he'd have hit his knees. Like Paul, he counted himself among the foremost of sinners, a man sorely in need of God's grace. With the laudanum calling to him, he needed that grace in abundance. It came in the tap of Adie Clarke's footsteps.

Bessie had left Josh a lamp, but she'd dimmed it to a haze that turned Miss Clarke into a shadow. Josh recalled her reddish hair and the glint in her gold-brown eyes. She'd struck him as young and pretty, though he wished he hadn't noticed. He'd dedicated his life to serving God with every thought and deed. He wasn't immune to pretty women, but he felt called to remain single. A man couldn't travel at will with the obli-gation of a wife and family.

Thoughts of children made him wince. Without Emily the family mansion in Boston had become a tomb. For the first

time, Josh had taken his meals alone. Listening to the lonely
scrape of his knife on fine china, he'd wondered how it would
feel to share meals with a wife, maybe children. Tonight he'd
envied the woman who'd fed the baby.

Adie Clarke studied him in the dim light. "Are you awake?"

"I am. I need something."

"Milk?"

"No," he said. "The laudanum…take it away."

Her gaze went to the bottle, then shifted to the cot where
Josh lay wrapped in a blanket and wearing a silk nightshirt.
Bessie had bandaged his shoulder, extracted the garment from
one of the trunks in the storeroom and helped him into the
shirt. Even in Boston, he hadn't worn anything so fine.

Miss Clarke stayed in the doorway. "Are you sure?
Bessie says—"

"Bessie doesn't know me."

"She's a good nurse."

"I don't doubt it, Miss Clarke." Josh felt ashamed, but the
truth set a man free. "Until a few months ago, laudanum had
a grip on me. I'll never touch it again."

"I'm sorry."

He didn't want her pity. "I'm over it."

"Of course." She walked to the nightstand, lifted the bottle
and hurried for the door.

"Wait," he called.

She stopped and turned, but her eyes clouded with reluctance. "Do you need something else?"

"Would you bring in my saddlebags?"

She froze like a deer sensing a wolf. Why would she
hesitate? Considering he'd been shot in her kitchen, fetching
his saddlebags seemed like a small favor. He could live
without the laudanum, but he desperately needed the Bible
packed with his clothes. "I'd get them myself, but—"

"No," she said. "I'll do it."

"Thank you."

As she headed down the hall, Josh rested his head on the pillow and stared at the ceiling. He hoped she'd hurry. His shoulder ached and his belly burned, but his soul hurt most of all. He thought of David writing Psalms in the midst of battle and loss.

Search me, O God, and know my heart… Love swelled in Josh's chest. He prayed for Emily, the women of Swan's Nest and the baby crying for milk.

Try me and know my thoughts… If an ulcer, a gunshot wound and a craving for opium didn't test a man, he didn't know what did. Would ever find Emily? Was she still alive? And her child… He grimaced.

See if there be any hurtful way in me… He prayed for purity of thought and a generous spirit.

And lead me in Your way everlasting. Amen.

As he finished the prayer, he looked expectantly at the door. Any minute Adie Clarke would be back with his Bible. More than ever, Josh needed the mercy of the God who'd walked the earth in a tent of human flesh. Jesus alone knew how he felt. He alone could bring comfort.

Adie ran to the carriage house. If she hurried, she could look in the saddlebags before giving them to Mr. Blue. On the other hand, she saw a risk. If she took too long, he'd wonder where she'd been. He also seemed more alert than she'd expected. If she rummaged through his bags, he might realize his things were in disarray and she'd have to explain herself.

As she entered the outbuilding, she considered another approach. Mr. Blue wouldn't be able to lift the heavy bags. He'd need her help. If she dumped the contents on the floor, she'd see everything *and* be able to gauge his expression.

Adie didn't like being sneaky, but her motives were pure. She'd do anything to protect Stephen.

Not bothering with a lamp, she found the saddlebags where she'd left them, draped them over her shoulder, picked up the rifle and went back to the house. She went down the hall to Mr. Blue's room where she leaned the gun by the door and set the bags against the wall. They'd be in his line of sight but not so close that he could see her expression.

He pulled himself upright so he could watch. "I'm not sure which bag it's in."

Adie didn't ask him what he wanted. The less information she had, the more reason she had to riffle through his things. She lifted the first bag, worked the buckle and dumped the contents on the floor. Pots, two plates and utensils clattered against each other, and a can of beans rolled away. She'd found his mess kit but nothing of interest. She put everything back, then unbuckled the second bag. She could tell from the softness that it held clothing. Before he could stop her, she removed trousers, a shirt and a frock coat, all tightly rolled and as black as coal.

"Keep going," he said. "What I want is at the bottom."

Adie removed dungarees, a denim shirt and two pairs of store-bought socks. She checked the edges for darning, found none and decided Joshua Blue was a single man and always had been. Wanting a reason to check his pockets, she picked up the clothing and stood. "I'll hang up your things."

"I'd be obliged."

Feeling like a fox in a henhouse, she went to a row of nails on the back wall. She turned her back, gave the coat a shake and searched the pockets. She felt a few coins, lint and a scrap of paper. A quick glance revealed notes about a man named Peter and something about catching fish. Seeing no mention of Maggie, Adie slipped the paper back in the coat and lifted a pair of trousers. She repeated her search and found nothing.

She went back to the saddlebag. "What is it you want?"

"My Bible."

She knew very little about Maggie's brother, but her friend had let it slip that he was a minister in a big city. Maggie had never said which one, though Adie had surmised she'd come from New England. Trembling, she looked up from the saddlebag. "Are you a preacher?"

"Of a sort."

"Do you have a church?"

"I do, but not like you mean."

Her hand shook as she checked a pocket. "I don't understand."

"I don't preach in a building," he explained. "I go from place to place."

Adie let out the breath she'd been holding. Maggie's brother had been wealthy. He'd have arrived in Denver in a private railcar, not on the back of a tired horse. He'd have never gone from town to town, preaching to the poor. She relaxed until she recalled his interest in Stephen. Not many men cared about hungry babies. Her nerves prickled with worry. Aware of his gaze, she reached into the saddlebag. She felt past a pouch holding shaving tools, found the book and lifted it from the bag.

The words *Holy Bible* caught the light and glowed like fire, taking Adie back to the evenings she'd spent with the Long family. Old Man Long had often read from the book of Jeremiah. Adie had felt sinful and condemned and confused by a God who treated people so poorly. She'd cast Maggie's brother in the same mold. Even without her promise, she'd have protected Stephen from such a man.

She stood and handed him the Bible. Their fingers brushed on the binding, but their hearts were miles apart. Adie believed in God, but she didn't like Him. Neither did she care for preachers. Carrying a Bible didn't give a man a good heart. She'd learned that lesson in Liddy's Grove. She let go of the book as if it had singed her.

Mr. Blue looked into her eyes with silent understanding and she wondered if he, too, had struggled with God's ways. The slash of his brow looked tight with worry, and his whiskers were too stubbly to be permanent. Adie thought about his shaving tools and wondered when he'd used them last. Her new boarder would clean up well on the outside, but his heart remained a mystery. She needed to keep it that way. The less she knew about him, the better.

"Good night," she said. "Bessie will check you in the morning."

"Before you go, I've been wondering …"

"About what?"

"The baby… Who's the mother?"

Adie raised her chin. "I am."

Earlier he'd called her "Miss Clarke" and she hadn't corrected him. The flash in his eyes told her that he'd assumed she'd given birth out of wedlock. Adie resented being judged, but she counted it as the price of protecting Stephen. If Mr. Blue chose to condemn her, so be it. She'd done nothing for which to be ashamed. With their gazes locked, she waited for the criticism that didn't come.

Instead he laced his fingers on top of the Bible. "Children are a gift, all of them."

"I think so, too."

He lightened his tone. "A boy or a girl?"

"A boy."

The man smiled. "He sure can cry. How old is he?"

Adie didn't like the questions at all, but she took pride in her son. "He's three months old." She didn't mention that he'd been born six weeks early. "I hope the crying doesn't disturb you."

"I don't care if it does."

He sounded defiant. She didn't understand. "Most men would be annoyed."

"The crying's better than silence…I know."

Adie didn't want to care about this man, but her heart fluttered against her ribs. What did Joshua Blue know of babies and silence? Had he lost a wife? A child of his own? She wanted to express sympathy but couldn't. If she pried into his life, he'd pry into hers. He'd ask questions and she'd have to hide the truth. *Stephen was born too soon and his mother died. He barely survived. I welcome his cries, every one of them. They mean he's alive.*

With a lump in her throat, she turned to leave. "Good night, Mr. Blue."

"Good night."

A thought struck her and she turned back to his room. "I suppose I should call you Reverend."

He grimaced. "I'd prefer Josh."

Adie preferred formality. She had her differences with the Almighty, but she'd been taught to respect God and honor His ways. Being too familiar with a man of the cloth seemed wrong. So did addressing a near stranger by his given name. She avoided the issue by murmuring good-night.

Before Mr. Blue could ask another question, she closed the door behind her and went to her bedroom. Too anxious to sleep, she stood next to Stephen's cradle and watched the rise and fall of his chest, treasuring every breath he took. Someday she'd tell him about Maggie Butler and pass on the things hidden in the trunk at the foot of her bed. Maggie's jewelry lay wrapped in a red velvet bag, untouchable, except in a matter of life or death. Adie expected to support herself and her son, though earning a living had proven more difficult than she'd expected. With the loan payment due on Friday, she would have to go to the bank where Franklin Dean would harass her.

Stephen hiked up his legs. Adie tucked the blanket across his back and thought of the other things in the trunk, particularly Maggie's diary. In the last weeks of her pregnancy, the two of them had spent their evenings on the porch of a Topeka boardinghouse. While Adie did piecework, Maggie had taken a pen to paper.

"It's my story," she'd explained. "If something happens to me, I want Stephen to have it when he's older."

Blinking back tears, she recalled the day Maggie had written the last words in the journal. She'd asked for the book, scrawled a final sentence and taken her last breath. Stunned, Adie had lifted the book from Maggie's still hands. Without opening it, she'd buried the journal deep in the trunk.

Looking at her son now, Adie thought of the diary and trembled. Maggie had lived with secrets. The book, Adie feared, held revelations that could tear Stephen out of her arms. She had no desire to read it. Instead she kept it hidden with the jewelry and the picture of his natural mother. Someday she'd give everything to her son. The book held truths he deserved to know, but its presence made Adie tremble. She had no intention of opening the trunk for a very long time.

Josh opened his Bible to the Psalms. Tonight he needed comfort and he'd find it in the words of David, a man with God's own heart but human inclinations. Josh understood that tug and pull. In Boston he'd been inclined to protect his own pride. He'd been an arrogant fool and he hadn't even known it. Others had, though. As the pages fluttered, he recalled preaching in front of a thousand people. Gerard Richards, the leading evangelist in America, had been in the crowd. Josh had been eager for the man's praise. Instead the famed minister, a stooped man with a squeaky voice, had looked him up and down and said, "You have a gift, young man. But you're full of yourself. You'll be better after you've suffered."

Josh had been insulted.

Now he understood. Emily's flight had knocked him to his knees. He'd fallen even lower when he'd lost everything in a river crossing. It had happened on the Missouri at the peak of the spring flood. The barge pilot had steered into an eddy and lost control. When water lapped the logs, the passengers had all run to the side closest to the shore. The raft tipped, sending everything—people, animals and their possessions—into the racing current.

Josh had made it to shore, but he'd lost the satchel he'd carried from Boston. The clothing could be replaced, but he'd grieved the Bible. It had belonged to his grandfather, the man who'd mentored Josh until he'd died of apoplexy. Even more devastating was the loss of Emily's letter and the tintype she'd had made a few months before she'd revealed her condition. Josh had tucked them in the back of the Bible for safekeeping, but the river had swallowed them whole.

Stripped of his possessions, he'd found work in a livery. That Sunday, he'd preached to a trio of bleary men who'd come for their horses after a night on the town. They'd each given him two bits for his trouble. Josh had put those coins toward the purchase of the Bible in his hands now. The men had come back the following Sunday and they'd brought a few friends. Josh had preached again. He'd used that collection for laudanum.

Recalling that day, he lingered on David's plea to the God who knew his deepest thoughts. He prayed, as he did every night, that the Lord would lead him to Emily. Before the river crossing, he'd shown her picture to everyone he'd met. Now he could only describe her. He missed the letter, too. The night she'd left, she'd put it on top of the sermon notes on his desk. He'd been preaching through the gospel of John and had reached the story of the adulterous woman and Jesus' famous words, "Let him whose slate is clean cast the first stone."

Sermons usually came easily to Josh, but he'd been unable to grasp the underlying message.

Now he knew why. He'd been a hard-boiled hypocrite. When Emily came to him for help, he'd berated her with words that bruised more deeply than rocks. Blinking, he recalled her letter. He'd read it so often he'd memorized it.

> I love you, Josh. But I don't respect you. You judged me for my sins—I admit to them—but you don't know what happened or why. You don't know me or my baby's father and you never will. I'm leaving Boston for good. Someday, Reverend Blue, you'll get knocked off your high horse. I'll pray for you, but I won't weep.
> Your sister, Emily.

That Sunday, Josh had taught on the same passage, but he'd changed the message. Instead of focusing on the woman and Christ's command to go and sin no more, he'd talked about throwing stones. In front of three hundred people, he'd admitted to his mistakes and resigned his position. A broken man, he'd packed a single bag and bought a train ticket. Based on Sarah's knowledge, he'd headed for St. Louis, worrying all the time that Emily would travel farther west. Josh hadn't found her in St. Louis, but he'd spotted a piece of her jewelry in a shop owned by a pawnbroker. It had given him hope. Over the next several months, he'd traveled far and wide.

Someday he'd find Emily. He'd hit his knees and beg for forgiveness. Until then, he had to live with his regrets. Exhausted, he blew out the lamp. As always he prayed for his sister's safety. Tonight, he added Adie Clarke to that list. He couldn't help Emily, but here at Swan's Nest, he saw a chance to do some good. What he couldn't give to Emily, he'd give to Adie Clarke and her friends. The thought put a smile on his face, the first one in a long time.

Chapter Four

"Don't let him inside!"

"I won't," Adie said to Pearl.

The two women were in the front parlor. They'd been on the porch when Pearl had spotted a carriage coming down the street. Terrified of Franklin Dean, she'd run inside with Adie behind her. Together they were peering through the lace curtain at a brougham that belonged to the banker. In the front seat sat Mr. Dean's driver, a stocky man dressed in a frock coat and black bowler.

Adie's gaze skittered to the back of the open carriage where she saw the banker folding a copy of the *Rocky Mountain News*. Some women would have found Mr. Dean handsome. He had dark blond hair, brown eyes, a mustache and what her mother had called a lazy smile, the kind that curled on a man's lips with no effort at all. In Adie's experience, smiles were rare and had to be earned.

She didn't trust Franklin Dean at all. She'd felt uncomfortable the instant they'd met, and those suspicions had been confirmed when she'd heard Pearl's story. A preacher's daughter, Pearl had been engaged to the banker when he'd taken her for a buggy ride. Dean claimed that they'd succumbed to temptation, but Adie knew otherwise. Pearl had told her about that horrible afternoon. She'd protested. She'd pushed him away. He'd pushed back and left her ashamed and carrying his child.

Adie put her arm around Pearl's shoulders. "Go upstairs. I'll see what he wants."

"I can't leave you."

"Yes, you can." Adie made her voice light. False courage, she'd learned, counted for the real thing if no one saw through it.

"But—"

"Go on." Adie pointed Pearl to the stairs. "I can handle Mr. Dean."

The carriage rattled to a stop. With her eyes wide, Pearl stared at the door, then at Adie. "I'll hide in the kitchen. If he tries anything, I'll scream for help. I'll get a knife—" Her voice broke.

Boots tapped on the steps. Adie nudged Pearl down the hall, then inspected herself in the mirror. She'd planned to walk to the business district to pay the mortgage and had already put on her good dress. Thanks to the rent from Reverend Blue, she had enough money for the payment *and* roast beef for supper. She'd put Stephen down for a nap and had been looking forward to a peaceful walk. Quiet afternoons were few and far between. She refused to let Franklin Dean steal her pleasure.

He rapped on the door.

Adie opened it. "Good afternoon, Mr. Dean."

He tipped his hat. "Miss Clarke."

It galled Adie to be pleasant, but riling him would only lead to trouble. She forced a smile. "What can I do for you?"

"May I come in?"

She stepped onto the porch and closed the door. "It's a lovely day. We can speak out here."

His eyes narrowed. "I've come to see Pearl."

"She's not accepting visitors."

"I believe I'm the exception."

No, he was the reason. The July sun burned behind him, turning the street into a strip of dust and giving his face craggy lines. Adie couldn't stand the sight of him. He'd hurt Pearl the way Timothy Long had tried to hurt *her.* He swaggered the way she'd imagined Maggie's brother strutted in his fancy pulpit. She had to convince him to leave.

"Pearl's resting," she said.

"You're lying, Miss Clarke." His lips curled into the lazy smile. "She was sitting by the window."

"How would you know?"

"Am I wrong?"

"It's none of your concern."

Her voice rang with confidence, but her insides were quaking. He'd been too far away to see Pearl through the glass. Had he been watching her house? She thought of the rock that had shattered her bedroom window. Fear gripped her, but she met his gaze as if they were discussing lemonade.

Dean rapped a walking stick against his palm. Over and over, he slapped his own flesh as if he didn't feel a thing. Adie had been beaten with bigger sticks and knew when to keep quiet. She also knew that Franklin Dean wanted to drive her out of Swan's Nest so he could sell the property for a higher price than she'd negotiated with his father. Between silver mines and gold strikes, farms, ranches and the arrival of the railroad, Denver had been dubbed the Queen City of the Plains. Adie's house stood on prime land and Dean wanted it back.

He couldn't have it. She forced herself to appear blasé.

He slapped the walking stick against his palm a final time. Gripping it tight, he smiled as if nothing ugly had passed between them. "I'm rather thirsty, Miss Clarke. I'd enjoy a glass of sweet tea."

"I'm fresh out."

"Water, then."

He wanted to get in the house and corner Pearl. No way would Adie open the door. "I was about to leave for town, Mr. Dean. If you'll excuse me—"

"No, Miss Clarke. I won't excuse you." His eyes burned into hers. "I want to see Pearl."

"Like I said, she's resting."

He glared at her. "The mortgage is due today, isn't it?"

"Yes."

"My timing's excellent," he said. "I'll collect payment and save you the trip to the bank."

"No, thank you." Adie never dealt with Dean when she made her payment. She always visited the same teller, asked for a receipt and stowed it in the trunk. They were that precious to her.

Craning his neck, Dean peered through the lace curtain hanging in the parlor window. Adie turned and followed his gaze to Pearl, her belly large and round, as she peered around the corner and out the window.

He rapped on the glass. "Pearl!"

Startled, the girl slipped back into the hall that led to the kitchen. Dean made a move for the front door, but Adie blocked him. He pivoted, went down the steps and turned down the path that led to the garden behind the house. Adie raced after him.

"Stop!" she cried.

"I have business with Pearl."

"You're trespassing!"

Ignoring her, he strode past the vegetables she'd planted in place of flowers and rounded the corner to the back of the house. He was headed for the door, but he hadn't counted on Joshua Blue blocking his path. The scarecrow in the garden had more meat on its bones, but the reverend had a fire in his eyes that scared Adie to death.

After two days in bed, Bessie's care and a gallon of goat's milk, Josh had felt the need for fresh air. He'd gone out the back door, taken in the garden and stepped into the carriage house. He'd been checking his horse when Pearl had run into the outbuilding. Shaking and out of breath, she'd closed the door and hunkered down behind a partial wall before she'd seen him.

Josh approached as if she were a downed bird. "Are you all right?"

She gasped. "It's Franklin Dean. He—" She burst into tears.

Josh didn't know a thing about Franklin Dean, but he knew about evil men. "Where's Miss Clarke?"

"He tried to get in the house," Pearl said, whimpering. "Adie stopped him."

Josh strode out of the carriage house. As he emerged in the sun, he saw a man headed for the back door of Swan's Nest. Adie was running behind him, ordering him to stop. One look at her face and Josh knew she'd fight this man. Pearl's fear explained why. Her belly testified to a deeper reason, one that made Josh furious. Stifling his anger, he looked the man up and down. The stranger didn't match Josh in height, but he weighed at least fifty pounds more. The difference came from both Josh's belly trouble and the man's indulgence. Whoever he was, he didn't skip dessert.

Josh blocked the path to the back door. "Can I help you, sir?"

"Who are *you?*" the man demanded.

"A guest."

He smirked at Adie. "I thought you didn't rent to men."

"I don't."

Dean huffed. "I see."

"No, sir," Josh said calmly. "You don't *see*. You're trespassing."

"I'm Franklin Dean."

He said it as if he expected Josh to bow down.

Adie interrupted. "Mr. Dean owns Denver National Bank. He holds the note on Swan's Nest."

Josh didn't care if he owned the entire town. "That doesn't give him the right to trespass."

"You have no business here, Mr.—"

"My name is Joshua Blue." Josh spoke with his richest Boston accent. "My family—"

"Has shipping interests," Dean finished.

"Among other things."

Dean's smile turned oily. "What brings you to Denver, sir?" He smelled money and it showed.

Josh found him revolting. "It's a private matter."

The banker's eyes narrowed. "So is my business with Miss Oliver."

Not in Josh's opinion. Her belly made the matter between them public. He didn't know the details, but he knew Pearl feared this man. At the sight of her, he'd recalled Emily and felt all the inclinations of a brother. Looking at Dean now, he wanted to deck the man for his arrogance. He settled for being direct. "It's time for you to leave."

"Not until I speak to Pearl."

Short of violence, Josh didn't see a way to get rid of the man. He'd have to outlast him. Josh had his flaws, but impatience wasn't one of them. He'd spend all afternoon with Dean if meant protecting Adie and her boarders.

"Fine," Josh said. "I'll wait with you on the porch until she's ready."

Dean frowned.

Adie interrupted. "I have a better idea, Mr. Dean. I'll tell Pearl you're concerned about her health."

"I am."

"If she's up for a visit, I'll send word to you."

Josh watched the banker's face. He didn't want to leave, but Adie had given him a way out that saved his pride.

"Very well," Dean said. "When you bring your loan payment, I'll expect a note from Pearl."

Adie gave a crisp nod. "I'll speak with her."

Dean glared at Josh, tipped his hat to Adie and walked down the path to the street. Josh followed him with his eyes, watching as he batted at a weed with his walking stick. When he rounded the corner, Josh turned to Adie. When he'd seen her chasing after Dean, she'd reminded him of a robin chasing down a worm. Now, in spite of the sun on her reddish hair, she looked subdued.

Josh raked his hand through his hair. "He's trouble, isn't he?"

"The worst kind."

"If there's anything I can do—"

"There isn't."

As she straightened her spine, Josh noticed her gown. Instead of the brown dress she usually wore, she'd put on a blue calico that made him think of the ocean. Adie Clarke, he decided, had the same sense of mystery. She seemed calm on the surface, but unseen currents churned in her hazel eyes and turned them green in acknowledgment of the dress.

The door to the carriage house creaked open. Pearl peeked from behind the heavy wood. "Is he gone?"

Adie hurried to her friend's side. "He just left."

"Good riddance!"

Josh thought so, too.

Adie put her arm around Pearl's huge waist. "If you'll excuse us, Reverend. Pearl needs to lie down."

"Of course." Except Adie had a need as well. She had to

deliver the mortgage payment. Josh decided he needed a walk. He fell into step with the women, held the door and followed them inside.

Adie gave him a harsh look. "Do you need something, Reverend?"

"No, but you do."

"I can't imagine what."

Josh liked her spirit. After the ordeal with Dean, some women—and men—would have been cowering in the closet. Not Adie Clarke. She'd walk on hot coals for someone she loved. So would Josh. Adie wasn't Emily, but for now he could treat her like a sister. "I'm going with you to the bank."

"That's not necessary."

Pearl dropped onto a chair. She looked exhausted. "He's right, Adie. You shouldn't go alone."

"And I need the fresh air," Josh added.

"But your shoulder—"

"It's much improved." He rolled his arm to test it. His belly still hurt, but he didn't pay attention. It *always* hurt, and it would until he found Emily.

Adie looked annoyed, an expression Josh found refreshing. In Boston, the members of his church had deferred to him. On the open trail, outlaws had put up with him. Adie didn't belong in either camp. She treated him with common sense, as if he were an ordinary man. He also admired her sweetness with Pearl. In spite of the pressure from Dean, she hadn't asked her friend to write a note.

Pearl looked at Josh. "She's stubborn."

He smiled. "I noticed."

"I am not." Adie wrinkled her brow. "I don't need company to go to the bank. Besides, I have errands to run."

"Good." Josh hooked his thumbs in the trousers. "I need to pick up a few things, like suspenders."

He'd hoped to lighten the mood and it worked. Pearl patted her tummy. "I don't have *that* problem."

When her friend smiled, Adie's face lit up with pleasure. "I'll bring you some peppermint candy. Would you like that?"

Pearl's eyes brightened. "I'd love some. It settles my stomach."

Josh had known expectant mothers in Boston. They'd all been wealthy and married, secure in love and protected by their husbands. Franklin Dean had robbed this sweet girl of that sanctuary. Someone else had robbed Adie of a husband. Emily had been robbed, too. Josh felt good about escorting Adie to town. He couldn't change the past, but he could help these women in the here-and-now.

"It's settled," he said. "I'm going with you to the bank."

Adie frowned. "You're pushier than Mr. Dean."

"Only for a good cause, Miss Clarke."

She sighed. "If you insist, but—"

Pearl interrupted. "*I* insist. This is all my fault."

Adie put her hands on her hips. "*Nothing* is your fault, Pearl. Do you understand?"

"Yes." Except she looked down at her toes.

Josh's mind flashed back to Emily asking to speak with him in his study. Like Pearl, she'd mumbled and stared at her feet. Josh would regret his first words until his dying day. He'd called his own sister a foul name. He'd ordered her to give the baby away. And for what? His pride…his reputation. What a hypocrite he'd been. In truth, he'd committed worse sins than Emily. By condemning her, he'd denied her the very mercy Christ had shown him and every other man.

Looking at Adie and Pearl, he felt the full weight of his failings. Men had a duty to protect the women they loved. Mothers. Sisters. Wives. He'd failed on two counts. Not only had he harmed Emily, but his mother had died two years ago when he'd been numb with laudanum. If he'd been clear-headed, he might have convinced her to see a doctor for her dizzy spells. As for the third kind of woman—a wife—Josh had vowed to never marry. Without a wife and children, he could pursue his work every minute of the day.

Even without the inclination to marry, he felt protective toward all females. That included Adie and her friends…especially Adie. Annoyed by the thought, he pushed it aside. So what if he liked red hair? He had a call on his life, and that would never change.

"I'll get my coat," he said to the women.

He went to his room, where he lifted the garment off a nail and put it on. After Adie made the payment, he'd excuse himself for a bath and a haircut. At the barber, he'd ask about pawnbrokers.

He went to the entry hall, where he saw Adie at a mirror, tying the ribbons of her bonnet. She'd lifted her chin, giving it a defiant tilt. She looked too young to be a mother, but Stephen was living proof. As she gave the ribbons a tug, Josh found himself admiring the way she faced problems. She didn't duck the truth, neither did she shy away from facts that couldn't be denied. He wished he'd had a friend like Adie in Boston, someone who'd have made him look in the mirror as she was looking in it now.

"I'm ready," he said.

"Me, too." She lifted a drawstring bag and clutched it with both hands.

Josh opened the door and let her pass. It had been a long time since a woman's skirt had brushed over his boots. In Boston, he'd put that awareness out of his mind. He tried to do it now but couldn't. Losing Emily had made him conscious of the simple things women did to soften a man's hard edges, things like smiling and noticing flowers.

As he followed Adie through the front door, he took in the walkway and manicured shrubs. He'd arrived at Swan's Nest in the dark and hadn't noticed the surrounding area. Another mansion stood catty-corner across the street. As they walked down the road, he saw a third home. Set back on a large parcel of land, it was half-demolished. He wrinkled his brow in surprise. "Why is it being destroyed? The house looks almost new."

"It's five years old."

"Seems like a waste."

Adie stared straight ahead. "It is, unless you plan to build five houses in place of one."

Josh put the pieces together. "That's why Dean's harassing you. He wants Swan's Nest so he can tear it down."

"That's right."

She glanced at the demolished remains, now three hills of ragged gray stone. "Mr. Dean bought that house last month. I knew the couple who owned it."

"What happened?"

"Bad investments." Her lips tightened. "The husband owned a silver mine. When it went dry, they lost everything."

"And Dean bought the house."

"For a song."

Josh thought of his cousin in Boston. Elliot liked money, but he wasn't a squirrel about it. He gave away as much as he kept. Sometimes more. A little competition might do Dean some good.

"Tell me more," Josh said.

"That's all I know." Adie made a show of inhaling and raising her face to the sun. "It's a beautiful day."

Small talk couldn't get any smaller than the weather. Josh gave her a sideways glance and saw the set of her jaw. In his experience, people were quick to talk about news and scandals. Considering Dean's visit and the demolished house, he found the change in subject odd, even suspicious, but he followed her lead.

"Summer here is dry," he said. "It's quite a change from Boston."

"I'd imagine so."

Was it his imagination, or did she look frightened? As they passed a third mansion, a stone monstrosity with turrets and a flat roof, she changed the subject again. She told him about the vegetables she'd planted and why she preferred beans to squash. In other words, she told him nothing. Women usually bragged on their children. Adie didn't mention her son once. Neither did she breathe a hint of how she'd come to Denver.

Josh knew about secrets. He'd kept his own. He'd also ridden with men who said nothing and others who told lies. Adie was intent on building a wall of words. Josh didn't mind. After months of gruff male talk, he was enjoying the singsong quality of her voice and the simple pleasure of walking by gardens filled with flowers.

As they neared the heart of Denver, her chatter faded to stray comments about the shops. She stopped talking altogether when they reached a church. Made of rusticated stone, the building had a tall bronze steeple and massive stained glass windows. He'd never seen such beautiful work, not even in Europe. He looked at the pitch of the roof and imagined a vaulted ceiling and the echo of a choir. He blinked and saw mahogany pews filled with people. He pictured a podium carved with an eagle. He'd used such a podium in Boston. He'd never use one again, but he could appreciate the beauty of the church simply as a man.

He glanced at the double doors, then at Adie. "Let's go inside."

"No, thank you." She clipped the words.

Josh would respect her wishes, but he needed to open the door for himself. He turned up the steps. "I'll just be a minute."

She kept walking.

The church could wait. Adie couldn't. He caught up to her in three strides and saw a glint in her eyes.

"What's wrong?" he asked.

"It's none of your business."

Josh had used the same tone when a church elder questioned him about the laudanum. "I don't mean to pry—"

"Then don't."

"You seem upset."

"Upset?" Her expression turned murderous. "Franklin Dean goes to that church. Pearl's father is the pastor."

He knew that Dean had harmed Pearl. Even if a woman welcomed a man's advances, he had an obligation to protect her, to say no for both of them until the benefit of marriage. As for Pearl's father, had he shunned his daughter the way Josh had rejected Emily? He needed to know. If he could spare Pearl a minute of suffering, he'd tell his story to her father.

"Tell me more," he said to Adie.

She stopped in midstride. When she looked into Josh's eyes, he knew he'd hear the truth and it would hurt.

"He raped her," she said in a dry whisper. "They were engaged. He took her on a buggy ride and he forced her."

Emily's face, tearstained and afraid, flashed in front of his eyes.

"Go on," he said.

Adie's voice quavered. "The next day, Dean went to Pearl's father. He 'confessed' that they'd gone too far and asked for permission to marry her immediately. Reverend Oliver ordered her into the parlor. He made her stand there and listen to that *snake* apologize. Her own father acted as if she'd been as sinful as Dean."

A year ago Josh hadn't listened to a word Emily said. He still didn't know who'd fathered her child, if she'd been raped or seduced by a scoundrel. Maybe she'd been in love. Josh had stayed beyond such feelings until the disastrous river crossing. Cold and shivering, he'd watched husbands and wives cling to each other, sharing tears and kisses. That night, he'd known the deepest loneliness of his life.

Looking at Adie Clarke, he felt that loneliness again. She had a way of standing up to people, including men like himself. He liked her spirit and wondered how it would feel to have her fighting at his side. He blocked the thought in an instant. He had no interest in marriage, no plans to settle down. He had to find Emily.

Adie's cheeks had faded back to ivory. "Pearl left home that night. I found her the next morning, throwing up in my garden."

"Did she ever tell her father?"

"She tried, but he wouldn't listen."

Poor fool, Josh thought. "He needs to know."

Adie huffed. "He said what happened was private and he didn't want the whole church gossiping about his daughter. He told her to get married and keep quiet."

Josh grimaced. "Dean committed a crime. What about the law?"

Adie glared at him. "Who'd believe her? They were engaged. She went with him willingly. Alone."

"But—"

"But nothing." Her cheeks flamed again. "Franklin Dean owns half of Denver. That's why he's still on the elder board. People are afraid to confront him, even the other elders. I don't know if *Reverend* Oliver tried to get him thrown off or not, but I doubt it. From what I can see, he cares more about his reputation than his daughter."

The same shoe fit Josh. "I see."

"Do you, Reverend Blue?"

He bristled. "I know about sin, Miss Clarke. I've seen arrogance, greed and male pride. None of it's pretty."

Her expression hardened. "You don't know what it's like to be Pearl. I do."

Her eyes turned shiny and she blinked. Josh had seen women cry. He'd visited sick beds and spoken at funerals, but he'd never been alone with a woman's tears except for the night he shunned Emily. He'd pushed his own sister away, but the urge to hold Adie flashed like lightning. It startled him. The lingering thunder unnerved him even more. A reaction, he told himself… A man's instinct to protect a woman and nothing more. He settled for offering his handkerchief.

"No, thank you." Adie frowned at the monogrammed linen. "I shouldn't have told you about Pearl."

"I'm not naive," he said gently. "My sister got in trouble, too."

Adie paced down the street, almost running to put distance between them. Josh didn't understand her reaction. She'd already revealed the truth of her son's birth, and he hadn't judged her for it.

He wanted to ask her about Emily, but he knew she wouldn't answer. Instead he caught up to her and walked in silence, recalling the times he'd asked strangers if they'd seen his sister. Most said no without thinking. He'd learned to ask less obvious questions. That's how he'd traced Emily to Kansas City. He'd shown her picture to a clerk in a St. Louis pawnbrokerage. The man had shaken his head. Later he'd recalled a woman asking for directions to the train station.

The bank loomed on their right.

"We're here," Adie said.

He stepped ahead of her and held the door. As he followed her inside, he saw a teller cage, a cherrywood counter and a clerk in a white shirt. To the right, a waist-high railing surrounded a massive desk. A leather chair resembled an empty throne, and a low shelf boasted artwork. Josh found himself staring at marble sculptures depicting Greek gods, cherubs and women. The mix made him uneasy. Franklin Dean was nowhere in sight, so he stood back as Adie made the payment.

As she tucked the receipt in her bag, he guided her to the door. The instant it closed behind them, she looked jubilant.

"Thank you, Reverend."

"For what?"

"Your rent helped to pay my mortgage."

She made him feel like an errant knight. "My pleasure, Miss Clarke."

"I'm making a roast for supper. I hope you'll join us."

Her hazel eyes shone with happiness. Josh liked roast, but he liked this woman even more. Common sense told him to avoid Adie and her autumn eyes, but supper would give him a chance to ask her boarders about Emily.

"I'd be grateful," he replied.

Concern wrinkled her brow. "Is your stomach strong enough? I could make you a custard."

Babies ate custard. Men ate meat. As kind as it was, Adie's offer irked him. "My digestion's much better."

"Good."

Having supper with five ladies made a bath a priority. "If you'll excuse me, I need to run an errand of my own."

"Of course."

As Adie retraced her steps down Colfax Avenue, Josh headed for the part of town where he'd find a bathhouse among saloons and gaming halls. Tomorrow he'd come back to this sorry place and ask about his sister, praying he'd find her and hoping it wouldn't be in an upstairs room.

Maybe she'd found a sanctuary like Swan's Nest. The thought cheered him. It also raised questions. Adie's dress, a calico with a high neck and plain buttons, spoke of a simple life. She worked hard to care for her boarders. How had she come to own a mansion, especially one with the air of old money? She kept one parlor closed, but the other had a marble hearth, cornices and wall sconces. An oriental rug protected the hardwood floor, and the latest flowery wallpaper lined the hall. While most of the Denver mansions were made of stone, someone had spent a fortune to haul in wood for siding.

Most notable of all, a stained glass window adorned the entry hall. Round and wide, it depicted a white swan with an arched neck floating on a lake of blue glass. Swan's Nest struck Josh as a perfect name, especially considering its owner and her female guests. Tonight he'd eat a home-cooked meal in the company of good women. They'd chatter, and he'd listen to their birdsong voices. He wouldn't be lonely for conversation, and he might glean news of Emily.

Two hours later, Franklin Dean entered the bank he'd inherited from his father. A review of the day's business showed Adie Clarke's payment. Irritated, he summoned Horace, his driver, and left for the Denver Gentlemen's Club.

As usual, he'd eat supper alone. He blamed the unfortunate state of his evening on Pearl. Didn't she know how much he loved her? He'd die for her. Sometimes, like this afternoon when he'd seen the foolish preacher at Swan's Nest, he thought he could kill for her.

He hoped the circumstances wouldn't come to that. He knew from experience that dead bodies raised questions. He hadn't meant to strangle Winnie Peters, but she'd started to scream. Why had she done that? Frank didn't know, and he didn't care. He'd left her body in a ravine and paid Horace to remove her belongings from the hotel. No one missed her. She'd come to Denver alone and hadn't made friends.

As the carriage passed through town, Frank considered today's visit to Swan's Nest. It hadn't gone well, and he'd missed Adie's visit to the bank. If it weren't for her, Pearl would be living at the parsonage. By now, her father would have forced her to marry him. Instead she'd found refuge in a mansion that should have belonged to the bank.

Frank scowled at his father's shortsightedness. Swan's Nest was on Seventeenth Street, a dirt road that led to the outskirts of Denver. As the city grew, that street would fill with businesses. In a few years, the land would be worth thousands of dollars. Frank's father had sold the mansion for a song, and Frank wanted it back.

He had to get rid of Adie Clarke and he had to do it soon, before Pearl had the baby and his son was born without his name.

"Horace?"

"Yes, sir?"

"Do you recall the job I asked you to do last month?"

"Of course, sir."

Frank had asked his driver to send Miss Clarke a message, so Horace had thrown a rock through her bedroom window. Miss Clarke had replaced the glass and said nothing, not even to the sheriff.

"It didn't accomplish what I'd hoped," Frank said.

"Another plan, sir?"

He thought of the garden he'd seen on the side of the house. A smirk curled his lips. "I believe Miss Clarke's vegetables need attention."

"Yes, sir."

Horace stopped the carriage in front of the Denver Gentlemen's Club. Frank exited the rig, then pressed a shiny silver dollar into his driver's hand.

Horace's eyes gleamed. "Thank you, sir."

With his walking stick in hand, Frank entered the club where he'd find fine food and drink. Tonight he had everything he needed…except Pearl. Only Adie Clarke stood in his way.

Chapter Five

"Good evening, ladies. May I join you?"

Adie had been about to carve the roast when she looked up and saw Reverend Blue, tall and lean in a black coat and preacher's collar, standing in the doorway. His cheeks gleamed with a close shave and his hair, dark with a slight wave, wisped back from his forehead. Adie nearly dropped the carving knife. The drifter who'd fainted on her porch was nowhere in sight. In his place stood a gentleman. His eyes, clear and bright, shone with mirth. He'd surprised her, and he knew it.

He'd surprised her boarders, too. Pearl's face had turned as pale as her white-blond hair. Mary, her cheeks red with anger, glared at him. Bessie beamed a smile, while Caroline stared as if she'd never seen a handsome man before.

Adie was as tongued-tied as Caroline but for different reasons. While walking to the bank, she'd chirped like a cricket to stop him from asking questions about Stephen. She'd kept her focus until they'd reached Colfax Avenue Church. She hated that building as much as she loved Swan's Nest. She felt that way about all churches, especially ones led by men like Reverend Honeycutt and Maggie Butler's brother.

Looking at Reverend Blue, she didn't see the trappings of such a man, but still felt more comfortable with the drifter.

She indicated the chair on her right. "Please join us."

As he approached, she glanced around the table. If he asked questions, her boarders would answer truthfully. The thought terrified her. They all knew she'd adopted Stephen after the death of a friend, but she'd never breathed Maggie's name. As slim as the details were, Adie didn't want a stranger, especially a preacher, knowing her business.

She positioned the meat fork, lifted the knife and sliced into the roast with too much force. As the cut went askew, the blade cracked against the platter.

Still standing, Reverend Blue indicated the roast. "May I?"

Caroline broke in. "Please do, Reverend."

Irritated, Adie set down the knife and took her seat, watching as his fingers, long and tanned by the sun, curved around the handle. Maggie's hands had been pale, but her fingers had been just as tapered. As he cut the meat into precise slices, her nerves prickled with an undeniable fact. Joshua Blue had carved a hundred roasts. Like Maggie, he'd sipped from fine crystal and knew which fork to use. Her stomach lurched. In the same breath, she ordered herself to be logical. Lots of men knew the proper way to carve meat.

Reverend Blue arranged the last slice on the platter and sat to her right. Adie had no interest in saying grace, but Bessie insisted on keeping the tradition. Tonight the older woman looked at their guest. "Would you give the blessing, Reverend?"

"I'd be honored." He bowed his head. *"Lord, we thank You for this meal, good friends and the gift of your son. Amen."*

He finished the prayer before Adie even folded her hands. Either he was hungry or he respected a woman's effort to serve hot food. She appreciated his quick words. Old Man Long's prayers had been lengthy and harrowing. She'd paid dearly for tonight's meal and wanted to eat it hot.

As she handed him the green beans, Caroline indicated the meat platter. "Take plenty, Reverend. You're still thin from your illness."

He blanked his expression, but Adie caught a hint of annoyance. No man liked being called scrawny, and that's what Caroline had done. He thanked her but still took a reasonable portion.

Bessie spoke over the plink of serving spoons. "How's your shoulder, Reverend?"

"Much better," he answered.

"You were in poor shape the last time we all met. Perhaps introductions are in order."

He glanced around the table. "I know Miss Clarke, and you're Miss—"

"Call me Bessie."

"Bessie it is."

Caroline said her name and beamed a smile. Mary answered with a scowl but introduced herself. Pearl, staring at her belly, spoke in a hush. They'd each offered their given names, expect for Adie. Reverend Blue turned in her direction. Not wanting to be different from the others, she shrugged. "You know my name. It's Adie."

"Short for Adelaide?"

"Yes."

He hadn't questioned the others about their names. Why her?

Caroline handed him the bowl of potatoes. "Where are you from, Reverend?"

"Boston. And you?"

"Virginia."

He turned back to Adie. "You're not from either of those places. I'd guess Missouri."

She would have lied, but her boarders knew bits of her history. "I was born in Kansas."

His interest was piqued. "When did you leave home?"

"Years ago."

He meant Kansas, but Adie thought of "home" as her mother's farm. Her stomach twisted. If Reverend Blue kept quizzing her, she wouldn't be able to eat. She sliced a bit of roast and started to chew. With her mouth full, she wouldn't have to answer his questions.

He lowered his fork. "This might be a good time to explain why I'm in Colorado. I'm looking for my sister."

Adie almost choked.

"She left home ten months ago."

"What's her name?" Caroline asked.

"Emily Blue."

The name meant nothing to Adie. Her stomach settled until the reverend drilled her with his eyes. "Emily was last seen in Kansas City, but I know she bought a train ticket for somewhere else."

Caroline turned to Adie. "Didn't you come here from Kansas City?"

Adie wanted to gag her with the napkin. Instead she blanked her face. "That's only where I got on the train. I was raised on a farm."

"But you've been there," Caroline insisted.

Adie tried to look bored. "It's a big city, Caroline. *Lots* of people pass through."

Mary gave Adie a sideways glance. Of all her boarders, she had the least in common with the former saloon girl, but that changed in a blink. Mary, too, lived with a secret. She saw the trepidation in Adie's expression and looked at the reverend.

"Your sister could be anywhere," she said. "The railroad goes to San Francisco now, or she could have gone to Chicago."

"That's true," he answered. "But I can't give up. I have to know she's safe, even happy."

Adie thought of how he'd considered Stephen's empty belly before the bleeding hole in his own shoulder. He couldn't possibly be the cruel man who'd driven Maggie from Boston.

He looked into her eyes. "It's worse than I've admitted. When Emily left Boston, she was unmarried and with child."

He'd said Emily, not Maggie. Except Adie recalled the day she'd met Stephen's mother. *I'm Maggie Butler now.* Adie had heard "now" and wondered about her past. Her friend, she realized, had changed her name. Adie risked a glance at Joshua Blue, saw Maggie's nose and decided fear was making her see things. She had to change the subject. "How's the roast?"

"Delicious," Mary replied.

Caroline snapped at her. "How can you think about food? I'm worried about Emily Blue."

"And the baby," Pearl whispered.

The reverend turned back to Adie. What did he see? She'd have sold her soul to protect Stephen, but she couldn't lie worth beans. Blood rushed to her cheeks.

"I'm desperate," he said to her. "Emily and I parted with unkind words. It was my fault."

Tremors raced from Adie's chest to her hands. Her throat went dry and the room started to spin. She needed water but didn't dare lift the goblet for fear of spilling it.

Bessie interrupted. "What will you do when you find her?"

"I'll take her home."

"And the baby?" Mary asked.

"Of course."

Pearl raised her chin. "What if she doesn't want to go?"

"I won't force her," he answered. "But I hope she'll listen to reason."

Adie knew all about "reason." Reverend Honeycutt had deemed it *reasonable* for her to leave Liddy's Grove while Timothy Long got nothing but a talking-to. She'd had to fight him off and had earned bruised ribs in the effort. Fuming, she managed a bite of bread.

Caroline's plate sat untouched. "What do you know about the baby's father?"

"Nothing."

"I hope you find her," Bessie said. "A single woman could have a hard time, especially with a baby. Do you have a picture of her?"

Adie went pale.

"Not anymore," he said. "I lost it in a river crossing."

The women mumbled condolences, even Adie though she felt like a liar. She was glad he'd lost the likeness of his sister. Without a picture she could dismiss the similarities between Emily and Maggie as coincidence. At least that's what she wanted to believe. In truth, she was already telling lies. Reverend Blue didn't have a picture of his sister, but Adie had one of Maggie Butler. The tintype, brownish in color, showed an oval of Maggie's face and was framed by white cardboard.

The picture had the potential to end this man's search. If Maggie and Emily were the same woman, it also had the power to rob Adie of her son. Concealing it made her feel dishonest, but she'd made a promise to Maggie. No matter the cost, she had to protect Stephen from his uncle.

"Adie?" Bessie's voice broke into her thoughts. "The reverend asked you a question."

"Your son," he repeated. "What's his name?"

"Stephen."

His eyes turned wistful. "That was my grandfather's name."

How many coincidences could she ignore? Desperate to avoid more questions, she raised her water glass to her lips and took a long sip. The liquid went down the wrong pipe and she choked.

"Raise your arms," Bessie ordered.

The coughing racked Adie's body. Bessie and Reverend Blue both shot to their feet. He was closer and reached her first. Both gentle and strong, he gripped her shoulder and thumped her back.

"I'm—" *Fine.* She choked again.

He patted harder.

Adie shoved to her feet. She needed air that didn't smell like roast and darkness that would hide her eyes as she weighed the facts. She signaled that she could breathe, then headed for the porch, where she coughed until tears streamed down her cheeks.

Josh hadn't meant to upset Adie. Since the trip to the bank, he'd figured she and Emily had walked a similar road. Now he was sure of it. Had she been shunned by her family? How had she come to own Swan's Nest? He also wondered about the father of her child. Any man worth his salt would have married her. Josh wasn't naive about the force of nature. He'd performed a shotgun wedding in Boston and two others since coming west.

He'd have performed one for Emily if he'd had the opportunity. Looking back, he saw signs that she'd been keeping a secret. For years she'd volunteered one day a week at the Greenway Home for Orphans. A few months before their argument, she'd been working three days a week and staying late. One day he'd expected her to be visiting Sarah and had paid a call. Sarah had been home, but Emily hadn't been with her. Three hours later she'd arrived home flushed and vibrant.

"Where were you, Emily?"

"Visiting friends."

"Who?"

"You don't know them."

It had been a clue, and Josh had missed it. He wished now that he'd shown more concern.

He wouldn't repeat that mistake with Adie. He wanted her to know he wouldn't throw stones. Even more important, God loved her. Because of her generosity, the ulcer had started to heal. He wanted to return the favor with food for her soul. He pushed to his feet. "If you'll excuse me, I'd like to speak to Adie."

"Of course," Bessie answered.

He filled Adie's water glass, then carried it to the porch, where he found her on the swing. He'd intended to call her Miss Clarke, but the name no longer fit. In his mind she'd become a friend, a sister like Emily.

"Adie?"

"Yes?" She sounded hoarse.

"I brought you water."

As she sipped, he ambled to the railing. The moon and stars bathed the porch in silver light. When he turned around, he saw Adie's watery eyes. Choking did that to a person, but she looked distraught for deeper reasons. He gentled his voice. "I'd like to tell you about Emily."

"Why?"

"Because you two have something in common."

Tears glistened on her cheeks. She looked terrified.

Guilt stabbed through Josh's chest. Had Emily sat on a similar swing, weeping with shame for what she'd done? He blinked and thought of the women of Swan's Nest. Pearl hadn't once looked up from her plate. Mary had scowled at him all through supper, a sign that she, too, had resentments. Bessie and Caroline looked like sisters who'd walked a hard road. Mostly, though, he wondered about Adie. The thought tripped him like a wire. He didn't want her to be special, but she was. She'd fixed his meals and offered him milk. She had a baby who needed a father, a kind heart and a head full of red hair that defied combs and pins.

Josh had never looked for a wife, nor had he met a woman who inspired such thoughts, at least not until now. Blinking, he flashed back to the times he'd hidden his laudanum bottle. If Adie had found it, she'd have spoken her mind and tossed it in the trash. She'd have held his feet to the fire in a way no one else had dared. Looking at her now, he wondered what it would be like to love a strong-minded woman.

Two seconds later, he squared his shoulders inside his coat and called himself a fool. Only Adie mattered tonight. Later he'd deal with his wayward thoughts. Hoping to appear relaxed, he leaned against the railing and got back to telling Adie about his sister. "Among other things, you and Emily are both alone."

Her lip quivered.

"You both lost families, either by choice or cruelty."

"You're right."

He barely heard the whisper. "I also know you're brave and kind. So is Emily."

She knotted her hands in her lap to hide the trembling. He couldn't stand being her enemy. "I don't know who hurt you, Adie. But I know God loves you."

"God?" Her mouth gaped.

"He's all-powerful. He's—"

"You came out here to talk about *God?*"

"Not exactly."

"Then why?"

"I could see Emily's story upset you."

"Just a little."

It had been a lot, but he let her keep her dignity. "People

judge a single woman with a child. I know, because I judged my sister. I'll regret it to my dying day."

"Don't pity me, Reverend."

She spat his title. If she didn't respect it, he didn't want her to use it. "Call me Josh."

She glared at him.

"Why not?" he asked. "It's my name."

"All right," she murmured. "I'll call you Josh."

He liked the hush of it, the way it hung between them like fog. In Boston, he'd avoided being alone with women. When he made calls, he'd brought his sister. He didn't feel that need with Adie. They were equals.

"You remind me of Emily," he said.

"How so?"

"In spite of being robbed of something, you both put others first. My sister worked in an orphanage. You take care of your boarders."

"Of course I do. They're my friends."

"It's more than that," he said. "I hurt Emily, but she didn't crawl into a hole and feel sorry for herself. She came west to make a new life. You've done the same, Adie. You're both survivors."

She put her hand to her mouth and coughed. "If you'll excuse me, I should do the dishes."

Josh had pressed her as far as he could. "I'll help."

She stood. "No, thank you."

"Really, I'd like—"

"No," she insisted. "You're a paying guest."

Josh knew about drawing lines. This one annoyed him. From what he'd observed, Adie worked harder than the Blue family servants. "Your other boarders help. So can I."

She looked peeved. "Not tonight."

"Then tomorrow."

"Fine." She stood and headed for the door. When she reached the threshold, she turned. Her shadow spoke to him in a hush. "I hope you find your sister."

"So do I."

She stepped into the house, leaving behind the scent of rosewater. Josh hadn't smelled rosewater in years. It took him back to his mother's sitting room where she'd read stories to Josh and Emily every night.

His sister felt close, or was it Adie's presence he sensed? Josh didn't know, but he had a confession to make. Deep down, he envied Adie Clarke. She had a home and a son, good friends and a belly that didn't hurt. Tonight she'd sleep in a clean bed. Tomorrow she'd bake bread. In the past year, Josh had ridden in the rain, slept in muddy caves and eaten snake for supper. He lived with an ulcer and a craving for opium. Like the Apostle Paul, he'd learned how to abase and abound, how to live well or humbly depending on the Lord's provision.

He wanted to say that he'd learned to be content in all things, Paul's declaration to the Philippians, but he couldn't make that claim. Tonight he felt a longing for the soft timbre of Adie's voice. He liked her far more than was wise for a man destined to leave. With an emptiness he didn't want to admit, he sat in the swing, bowed his head and prayed for Adie, Emily and all the women of Swan's Nest, but especially for Adie.

Adie went to the kitchen, saw that her friends had done the dishes and headed to her room. She needed to hold her son to chase away thoughts of Emily Blue. As she climbed the stairs, she thought about Josh's description of his sister and how he'd compared Adie to Emily, calling them both survivors. Maggie had called herself a survivor with pride. Adie would have described her just as Josh had described his sister. Her friend had overcome everything except death.

As Adie neared her bedroom, she heard a creak from down the hall. She turned and saw Pearl looking pale and afraid.

"Are you okay?" Adie asked.

"Can I speak with you?"

"Of course." She went to her room with Pearl, lit the lamp and checked Stephen. His little chest rose and fell in a soothing rhythm. No colic tonight. Relieved, she turned to the bed where Pearl was lying on her side to ease the pressure on her back. She looked as round as the moon.

"I'm scared," she said.

"Of what?"

"Giving birth."

"You'll do fine." Adie sounded confident, but she knew the risks. So did Pearl.

"I want you to promise me something."

Adie flashed to Maggie lying on soiled sheets. Ashen and weak, she'd made the same request as Pearl. She'd asked Adie for a promise. "What is it?"

"If something happens to me—"

"It won't."

"It could and we both know it." Pearl sounded strong, even wise. "If I don't survive the birth, I want you to give the baby to my father. I don't want Frank to even *see* my child."

Adie gripped her hand. "I promise."

"My father's a good man."

Adie wasn't so sure. Reverend Oliver had taken Dean's word over his daughter's. He struck her as stern, but Pearl loved him. "I'll do whatever you ask."

"Thank you." Pearl tightened her grip. "I'm scared."

"It's natural."

"There's more," she said. "Tonight at supper, I saw the reverend's expression when he talked about his sister. He won't stop until he finds her."

Adie thought of Josh's words on the porch. "You're right."

"As long as I'm in Denver, Frank won't leave me alone. If I left—"

"Don't even think about it." Adie recalled her earliest days with Stephen. She'd had Maggie's jewelry but no friends. No mother to take a turn rocking the colicky child. No husband to shoulder the load of food and shelter. "Being alone is harder than you know."

Pearl rested her hand on her belly. "But if I left, no one would know me. I'd have some peace."

"Maybe," Adie said gently. "But you'd have other problems, like paying rent and buying food." *And living a lie.*

Pearl sighed. "Do you think Frank would follow me?"

"I don't know."

"I *hate* it here." Her voice wobbled. "People think the baby is my fault, but he forced me. He—" She clenched her teeth, but tears still rose to her eyes.

Adie gripped Pearl's hand in understanding. Timothy Long had abused her in the Long family's attic, but she'd escaped with her purity and a shred of pride. Thanks to Maggie Butler, she'd been given a fresh start. Pearl deserved the same chance. Adie flashed on the jewelry in the trunk. Maggie would have approved of giving Pearl a nest egg, but Adie couldn't risk selling even a brooch. If the Butler family had hired a detective, pawnbrokers would be the first place he'd look for clues.

Pearl heaved a sigh. "Maybe I'll write to my cousin. She might take me in."

"Where is she?"

"Wyoming." Pearl told Adie about Carrie Hart, the daughter of her mother's sister. Carrie was about Pearl's age. When her parents passed away last year, she'd chosen to stay in Cheyenne where she taught at Miss Marlowe's School for Girls. Pearl hadn't confided in Carrie, but they exchanged occasional letters, and she knew her cousin missed having family close by.

Adie liked her. "Going to Wyoming might be smart."

"Maybe." Pearl bit her lip. "I'd still have to earn money somehow."

"If someone could watch the baby, you could teach."

"Or I could sew at home."

Neither occupation would give Pearl security, but she'd have her dignity.

"Think about it," Adie advised.

"I've been praying for *months*." Pearl wrinkled her brows. "God isn't answering."

Adie knew the feeling.

"I believe, though." Pearl wiggled to a sitting position. "And I like Reverend Blue. You have to admire a man who cares so much about his sister."

"I suppose."

"He's handsome, too."

Adie's cheeks turned pink. "I didn't notice."

"Caroline did." Pearl's eyes twinkled. "She's looking through her recipe book this very minute. She's going to bake him a pie."

The thought irked Adie beyond reason. With his weak stomach, Josh needed simple food, not a crust made from lard. Even more upsetting was the possibility that he'd like Caroline and her pie. What if he stayed in Denver? She thought of Caroline charming him and frowned. "I wish she wouldn't do it."

"Why not?"

"He doesn't belong here."

"I'm glad for it." Pearl patted her belly. "I'm as big as a horse. I might as well eat like one."

Adie smiled. "You don't look anything like a horse. You're beautiful."

With her pale hair and blue eyes, porcelain cheeks and perfect nose, Pearl had the luster of her name. She also had tears in her eyes as she touched the hard roundness of the baby.

"I'm ruined, Adie. What man would want me now?"

"A very special one."

"Do you really think there *is* such a man?"

"I do."

For the second time that night, Adie had lied. She'd told Josh she hoped he found his sister. She did, but only if the woman wasn't Maggie Butler. As for Pearl's question, Adie doubted a man that special walked the earth.

Pearl yawned. "I'm off to bed."

As the women stood and hugged, Adie felt Pearl's belly and thought of Maggie. What would she say about Swan's Nest? Adie hoped she'd be proud.

Thoughts of Stephen's mother led to an awareness of the trunk. As soon as Pearl left, Adie looked at the walnut case with its brass lock. Did Maggie's picture hold the answer to Josh's search? Adie didn't know and was afraid to find out. For now, the trunk would keep its secrets.

Chapter Six

Five days later, a noise in Adie's garden woke Josh from a fitful sleep. Living among outlaws had made him wise to danger and he felt that prickle now. He pushed aside the blanket, dressed and strode down the hall to the back door.

A sweet fragrance made him wince. Caroline had baked another pie, her third this week. Josh had endured baking sprees before, but he'd never been caught under the same roof as the woman doing the baking. Not once in Boston had he felt even a spark of interest. He did now, though not for Caroline. It was Adie who filled his thoughts.

Two days ago, she'd been working in the garden. He'd stood by the carriage house, watching from afar as she arranged the tomato vines. He'd seen her lips moving and he'd smiled. Adie talked to her plants in the same tone she spoke to Stephen. She crooned to them. Josh didn't think the plants felt a thing, but he did. Just looking at her made him feel sharper, more alive. More everything.

Being with Adie brought out Josh's humanity in the best possible way. He enjoyed the way she took care of others, the way she'd cared for him when he was ill. Her independence, a trait he suspected had been honed by loss, made him want to shield her from life's hurts. She stirred him up in a good way, but he hadn't missed the obvious. The sooner he left Denver, the better off he'd be. Yesterday he'd visited several pawnshops, but he hadn't quizzed the patrons of local saloons. He'd do it soon, though. Maybe tomorrow.

In the meantime, he wanted to know more about the noise in Adie's garden. He went out the back door, heard thumping and strode toward the noise, pausing at the woodpile to arm himself with a split of wood. He believed in turning the other cheek but only for himself. If an intruder had plans to hurt Adie, he'd do it over Josh's dead body.

Tense and wary, he rounded the house and saw a bulky shadow trampling Adie's vegetables.

"Hey!" he shouted.

The man bolted for the street. Josh dropped the wood and sprinted after him. He chased the stranger to the end of the block, but he didn't have the wind to catch him. Annoyed, he slowed to a walk, then headed back to the garden.

Moonlight revealed a methodical assault. The man had started in the corner, where he had kicked down the stakes supporting the tomatoes and trampled the vines. Next he'd flattened most of the cornstalks. The strawberries made Josh even angrier. He knew how much Adie liked strawberry jam. Red and ripe, they'd been ready for picking.

Looking at the mess, he felt a strong need for vengeance. Not only did Adie need the garden for food, but she loved it. He'd seen her on her knees, working the loamy earth with her small, pretty hands. At supper she talked about her squash and beans. The man who'd destroyed her garden had done it out of malice, and he'd done a good job.

Josh worshipped the God of mercy. He also revered the God of justice. Looking at the damage, he wanted to see

Adie's assailant—or the man who'd hired him—pay for his crime. Was Dean behind the vandalism? Josh's neck hairs prickled. Unless he found a sign that Emily was in Denver, he had no reason to stay. He'd been considering where to go next, San Francisco or maybe Chicago. Tonight's assault changed his priorities. He wouldn't leave Swan's Nest until the vandal was caught.

He looked again at the damage, then fetched a rake from the toolshed. He didn't know much about gardening, but he could spare Adie the sight of the crushed vines.

After an hour, he'd swept the mess into a pile and had shoveled it into the compost heap. By the time he finished, the eastern sky had a lavender glow. Birds were chirping in the lush cottonwoods and he smelled the freshness of a Colorado dawn.

The slap of the back door broke into his thoughts. He turned and saw Adie walking to the carriage house where she'd milk Buttons. He dreaded telling her the bad news, but it had to be done. He put the tools in the shed, then went through a side door that led through the tack room to the main part of the building. Adie had her back to the door. She didn't see him, nor had she heard his footsteps. Josh paused. Buttons could be trouble and he didn't want to startle her.

Neither did he want to take his eyes off Adie. After a scratch and pat for the goat, she dropped to her knees at the animal's side. Her dress, a faded calico with tiny flowers, made a circle on the floor. A high window sent a slice of dawn across her shoulders and neatly pinned hair. Her red hair…even restrained by pins, it looked as spirited as Adie.

When was the last time he'd appreciated the simple beauty of a woman? Maybe never. He'd prided himself on being above such things, but looking at Adie he saw God's handiwork. She had a heart and soul, eyes that changed with her moods and a knack for being wise. The Lord himself had knit Adie in her mother's womb and He'd done a fine job of it.

Even so, Josh couldn't stand by the door and stare. It was unseemly, even rude. Buttons would have to cope. He cleared his throat. "Adie?"

Gasping, she pressed her hand against her chest and faced him. "You startled me!"

"Sorry."

Her brows snapped together. "Is something wrong?"

He stepped closer so he wouldn't have to shout. "Someone vandalized your garden."

"My *garden?*"

He told her about the damage. "I stopped him before he could finish it off. You still have beans and squash."

Her eyes burned. "If Dean's behind this—"

"I saw the man who did it," Josh said. "He was too stout to be Dean, but he could have been paid."

Adie rocked up from her knees. Josh stepped forward and offered his hand. As she took it, Buttons grabbed a mouthful of his shirt and pulled. Instinctively he stepped back, taking Adie with him. They ended up in a tangle with Buttons tearing his shirt. Adie stumbled into his arms. They were face to face, hands gripping each other's elbows. When she gasped, he felt the breath of it.

They stepped back at the same time. Adie grabbed Buttons by the collar and pulled. "Stop that!" she said to the goat.

As Buttons bleated a complaint, Josh looked down at the rip in his shirt and chuckled. "That's a first. I've been attacked by a goat."

She scowled at the tear. "I'll mend it for you."

"Thanks." When he left Denver, he'd have a reminder of Adie's hands working a needle and thread. The thought warmed and saddened him at the same time.

Adie led the goat back to the milking spot. "I'll finish with Buttons, then check the garden."

As she dropped to her knees, Josh walked to the door to wait. Slouching against the frame, he took in her profile. She had to be frightened, but the fear didn't show as she calmed Buttons and finished the milking. As her shoulders moved, he thought of her stumbling into his arms. Awareness had flashed in her eyes. He'd felt it, too, and he'd wondered again what it would be like to court her properly.

Had Adie wondered, as well? Guilt welled in his belly. He had no business thinking about a future with Adie Clarke. As soon as the vandal and his cohorts went to jail, Josh would leave Denver. Somewhere, Emily needed him.

Adie pushed to her feet. "I'm done."

Josh opened the door. As she walked through it, her skirt dusted his boots and the sun reflected off the crown of her head. With the scent of cotton filling his nose, he waited while she walked to the house. She left the bucket on the first step, then returned to the carriage house. As she looked toward the garden, her eyes dimmed. "I better see the mess for myself."

"I cleaned up," he said as they walked down the path. "But it's not pretty."

"Thank you."

"I wish I'd caught whoever did this."

When the damage came into view, Adie gasped. Leaving Josh at the edge of the plot, she went to the corn, dropped to a crouch and touched a broken stalk. She stood, propped up a stake and arranged a single tomato vine. When she looked at the remains of the strawberry plants, she pressed her hand to her lips and whimpered. A woman's tears had never dampened Josh's shirt, but he didn't think twice about stepping to Adie's side.

He touched her back. "I'm sorry. I know what the garden means to you."

Instead of turning to him, she stiffened. "I have work to do. I have to replant."

"I'll help." When a tremor shot up her spine, he wanted to bloody Franklin Dean's nose. He settled for glaring at the corn. "We need to call the sheriff."

"No!"

Her reaction didn't make sense. "Why not?"

Adie took three steps away from him. She seemed to be staring across the street, but Josh sensed she was hiding her eyes. "There's no point," she finally said. "Dean owns Denver and everyone in it."

"He doesn't own *me*. I'll hire an attorney. I'll—"

"You'll do *nothing*."

"Adie—"

She faced him. "Pearl's involved, too. She wants her privacy."

"But—"

"But nothing!"

Josh didn't care for one-sided conversations, but he couldn't force Adie to share her thoughts. "All right," he said. "I'll respect your wishes."

"Good."

"I don't like it, though."

She glared at him. "It's none of your concern. You'll be leaving soon."

"No, I'm not."

Her mouth gaped. "But—"

"I won't leave until you're safe…Pearl, too."

Josh didn't want to butt in to Pearl's life, but someone had to speak candidly with her father. When the time was right, he'd visit Colfax Avenue Church.

Adie stood glaring at him. "There's another problem."

"What's that?"

"You can't stay here indefinitely."

"Why not?"

"Our agreement was for two weeks."

"So we can change it."

"I don't want to. As I said, I don't rent to men. I made an exception, but it's awkward."

Josh couldn't disagree. Between his feelings for Adie and Caroline's baking, he felt like a black swan among five white ones. He had to stifle his tender feelings for Adie but not the urge to keep her safe. "Dean wants to harm you," he said in a sure voice. "If you think I can leave now, you've misjudged my character."

No, she hadn't. Josh had washed dishes and fixed the roof. He'd cleaned up after Buttons and filled the wood box. He had a good heart. He hadn't asked about Emily again, and Adie could almost believe he wasn't Maggie's brother. She'd decided to let sleeping dogs lie, but if Josh stayed in Denver, those dogs would wake up and bark. She had to convince him to leave.

Apart from her worries about Stephen, she didn't like the way he made her feel. When he looked into her eyes, she saw a man full of hope and kindness. He knew how to laugh and when to cry. He didn't resemble Reverend Honeycutt in the least, but he still wore a black coat and believed in God. Adie believed in God, but she wanted nothing to do with Him.

She and Josh lived on opposites sides of an endless fence and she didn't see a gate. Never mind his blue eyes, bright with anger and ready to fight. Never mind the sight of his arms laced stubbornly across his chest. She couldn't let this man fight her battles. Franklin Dean posed a threat to Adie's house, but Josh could take her son. The sooner he left Denver, the safer she'd be. She squared her shoulders. "I still want you to leave."

"I can't."

"Find a hotel."

He lowered his chin. "I'll pay triple."

Oh, how she needed the money…. "No."

"Four times."

Her mouth gaped. The amount would cover half the mortgage. She could afford a new dress.

"Five—"

"Stop." Her greed shamed her. Stephen mattered more, but she desperately needed the money. Every month she lived in fear of selling Maggie's jewelry and being discovered. If Josh stayed at Swan's Nest, she could keep the trunk closed a little longer.

"You win," she said. "You can stay."

He looked pleased.

"But four times the rent is too much."

"I don't think it's enough." His eyes locked with hers. "Our deal was for two meals a day, but I'm getting breakfast, lunch and supper. I have a place to sleep, company in the evenings. I've never had it so good."

Maggie's brother, a wealthy man, wouldn't have been impressed by Swan's Nest and her humble meals. Josh enjoyed simple things as she did. He'd also saved her garden from total devastation. She owed him her gratitude, if not the truth.

"All right," she said. "We'll keep the current deal."

She considered telling him not to pay double, but she knew he'd argue.

"Agreed," he said.

Why did she feel light-headed? "Are you hungry?"

"Bacon and eggs?"

She smiled. "Biscuits, too."

Together they walked to the house. When they reached the steps, Josh lifted the milk bucket and held the door. As they stepped inside, Caroline came into the kitchen holding Stephen. Adie reached for the baby. Aware of Josh's eyes on her back, she felt goose bumps rising on her back and arms. The less Josh saw of Stephen, the safer she'd feel.

Caroline greeted her, then turned to Josh. "Good morning, Reverend. You're up early."

"It's a fine day."

Caroline beamed. "'This is the day the Lord hath made. We will rejoice and be glad in it.'"

Adie didn't need Caroline to quote Bible verses. Neither, apparently, did Josh. He looked uncomfortable.

Caroline gave a too-cheerful smile. "Would you like breakfast, Reverend? I'd be happy to fry some eggs."

"I'm doing it," Adie said.

"You have Stephen." Caroline lifted a fry pan from the rack on the wall. "He's hungry, plus he'll need a fresh nappy."

Josh gave Adie a look she could read like her own thoughts. He had no interest in Caroline and her fried eggs. Neither would he be the rope in a tug-of-war. "Milk and bread would be fine."

With Stephen on her hip, Adie set the bucket on the counter, then poured a glass of milk for Josh from the pitcher. The baby smelled food and cooed. She would have treasured the moment, except Caroline was buttering bread for Josh. She also had to tell her friend about the garden.

She looked over her shoulder at Caroline. "I have some bad news."

"What happened?"

Adie told her about the vegetables and how Josh chased off the vandal. When she finished the story, Caroline looked at Josh as if he could walk on water. "You're a brave man, Reverend. You could have been hurt."

He looked more annoyed than before. "It was nothing."

"*I* don't think so!" She set a plate of bread in front of him. "Whoever did it could have turned on you."

Mary walked into the kitchen. "What happened?"

Caroline faced her. "Someone trampled the garden. The reverend chased him off." She turned to Adie. "We have to go to the sheriff."

Mary huffed. "It won't help."

"It might," Caroline insisted.

Adie felt Josh's gaze on her cheek. She couldn't protest without sounding desperate. She looked to Mary for help, but Mary shrugged. "I guess it's worth a try."

"I'll go this morning," Josh said.

He looked to Adie for approval. She didn't want to give it, but how could she say no? She thought of using Pearl but felt terrible for the thought. Deep down, she knew Dean had to be stopped and Pearl couldn't do it alone. If Adie didn't step up, who would? As much as she wanted to go to the law, the thought terrified her. What if a Pinkerton's detective had visited the sheriff with questions about Maggie Butler? For all Adie knew, Maggie's brother could have distributed posters with his sister's likeness. Adie held Stephen tighter. With a little luck, nothing in the sheriff's office would link Maggie Butler and Emily Blue. If it did, she might have to flee Denver.

Barely breathing, she watched as Caroline poured coffee for Josh and then herself. She loved her house and her friends, but she loved her son more.

Shortly after breakfast, Josh changed into his black coat and left Swan's Nest. The milk and toast had settled nicely, but he regretted the coffee. His stomach burned as he walked into the flat-front building that housed the Denver sheriff's office.

A man in a leather vest with a badge stood up behind the desk. "Good morning, Reverend. Can I help you?"

"I hope so." Josh introduced himself. "Someone vandalized Swan's Nest last night."

"The boardinghouse on Seventeenth?"

"That's it."

The deputy offered his hand. "I'm Beau Morgan." He indicated a battered chair. "Have a seat."

Josh sat on the wood, then told the story. "I'm worried, Deputy. Someone wants to harm Miss Clarke."

"Any thoughts on who?"

"Franklin Dean paid a call recently. To put it mildly, he forgot his manners."

Morgan's brow furrowed. "He owns the bank."

As if that mattered, Josh thought. Evil men came in all shapes and sizes. Some had money. Others didn't. "He also trespassed on Miss Clarke's property. I saw it." Josh left Pearl out of the conversation. He wanted to see Dean punished, but he didn't have the right to tell her story.

The deputy wrinkled his brow. "Anyone could have vandalized the garden, but I could have a chat with Mr. Dean."

"I don't think that's wise," Josh answered. "If he's pressured, he might do something even worse."

"Personally, I don't care for the man." Morgan looked as if he'd gotten a whiff of bad meat. "Rumor has it Dean roughed up one of Miss Elsa's girls. I'll ask around town, quietly of course. Can you describe the man you saw?"

"Average height. Stocky build." Josh thought of the chase down the street. "He's fast on his feet."

"Anything else?"

Josh had two missions today. He'd done his best for Adie. Now he could focus on Emily. "It's unrelated, but I'm looking for my sister." He described her and mentioned she had a baby. For the hundredth time, he wished he had the oval tintype.

"I can see why you went to Swan's Nest," Morgan said. "Miss Clarke's new in town, but she's got a reputation."

"For what?"

"Helping women in trouble." The deputy chuckled. "I'm surprised she gave you a room."

"Why?"

"She chased Clint Hughes off with a shotgun. He had it coming, though. The drunken fool nearly busted down her door."

Josh was glad he'd faced Mary's pistol instead of Adie and two barrels of buckshot. He focused back on Emily. "If you see anyone resembling my sister, I'd like to know."

"Sure."

The men shook hands and Josh went back to the street. He climbed on his horse and rode to Fourteenth Street where he hoped to find a quality jewelry shop. Emily's jewels were worth a fortune but only if someone had the money to buy them. If she'd come to Denver, she'd been wise. What with mining interests, the railroad, commerce and cattle, the city had men who'd want fancy jewels for their wives.

As Josh approached the corner of Broadway and Colfax Avenue, he saw the steeple of Colfax Avenue Church. On a whim, he turned and rode past the magnificent building. He wanted to go inside, but today the doors looked intimidating. Entering the church would send him back to Boston. He'd recall the crowds and the rapture of the choir. He'd also hear the ring of his own voice.

Josh was certain he'd been born to preach. He'd felt the call at a young age and had flourished under his grandfather's mentoring. The question had never been *should* he preach, but where? Not in a church like this. Not anymore. Feeling bittersweet, he clicked to his horse and headed for a row of shops. He spotted a jewelry store and went inside. A balding man came out from behind a black curtain.

"Good morning," he said in a German accent.

Josh glanced around the spartan room with a sinking heart.

He saw gold, silver and turquoise but nothing like Emily's pearls or other pieces.

"I'm looking for fine jewels," he said.

"A diamond, perhaps?"

"Possibly. May I see what you have?"

The man came out with a tray of rings on black velvet. Josh didn't recognize a single one, but he felt the heartache shining in the stones. What made a woman sell a precious ring? Need and desperation… His heart pounded for Emily's suffering.

"Thank you, sir." Josh wrote his name on a card. "I'm staying at Swan's Nest. If something new comes in, would you contact me?"

"My pleasure."

Josh left the store and headed into the heart of Denver where he visited three pawnbrokers but saw nothing of interest. The next stop tore him up inside, but it had to be made. He walked into an establishment called Brick's Saloon where a burly man was sweeping the floor. Judging by his size and red hair, he had to be Brick.

The man looked Josh up and down. "Kind of early for preaching, ain't it, Reverend?"

"I'm not here to preach," Josh said. "I'm looking for a woman."

Brick kept sweeping.

"She's got dark hair, the same as mine."

As Josh had hoped, Brick looked him in the eye. "Why do you want her?"

"She's my sister."

The man set the broom against the wall, stepped behind the counter and poured Josh a glass of water. "Here."

Josh took a sip and waited. He'd learned to let people tell their stories in their own time. The barkeep busied his hands by wiping the counter, but his mind seemed to be a hundred miles away. When he'd wiped the last inch of the wood, he looked at Josh. "I have a sister, too."

"What's her name?"

"Jenny."

"Is she in Denver?"

"Nope. Don't know where she went." The man looked as broken as Josh felt. "She ran off with a two-timing rat. My little sister—" The man cursed.

"I'm sorry."

"Me, too." Brick looked at Josh. "You gotta picture of your sister?"

"Not anymore." Josh gave Emily's description.

Brick kept wiping the counter. "Miss Elsa's Social Club is on Walnut, just past Fifteenth Street. If your sister's gone down that road, that's the place to look."

Josh headed for the door.

The barkeep called after him, "Come back again, Reverend. Coffee's on the house."

"I'll do that," Josh replied.

He felt at home with men like Brick. On a whim, he looked back and saw the barkeep neatly folding the towel. "Are you open on Sunday morning?" he asked.

"No, sir."

"Mind if I hold a church service here?"

Brick scowled. "I don't see why. There's lots of churches in Denver."

"And lots of people," Josh added. "Not everyone's comfortable in the same place."

The barkeeper grunted. "I know how it is."

Unfortunately, so did Josh. His Boston congregation had been well heeled and as proud as he'd been. Josh no longer saw "church" as four walls and twenty rows of mahogany pews. Now he held services anywhere, anytime.

Brick shrugged. "I guess there's no harm."

"Then spread the word," he said. "I'll be here on Sunday. The service starts at ten."

Brick grinned. "I'll do that."

Josh left the saloon, climbed on his horse and headed to Walnut. His spirits sank as he neared a mansion built in the style of the South. White and proud, Miss Elsa's Social Club had tall columns, long windows and a veranda where he saw four women sipping tea. He spoke from atop his horse. "Good morning, ladies."

Another woman came through the door. Tall and slender, almost emaciated in Josh's opinion, she wore a gold silk gown. In spite of her rouged cheeks and dyed hair, she looked several years older than the girls on the veranda.

"Good morning, Reverend. I'm Miss Elsa."

He tipped his hat. "I'm Joshua Blue, out of Boston."

"What can I do for you?"

The invitation in her voice was unmistakable. Before he left, Josh vowed to make an invitation of his own. "I'm looking for someone."

The girls on the veranda stared with desperation, as if they were hoping he'd come for them. In a way, he had. Every time he reached out for Emily, he prayed for women in her predicament.

"My sister's name is Emily," he said to the girls. "Maybe you've seen her." For the third time that day, he described her dark hair and eyes.

Miss Elsa's expression revealed nothing. "I can't help you, Reverend. We keep secrets here."

She paused to let her meaning sink in. If Emily had been inside, the madam wouldn't tell him. She'd also implied that she'd keep secrets for Josh. If Miss Elsa thought she could tempt him, she was flat-out wrong. He didn't see pleasure sitting on her porch. He saw four Mary Magdalenes in need of rescue. Josh focused on the girls. They ranged in age from young to bitter. He didn't know which broke his heart more.

He looked each one in the eye, then said, "I'm starting a church. You're all invited to Brick's Saloon on Sunday at ten."

Two of the women sneered. One stared at her toes. He looked at the fourth girl and saw hope.

He focused on the girl with the hopeful eyes. "I hope to see you there."

After a nod to Miss Elsa, he turned his horse down the road and headed back to Swan's Nest. He had a sermon to write. He also needed someone who could carry a tune. He'd sing if he had to, but it wasn't pretty. As he neared Swan's Nest, he thought about refreshments. He wouldn't ask Caroline to bake cookies, but she'd probably think of it herself.

Would Adie come? He hoped so, but he didn't think she would. Last night at supper, Caroline and Pearl had asked him to lead a Bible Study. Josh had agreed and they'd made plans for Thursday. Bessie liked the idea and even Mary said she'd attend. Adie hadn't said a word. She'd made it clear that she didn't think much of churches and the men who ran them. Josh wanted to know why. When the time was right, he'd ask.

Chapter Seven

Alone in the kitchen with Stephen on her hip, Adie tapped her toe as she waited for his milk to warm. Laughter filtered down the hallway from the parlor where her boarders had gathered for Josh's Bible study. He'd stepped outside and would be back any minute. Adie wanted to be upstairs before he came through the door.

As she tested the milk, Mary walked into the kitchen. "You're not going to hide in your room, are you?"

"I'm not *hiding*," Adie replied. "I'm going to feed Stephen and put him to bed."

"Feed him downstairs."

"He'll make too much noise."

"Nonsense!"

"No, it's not," Adie insisted.

Mary's eyes twinkled. "You know what I think?"

"No, but you're going to tell me."

"I think you like the reverend…a lot."

"Mary!"

"See?" The saloon girl sounded wise. "Women only avoid men they care about. It can be love, hate or fear. No one hates

Josh. He's a gentleman. Even *I* like him. There's no reason to fear him. That leaves—"

"Don't be ridiculous!"

The back door opened in the middle of her protest. Smiling, Josh looked from Mary to Adie. "What's ridiculous?"

Adie turned to the stove to hide the pink stain on her cheeks.

Mary nudged her elbow as if they'd been sharing a joke. "It's girl talk, Reverend. I'm trying to get Adie to stay for the Bible study."

Of all the confounded choices… If she said no, Mary would think she had feelings for Josh. If she said yes, she'd have to sit through a harangue with Stephen in her lap. Adie had heard enough scripture from Old Man Long to last a lifetime. At night the family would sit in a circle while he read. Sometimes he thundered just at her.

Adie couldn't see Josh thundering at anyone. On the other hand, she could imagine Mary teasing her for days. She needed a way out.

She looked to Josh for an excuse. "What if Stephen cries?"

"So what?"

"Babies fuss. Back in Kansas—" Adie sealed her lips. She'd slipped, badly. Emily had been in Kansas.

Mentioning it had to rouse his curiosity, but he looked disinterested. "This isn't Kansas."

Without a bit of hesitation, he walked out of the kitchen, leaving her alone with Mary. Without an excuse, Adie shrugged. "I'll go, but I warned you about Stephen."

Mary's eyes twinkled with mischief, but she kept silent.

Adie lifted the bottle from the pot of water and followed her to the parlor. She saw Caroline and Bessie on the divan and Pearl on a hard chair from the dining room. She preferred it for her back. Josh was sitting in the armchair. Mary gave Adie the rocker next to him and squeezed onto the divan.

When the women were settled, he opened his Bible. "Ladies, shall we pray?"

Adie thought of Old Man Long. She wished she hadn't come, but she couldn't leave now.

The women bowed their heads. Adie followed their lead, but her neck ached with old resentments. In the Long home, she'd worked from dawn to dusk. Once she'd fallen asleep during the Bible reading and Old Man Long had slapped her for showing disrespect. As Josh asked the Lord to open their hearts, Adie's chest ached. She'd been eight when her father went to pan gold and never returned. She'd been twelve when her mother died and sixteen when Timothy Long had trapped her in the attic. Where was God on that miserable night?

"Amen." Josh's voice rang with a joy Adie didn't feel. He looked at her, then scanned the other faces. "Before we start, I have an announcement. This Sunday at ten o'clock, I'm holding a church service."

Pearl looked pleased. "Where?"

"At Brick's Saloon."

"A saloon!" said Caroline.

Mary raised an eyebrow. "What's wrong with that?"

"I'm just surprised," Caroline answered.

So was Adie.

Bessie smiled. "It sounds like you're putting down roots, Reverend."

"No," he said. "I'm just planting seeds. Someone else will tend them when I'm gone." He scanned their faces, stopping when he reached Adie. "You're all invited. In fact, I'm hoping for a little help."

"What do you need?" Caroline asked.

"Cookies would be nice."

"I'll make macaroons."

"Can anyone sing?" Josh asked.

Mary's face lit up with interest, but just as quickly her smile sagged. "I used to."

"Then you still can," he said. "Any hymn would do."

"Can I think about it?" she asked.

"Sure."

He looked at Adie but said nothing. She hid her eyes by staring at Stephen's nose.

Josh went back to business. "I thought we'd talk about a Psalm tonight. Any suggestions?"

Caroline, seated on Josh's left, looked poised in a blue dress with a lace scarf draped around her neck. She'd washed her face and repinned her hair. Across from her, Adie felt like an out-of-place sparrow. Her brown dress had a spot on the bodice, and her hair had become untidy.

Caroline smiled demurely. "You pick, Reverend. I'm sure you have a favorite."

"I do."

Josh closed the Bible and recited words that Adie had never heard.

"O Lord, Thou hast searched me, and known me.
Thou knowest my downsitting and mine uprising, thou
understandeth my thoughts afar off."

His voice went deep and low, slowing as the psalmist described his inability to hide himself from God, then soaring with the awareness of God's infinite presence. He spoke about darkness and light being alike to God, how the writer had been fearfully and wonderfully made in his mother's womb. How many times had Adie marveled at Stephen's toes? She had no trouble believing in God, but she didn't believe He loved His children like an earthly father. She'd lived through too much heartache.

Josh, though, spoke with power and compassion. Adie imagined him in a Boston cathedral and felt both awed and afraid. With the next verse, he focused on her.

"Search me, O God, and know my heart. Try me and know my thoughts."

Adie didn't want anyone to know her thoughts. She feared being found by Maggie's brother and dreaded losing Stephen. Still focused on her face, Josh's eyes filled with compassion, as if he were confessing his own anxious thoughts, his own worries. His voice gentled to a plea.

"See if there be any hurtful way in me, and lead me in Your way everlasting."

Still holding her gaze, he whispered, "Amen."

Adie didn't want to hurt anyone, especially not Josh. Sometimes he reminded her so much of Maggie that her stomach knotted. Other times she felt certain that this good man couldn't possibly be the ogre who'd driven Maggie from her home. The trunk held the answer, but she couldn't bear the thought of opening it and losing her son.

Mary looked thoughtful. "Tell us, Reverend. Why is this Psalm your favorite?"

"It keeps me humble."

Maggie's brother didn't know the meaning of the word. Feeling safer, Adie dared to look at his face.

His eyes glistened with the lamplight. "Back in Boston, I was an arrogant know-it-all. Deep down, I'm still that man."

"No, you're not!" Caroline insisted.

When Josh gave her a firm look, Adie felt oddly pleased.

"No, Caroline," he said gently. "I *am* that man. Left to

myself, I'm as prideful as ever. This Psalm reminds me that God knows me inside and out. He's with me, even when I stumble. He's with each of you."

Bessie looked wise and Mary seemed hopeful. Pearl was rubbing her belly as if to caress the baby, and Caroline had a worshipful expression Adie found irritating. As for herself, she didn't believe a word Josh had said. Where was God when her mother died in the middle of the night? Adie had been alone at her bedside. She'd tried to dig the grave herself, but the task had been too great. She'd gone to Reverend Honeycutt for help and her life had turned wretched. And what about Maggie? She'd endured a hard labor and then died for her effort. Adie looked down at Stephen. She hadn't been paying attention and he'd chugged half his bottle. He needed to be burped, so she raised him to her shoulder.

Josh watched the baby with stark longing. "God loves my sister, too."

Adie wondered.

"Have you heard anything?" Bessie asked.

"No, but I've been asking around town." He told them about his trip to the saloon and vaguely mentioned Miss Elsa's Social Club. "At least I know where she's *not*."

"That's a help," Mary said.

Caroline looked concerned. "Did she have money when she left?"

"Her jewelry."

Adie's hand froze on Stephen's back.

"Did you check the pawnbrokers?" Mary asked. "That's what I do. I'd sell it and start over."

"I hope she did," Josh answered. "I left word around town that I'm looking for certain items."

"Like what?" Caroline said.

Before Josh could answer, Stephen let out an angry cry. As

Adie shifted him to her other shoulder, he lost the contents of his tummy. Sour milk dripped down the front of her dress.

"Ick," said Mary.

Pearl turned green.

Bessie headed for the kitchen. "I'll get a towel."

Caroline stood to help her, but Josh stepped in front of her. "I'll hold him. You go change."

Before Adie could protest, he lifted the stinky, crying baby into his arms and held him as if he'd been given a precious gift. Still in the chair, Adie looked up at Josh, watching as he focused on Stephen and crooned. Would he see Maggie's nose? Her heart-shaped face? Breathless, she waited for a glimmer of recognition. Instead she saw the most generous kind of love. There was Stephen, reeking of spit-up, kicking and crying. Yet in Josh's eyes she saw nothing but joy. Compassion, too. The man knew about stomach trouble. Standing tall, he swayed with the baby in his arms, making silly talk until Stephen quieted.

He looked down at Adie. "He's beautiful."

"Thank you."

"He has your eyes."

Icy tingles ripped down her spine, leaving her numb with fear. Her boarders knew she'd adopted Stephen. Once, during a thunderstorm, they'd each shared a secret. Stephen's adoption had been hers. She'd never described Maggie or told her friend's story, but they knew Stephen's eyes would never match hers.

Mary and Pearl didn't react, but Caroline stared at her.

"Go change," Josh repeated. "We'll wait for you."

Adie wanted to grab her son and run. Instead she calmly walked to her room, where moonlight poured through the window. When she reached the trunk, she fell to her knees and wept. "Help me, Maggie. I don't know what to do."

She'd spoken to her friend's memory, but Adie felt the presence of the God in Josh's Psalm. He could see her now, on her knees and torn to pieces. Adie didn't feel fearfully and wonderfully made. She felt wicked and deceitful for what she'd done.

She touched the lock with her fingertips, pressing until the brass felt warm. If she stood, she could fetch the key from the drawer. With a turn of her wrist, she could be free of her guilt. She'd show Josh the picture, he'd shake his head no and her worries would end. But the risk… If Maggie Butler and Emily Blue were the same woman, Josh would take his nephew home to Boston. Adie would lose her son. She'd purchased Swan's Nest with Maggie's money. He'd have the right to take her home. Where would Pearl go? What would happen to her friends? To her?

Her fingers slid away from the lock. The risk was too great. Determined to compose herself, she stumbled to her feet and put on fresh clothes, dawdling with the hope that Josh would give up and go to his room. She'd heard enough Bible reading for tonight…enough for the rest of her life. After several minutes, she went downstairs to fetch Stephen.

"Adie's taking her sweet time," Caroline said irritably.

Josh barely heard her. He was holding Stephen and couldn't take his eyes off the boy's face. In Boston, he'd christened babies in front of huge crowds. He'd enjoyed the moment, but his heart hadn't stirred the way it did for Adie's son.

Earlier Bessie had cleaned the child up. She'd wiped his face with a damp rag, then changed him into a baby gown she'd fetched from the laundry room. She'd offered to hold him, but Josh had said no. He hadn't felt this peaceful in months, maybe never. He thought of Adie alone in her room. The Psalm had touched her, he felt sure of it. He hoped it touched everyone. Of the five women at Swan's Nest, Bessie had the calmest disposition, but she also had an air of sorrow. Pearl was the most anxious. Caroline desperately needed someone to love and Mary needed someone to fight. That left Adie. What did *she* need?

A husband.

A friend.

Someone who'd protect her from Franklin Dean and pay the mortgage, a man who'd teach Stephen to fish and to read, to respect all men and fight for the people he'd come to love. Not once in Josh's life had he wanted to be a father, but he did now. Looking at Adie's son, he felt a connection that defied logic. The feeling stretched to Adie, too.

He'd glimpsed her face just before Stephen lost his supper. She'd gone pale. Why? He'd been talking about Emily, but he hadn't been critical of anyone but himself. If he'd hurt Adie's feelings, he wanted to apologize. As a man, he couldn't stand the thought of her tears. As a minister, he wanted her to be at peace with herself and the Lord. He wanted to speak to her but not tonight. He'd had an upset of his own. She'd looked lovely in the lamplight and he'd caught himself looking twice, even a third time. Adie made him weak in the knees. Before he spent time with her, he had some praying to do.

"Let's call it a night," he said to the group.

Caroline frowned. "We could start without Adie."

Josh held in a groan. Caroline had many fine traits, but he had no interest in her as a woman. Yesterday she'd offered to mend his shirts. He'd said no. He'd also imagined Adie's fingers sewing the tear made by Buttons. Looking at her tonight, covered with the mess from Stephen, he'd imagined the joys he'd forsaken for the benefit of his calling. A wife…a child. He couldn't go down that road, not with Emily missing and his history of pride.

"We'll continue next week," he said to the women.

Caroline smiled demurely. "It's a lovely Psalm, Reverend."

Lovely wasn't how Josh would have described the words he'd just read. David, a gifted poet and powerful king, had known the torment of bad decisions.

Caroline said good-night and headed for the stairs. Mary and Pearl followed. Bessie watched them leave, then faced Josh. "May I speak with you, Reverend?"

"Of course."

"It's about Adie."

He avoided gossip, but people often spoke to him in confidence about family members. The women at Swan's Nest were sisters. "You sound worried."

She lowered her voice. "Be kind to her."

Had he been *un*-kind? "I don't understand."

"I know you don't, but you will. She and Stephen had a hard beginning. Your sister's story hits close to home."

"That's what I thought."

"She's afraid."

"Of what?"

"You, I think."

Josh had seen that same fear in outlaw camps. It lived in the eyes of men who'd murdered and thought they were beyond mercy. Guilt wore a person to bare bones, and he feared Adie lived with that despair. He couldn't stand the thought, especially while holding her son.

"When the time's right, I'll speak to her," he said to Bessie.

"Don't wait."

He felt the same urgency. "I'll do it tomorrow."

"Tonight," she insisted.

Before he could reply, Adie entered the parlor. She'd changed from the brown calico into the coppery dress that matched her hair. The color reminded him of maple leaves.

Maples reminded him of home—not the mansion in Boston, but the home in his heart, the place he went when he closed his eyes and laid his humanity at God's feet. Somehow Adie and home had become one thought. The realization shocked him to the core. He had no business thinking of Adie in that way. He had to find his sister and the search might never end.

Looking at her now, Josh knew he wasn't the only troubled soul in the room. Her eyes had a dullness he'd never seen before, and her skin had gone from rosy to pallid. Bessie was right. He had to speak with her tonight.

Stephen had fallen asleep. Without meeting Josh's gaze, Adie reached for her son. "It's his bedtime. I'll take him upstairs."

Bessie cut in front of her. "I'll do it."

"No," she insisted. "You've done enough."

Josh maneuvered Stephen into the nurse's arms. "If you don't mind, Adie. I'd like a word with you."

She looked ready to grab the baby and bolt, but Bessie had a firm hold. As the women locked eyes, Josh saw compassion in Bessie's gaze and fear in Adie's. The nurse didn't give an inch. Defeated, Adie lowered her arms and turned to Josh with a hard look in her eyes. She was poised for a fight, which he didn't mind at all. When it came to Adie, he welcomed the challenge.

As Bessie climbed the stairs, he turned up the lamp. He couldn't change darkness to light, but the wick did a fair imitation. He indicated the divan. "Please, sit down."

Adie stepped by him and turned down the lamp. "If you don't mind, it's too bright for my eyes."

Josh *did* mind, but for all the wrong reasons. Darkness and light were alike to the Lord but not to Josh. He didn't want to be alone with her in the shadows. The dark kept secrets. It hid the truth and led down a dangerous road. He considered postponing their talk, but Adie looked like a bird caught in a net, as if she wanted to escape but had nowhere to go.

He sat on the armchair. "You have a beautiful little boy."

"Thank you."

"It's none of my business," he said gently. "But you seem troubled whenever I mention Emily."

Her eyes narrowed. "What do you mean?"

"When I say her name, you look pained."

"I do?"

"Every time. I'm wondering why."

Chapter Eight

How much did Josh know? Was he toying with her? Maggie's brother would have done such a thing, but Josh wouldn't. From the day he'd arrived, he'd treated her with respect, even kindness. He also wore a black coat and carried a Bible, signs that he couldn't be trusted. Looking at him now, Adie felt more confused than ever. His mouth had settled into a gentle curve, and his eyes held only compassion. No wonder Caroline had baked six pies and three cakes. Josh was a handsome man. Even more frightening, he inspired trust.

So had Timothy Long.

So had Reverend Honeycutt.

Adie prepared herself for a fight. She'd do anything to keep her promise to Maggie Butler. She had to protect Stephen at all costs, even Josh's peace of mind. She homed her gaze to his too-blue eyes. "Emily's story upsets me. I can't imagine."

Except like Emily, she'd been deceived by a minister and forced to leave the town she'd called home. She knew exactly how Josh's sister had felt. She'd lied again.

Judging by the look in his eyes, Josh knew it, too.

She folded her hands in her lap. "I guess I can *imagine* it, but I haven't *exactly* been in that position." With her cheeks flaming, she jerked her eyes away from his. She'd done it again—said too much and raised questions.

"Adie?"

She said nothing.

"Please," he said gently. "Look at me."

She couldn't, not with lies still sour on her tongue. She closed her eyes, but she couldn't escape the sense of Josh's gaze. She heard the slight rustle of his coat, then felt the warmth of his fingers on her chin, urging her to look up. When she finally gave in, she found herself staring into his eyes and feeling a kinship she'd never known. Not with her father... Not with anyone.

He held her gaze but lowered his hand. The warmth of him lingered like the scent of bread. He looked as unsteady as she felt. "I want to tell you about the night Emily left."

Her heart cried no, but she nodded yes. She hurt for this man. She also feared him. Of the two, the hurting weighed more than the fear, at least for now. "I'm listening."

He sat back in the chair. "Talking about Emily hurts worse than giving up laudanum."

"Then it hurts a lot."

His face went rigid. "The story begins three years before Emily left. I'm not bragging when I say I had everything— the biggest church in Boston, respect from my peers. I felt God's hand on my life in a way I can't describe."

"In a good way?" She couldn't imagine.

"The best."

"What happened?"

"I got prideful. Greedy, too. If fifty people came to hear me preach, I wanted a hundred. I worked to make it happen. I told myself I was doing God's work, but somehow I lost my way. I prayed but didn't listen for answers. I told God what I thought and assumed He'd agree."

Adie couldn't imagine anyone talking to God. Old Man Long had bellowed about sin and salvation in the same tone he used to call the pigs. Josh's faith fascinated her. So did the hard line of his jaw and the hint of whiskers. She saw a man with feelings, hopes and failures, a man who also wore a preacher's collar.

He gave a half smile. "My downfall started with a bellyache."

"The ulcer?"

"A small one, but I refused to slow down. I didn't eat right. Didn't get enough rest. When the pain became intolerable, I went to a doctor. Not to our family physician, but to a man who didn't know me. I didn't want anyone in the church to know I had a weakness." Josh looked her in the eye. "Secrets are dangerous. They're a sign that something's amiss with a person's soul. I know, because I've kept my own."

Her insides started to quake.

"I don't know what your secret is, but I suspect it has to do with Stephen and how he came into this world."

She struggled to breathe evenly. "What do you mean?"

"Emily left home because I shamed her. I cared more about my reputation than I did about her." He raked his hand through his hair, leaving furrows. "She left because I told her to stay with cousins in Providence. I wanted her to give her baby away."

Maggie…Emily… The stories matched again in perfect, undeniable detail.

"I didn't ask her about the father," Josh continued. "For all I know, she'd been attacked and was afraid to tell me. Or maybe she was in love. I hope so. The thought of violence—" He sealed his lips. "I'd rather think she was in love and fell to the oldest temptation in the world."

Adie didn't know Maggie's whole story, but she knew her friend had loved the father of her child. He'd died and she'd been grieving when they'd met. She wanted to offer Josh that comfort, but she couldn't do it without opening the trunk. She didn't want to hear another word about Emily, but she felt compelled to reach out to Josh. "How old is your sister?"

"Twenty-four."

Maggie had been twenty-three when they'd met. Her birthday would have been in April.

"Emily had suitors," Josh added. "But she never said yes to marriage. Before our mother died, she made sure Emily met suitable men. She encouraged her to find a husband, but I didn't. I had the benefits of a hostess without the complications of a wife."

"Maybe she didn't want to marry."

"I doubt that."

"Why?"

"Emily loved children."

So had Maggie. The two women had sometimes talked of marriage. Adie felt intimidated by it, but Maggie had no such reluctance. In spite of her grief for Stephen's father, she'd told Adie that she didn't regret falling in love, only the mistakes that followed. If she'd lived, she'd have married and had more children.

Adie looked for another consolation for Josh. "Maybe she went to the baby's father."

"Or else she's alone somewhere."

"You don't know that."

His eyes burned into hers. "What about you, Adie? Were you alone when Stephen was born?"

Blood drained from her face. "No."

"Losing my sister changed me." He leaned forward in the chair. "I failed Emily. I won't fail you and Stephen."

"I don't need your help."

"I think you do," he said. "Someone trampled your garden. I see you counting pennies."

"Thank you, but I can manage on my own."

She pushed to her feet. Josh stood, too. When she turned, he pinned her in place with his eyes. "I don't know who hurt you, Adie. But I know God loves you. Whatever it is that upsets you when I say Emily's name, put it down."

She wanted to run from the room. She settled for looking down at his boots. She saw creases in the leather, a sign of the miles he'd traveled for Emily.

He shifted his weight. "No matter what happened, you don't have to carry that shame."

The shame of an out-of-wedlock child was small compared to the guilt she felt now. She felt certain Maggie and Emily were the same woman. If her fears proved true, he'd take Stephen back to Boston.

He laced his hands behind his back. "I'm sharing this story for one reason."

Her throat hurt. "What is it?"

"I was a hypocrite and a fool. I've been addicted to laudanum, told lies and had thoughts so hateful they still shame me. In spite of my failings, Christ died for me. He paid the price for *all* of us."

He shifted his weight again. "I don't know who fathered your son, Adie. I don't know what happened to you. But I know this… No one has the right to throw stones at a woman who's made a mistake."

Realization stole Adie's breath. Josh had no idea that she hadn't given birth. Her secret was safe, but that security came at the cost of her integrity. By staying silent, she was lying. Josh had told the truth about secrets. Knowledge of Maggie's diary weighed like a millstone. She couldn't bear his compassion. She didn't deserve it. Fighting panic, she broke from his gaze and headed for the door.

"Adie, wait." He cut in front of her. "I did it again. I hurt you. That's not my intent. I—"

"Stop! Don't say anything else."

She looked up and saw the shadow of his day-old beard. His black hair wisped over his ears and his jaw jutted with determination. He didn't look a thing like Maggie…except for the shape of his eyes and the slant of his nose, the line of his brow and the curve of his mouth. Adie's heart cried no, but her common sense said yes. She stepped around Josh and raced up the stairs. She heard his boots in the hallway, but they halted at the first step. As she fled into her room, the words of the Psalm played through her mind.

Wither shall I go from Thy spirit?

And wither shall I flee from Thy presence?

Josh hadn't come up the stairs, but she felt as if he were hearing her thoughts. With nowhere to hide, she checked Stephen. Instead of calming her, the sight of the sleeping baby made her tremble. Soon she'd have to pay the mortgage. If she had to sell one of Maggie's brooches, Josh would see it in the jewelry shop and he'd know. She also feared that Bessie would tell him about Stephen's adoption. Looking back, she realized why the older woman had thrown them together. She suspected the truth and wanted Adie to be honest. If Bessie suspected the connection, so did Caroline.

Feeling trapped, Adie stared at the open window. "Talk to me, Maggie."

Adie waited for a flash of memory, a sense of what Maggie would say about Josh now. None came, but Adie didn't need her friend to guide her. She knew right from wrong. She also loved her son enough to die for him and she'd made a deathbed promise to the boy's natural mother. Did that promise give Adie the right—the obligation—to hide the journal? Did a secret do harm when it protected an innocent baby? Or was she protecting herself?

She touched her son's cheek. No one could love him as

much as she did. Not an uncle or cousins. Nothing mattered more than love… Not money. Not blood. Someday Stephen would ask questions. When that day came, she'd answer them truthfully. Until then, she'd hide the facts of his birth.

The decision calmed her but only until she looked out the window. A month ago someone had hurled a rock into her room. Three days ago a man had stomped her tomato plants. She felt as unsafe as she had with the Long family. Adie didn't know whom she feared more—Josh with his good intentions or Franklin Dean, who wanted her out of Swan's Nest.

Either way, she had everything to lose and nothing to gain from opening the trunk. Some truths, she decided, were best left buried.

At precisely midnight, Frank left Miss Elsa's Social Club through the back door. As instructed, Horace met him with the carriage. Frank smelled liquor on his driver's breath and frowned. He didn't care how Horace passed the evening, but the man had to be discreet. If liquor loosened his tongue, he'd become untrustworthy, a fearful possibility considering the secrets he kept.

Frank didn't need the details, but he had to be sure Horace hadn't taken to blabbing at Brick's Saloon.

He made his voice jovial. "Where have you been, my friend? In good company, I hope."

"At Brick's Saloon, sir."

"I smell whiskey."

Horace chuckled. "I downed a shot or two, but I think you'll be pleased with what I gleaned."

"Regarding Miss Clarke?"

"In a way, sir." Horace turned on Broadway where Frank lived in a new mansion. Made of stone with turrets on the corners, it resembled a castle. Other homes on the street had the same look, but none of them matched his house in size.

"Tell me what you learned," he said to Horace.

"It's about the reverend."

"Joshua Blue?"

"He's starting a church, sir."

Frank wrinkled his brow. "Whatever for? Denver has more churches than it needs."

As an elder for Colfax Avenue Church, the biggest church in Denver, Frank kept track of attendance and collection records. Another church would take a slice of the pie.

Horace chuckled. "It's not *your* kind of church."

"Oh?"

"The reverend's holding services in the saloon. He told the barkeep to spread the word."

"I see."

Aside from objecting to another church, Frank didn't want Joshua Blue lingering at Swan's Nest. The reverend had done more than protect Pearl at Franklin's last visit. He'd declared war. The banker could play that game, too. Horace knew better than to mention Adie's garden, but Frank had heard talk at the café where the blonde named Mary waited tables. Swan's Nest had been vandalized. Adie Clarke had cleaned up the mess and replanted.

What would it take to drive her away? If Miss Clarke left town, Pearl would have to move back to the parsonage. Her father could marry them in a private ceremony. Frank would have possession of his son and of Pearl. He wouldn't need to visit Miss Elsa's Social Club. As always, tonight's visit left him feeling cheated. It was Pearl's fault. If she'd only coop-erate, he'd be a good husband. But Pearl wouldn't listen. Not with Adie Clarke filling her mind with lies about respect and love and female independence.

As Horace steered the carriage to the back of the house, Frank looked at the windows, all dark except for his bedroom where a maid had lit a lamp. He couldn't live this way. He needed Pearl.

Horace climbed down from the high seat. Frank got out by himself and faced his driver. "It's time to do more." He didn't need to explain what he meant.

"Any ideas, sir?"

"A fire, perhaps."

Horace raised his brows. "The whole house?"

A fire had hidden benefits. As soon as Franklin took possession of Swan's Nest, he intended to tear it down and build a row of houses he'd sell to entrepreneurs flooding into Denver. If Swan's Nest burned to the ground, the demolition job would be simpler. On the other hand, he didn't want to endanger Pearl.

"Use your judgment," he said. "But Miss Oliver mustn't be harmed."

"What about the others?"

Frank shrugged.

When Horace grinned, moonlight showed his yellow teeth. "You won't know a thing until it happens."

"You're a smart man, Horace."

"That's what you pay me for."

Frank took the hint. Arson cost more than stomping tomatoes. He slipped a five-dollar gold piece into Horace's hand. "Remember. No harm to Miss Oliver."

"Yes, sir."

As the driver led the horse to the stable, Frank had another thought and turned. "One more thing, Horace."

"Sir?"

"When was the last time you went to church?"

Horace snorted.

"It wouldn't hurt you to attend services this Sunday." Frank gave a sly smile. "I hear Reverend Blue is preaching at Brick's Saloon."

The driver smiled back. "That he is, sir. In fact, I think I'll attend."

"Good idea."

As Horace led the horse away, Frank heard the hollow clop of hooves on the dirt path. He entered his house, then headed up the stairs to his empty bedroom, where he blew out the candle and dreamed of Pearl.

Chapter Nine

On Sunday morning Josh strode into Brick's Saloon, saw seven people and rejoiced at the size of the crowd. Brick had arranged the chairs into a square. The barkeep and the girl from Miss Elsa's sat in the second row. Caroline and Bessie had come, but Mary had woken up with a fever. Behind Brick sat three men. Two of them were cowpokes. The third man, a stocky fellow, wore a frock coat and had set a black bowler on the chair next to him. Josh greeted him with a nod. He smiled back, revealing yellow teeth.

Adie's presence would have made him even happier, but he hadn't expected to see her. She'd avoided him since the Bible study and he was worried. For now, though, he had seven souls in his care.

Josh stepped to the counter that Brick had polished. The barkeep had also tacked a sheet over the racy painting above the bottles, a gesture Josh appreciated. As he set down his Bible, he prayed for God to keep him humble.

"Good morning," he said in a hearty voice.

The ladies answered. The men didn't. In some ways,

churches were all alike. No one had sat in the front row. No one ever did, not even in Boston.

Josh felt at home. "Anyone here ever make a mistake?"

The cowboys both grimaced. Josh had never been drunk, but knew a headache when he saw one. Brick looked chagrined, and the girl from Miss Elsa's clutched a hankie. Bessie and Caroline both nodded in support. Josh glanced at the man with the yellow teeth and saw a sneer. Preaching to outlaws had made Josh wise. He judged no man by his appearance, but neither did he turn his back on strangers. He looked straight at the man in the frock coat.

"I've made mistakes," Josh continued. "I make them every day. A year ago I made one so bad it cost me everything. What I'm here to say, friends, is that there's hope. If God can take a man like me—a man who, figuratively speaking, murdered his sister with his anger—then He can touch *you* right where you're sitting today."

The girl from the brothel had tears in her eyes. Brick and the cowboys merely blinked, but Josh rarely saw emotion in the faces of hardened men. Bessie sat with her usual calm, but Caroline, her eyes shimmering with admiration, worried him. She looked like a woman in love and not just with the Lord. As for the man with the yellow teeth, he looked amused.

In Josh's experience, mockers came from two camps. Some had chips on their shoulders. They knew their Bible but had been hurt and wanted to fight. Josh gladly took them on. The second group made his blood run cold. They were hard men who bullied others. Before arriving at Swan's Nest, he'd spent time with the Johnson gang. He'd seen Clay Johnson shoot a dog for wagging its tail at him. Josh didn't know where the fellow with the bad teeth stood, but his instincts told him to be careful. Before he went back to Swan's Nest, he intended to speak with the man. First, though, he had a sermon to give.

The words came to him easily. He told whatever Bible

stories came to mind and trusted the Holy Ghost to make them real. Today he told the story about the prodigal son. By the time he finished, Brick and the cowboys were sitting tall and Miss Elsa's girl looked alive with hope. The fourth man yawned.

"We'll close with a hymn," Josh said. "Who knows 'Rock of Ages'?"

Four hands went up.

Josh got ready to embarrass himself. As Wes Daniels once said, he couldn't carry a tune in a bucket. In Boston, he'd had a choir to fill the gap and he had refused to try. Here he had only himself. With no room for pride, he made a joyful noise to the Lord. Noise, he knew, was being charitable.

As the group sang the last verse, the man with the yellow teeth left the saloon. After the final note, Bessie greeted the girl from Miss Elsa's. As Caroline served cookies, Brick filled mugs with strong coffee. The small group lingered, chatting in the awkward way of strangers.

Josh motioned for Brick to step to the side. "Do you know the fellow who left?"

"Sure do. His name's Horace."

"Is he a regular?"

"On and off," Brick answered. "He's Franklin Dean's driver. Dean owns—"

"The Denver National Bank," Josh said dryly.

"That's him."

Josh thought of the man he'd chased out of the garden. They had similar builds.

"He doesn't say much," Brick added.

In Josh's experience, snakes lay in wait. One had spoken to Eve, but most of them struck without warning.

"Hey, Reverend."

Josh turned and saw the two cowboys. The younger raised his voice. "Thanks for the story."

"You're welcome."

Caroline approached him with a smile. "Are you ready to go back to Swan's Nest?"

Yes, but not with Caroline at his side. Josh had never been in this position. In Boston Emily had run interference for him. If she were here now, she would have spoken to Caroline without embarrassing her.

Bessie approached. "Wonderful sermon, Reverend."

"Thank you."

After giving Josh a knowing look, she turned to Caroline. "It's time for us to go."

Caroline frowned. "I thought Josh might like some company."

Until now he'd been Reverend Blue.

"He doesn't need us," Bessie said lightly. "Do you, Reverend?"

Josh didn't want to hurt Caroline's feelings, but he had to discourage her. "Go on ahead. I'll see everyone at supper."

Caroline looked dismayed, but she followed Bessie out the door.

Josh looked in the basket he'd set on the counter. He hadn't taken an offering, but he knew people would give. He saw a surprising amount of money, including two silver dollars. He didn't care about the amount. What blessed him was knowing people valued the message. He picked up the basket, approached Brick and put some coins on the counter. "For the coffee."

The barkeep shook his head. "You don't have to pay me, Reverend. It's my pleasure."

"I'm not paying you. The congregation is."

"I guess they did." Brick smiled. "Will you be back next Sunday?"

"Definitely."

No way could he leave Adie alone in Denver. Dean had sent a spy. Josh took it as a warning of trouble to come.

He put the rest of the offering in his pocket, then headed for Swan's Nest. He knew exactly what to do with the remaining money. He'd give it away to people in need. Right now, Adie and her mortgage payment were at the top of the list. He had a hunch she'd argue with him. Her cheeks would turn pink and her eyes would flash. She'd act tough, but she didn't stand a chance against Josh's good intentions. Just for the joy of it, he added a gold coin of his own.

For the third time that morning, Adie lifted the sugar bowl from the cupboard and counted the money she'd set aside for the mortgage. She needed twenty-two dollars. She had sixteen and some change. Josh had already paid his rent. Without it, she would have been impossibly short. Both Caroline and Bessie owed for the week, but yesterday Caroline had said she'd be short. Adie had fumed. If the woman hadn't been buying sugar for pies, she could have paid her rent. Bessie worked for Dr. Nichols. Sometimes he paid her a wage. Other times he shared what his clients gave him. A chicken, even a plump one, wouldn't pay the mortgage.

Pearl paid nothing. Mary would contribute, but she'd missed two days of work because of a fever.

Barring a miracle, Adie would have to sell a piece of jewelry to meet her obligation. A single brooch would pay the mortgage for months, but Josh checked the jewelry stores every day. She knew his habits because of Caroline. Every night at supper, she asked if he'd learned anything about his sister. Every night, he gave the same answer.

"Not yet," he'd reply. "But I won't give up."

Adie believed him.

With her stomach churning, she put away the money and looked at Stephen, asleep in the wicker basket she'd lined with cotton. He'd gone three days without colic. Every day Adie looked at his eyes for signs they'd turn brown like Maggie's. They were still blue…like Josh's.

Sighing, she stirred the soup. It looked thin, but she didn't want to sacrifice another chicken. She needed the eggs. She'd saved some carrots from her trampled garden, but they didn't make up for meat. Even if she scraped together the mortgage money, she needed feed for Buttons, shingles for the roof and food for six adults.

Footsteps padded down the hall. She looked up and saw Mary, dressed in faded calico with a shawl on her shoulders.

"You should be in bed," Adie scolded.

"I'm better."

"The fever could come back."

If Mary's illness returned, she wouldn't be able to work. If she couldn't work, she couldn't pay her rent. Adie instantly felt selfish for the thought. What had happened to her good-will? She wanted Swan's Nest to be a haven for women in need, not a place of disgrace.

Mary reached into the side pocket of her dress. "The mortgage is due in a few days, isn't it?"

"On Tuesday."

"Here." She set a handful of coins on the table. "It's all I've got, almost three dollars. I know things are tight."

Adie did some quick arithmetic. She needed another three dollars for the mortgage and spending money for the week. Maybe she could sell some of the linens stored in Josh's room, though she'd tried before and had gotten pennies.

"Will we make it?" Mary asked.

"I think so." Adie stirred the soup. Her boarders knew she struggled to make ends meet, but no one knew about the jewelry.

Mary glanced at the pot on the stove. "It smells good."

"Would you like some?"

"Just a little."

As she sat, the back door opened and Josh walked into the kitchen. "Good morning, ladies," he said as he hung his hat on a hook.

"Hello, Reverend," Mary answered.

Adie focused on the soup. Since the night on the porch, she hadn't been able to look Josh in the eye. Good manners demanded that she offer him a bowl, but she didn't want him to stay in the kitchen. She mumbled a greeting as thin as the broth.

"How was the service?" Mary asked.

"Good."

"I hear Bessie and Caroline enjoyed it."

Josh chuckled. "Maybe the preaching, but we need someone who can sing."

Mary gave a wistful sigh. "I used to sing every Saturday night. People came to the Ridgemont Canary just to hear me."

As Adie ladled soup for Mary, she heard chairs scraping against the floor, then the rustle of cotton as Mary sat first, then Josh. She didn't dare look up. If she kept her eyes down, she stood a better chance of avoiding conversation. Feeling invisible, she listened as Mary revealed to Josh that she'd sung in a fancy music hall in Texas and had come close to joining a traveling revue. Adie wondered what had stopped her.

If Josh wondered, he kept the question to himself. "If you're free next Sunday, I hope you'll sing for us."

Adie had filled the bowl to the brim. She didn't want to look Josh in the eye, but she had to bring the soup to Mary. As she turned, she heard a tremor in Mary's voice.

"Are you sure, Reverend? I'm not exactly…you know."

"I know, all right." He focused solely on Mary. "I'm not 'exactly,' either."

Neither was Adie.

The bowl dipped in her hand. Josh, tall and dark in his black coat, pushed up from the chair and steadied her grip with his long fingers. The sight of him should have filled her with resentment. Instead she saw his clear eyes and felt as if he truly understood the shame of her deception. His hair, slightly mussed from the hat he'd hung by the door, wisped over his ears and collar. The coat matched the raven color and made his features even sharper.

He lifted the bowl from her hands. "I've got it."

As he served Mary, Adie felt shaken to the core. Surely Maggie's brother wouldn't sit in a kitchen with a saloon girl and an unwed mother. He'd been a Boston muck-a-muck, not a man who'd hold church in a saloon. Oh, how she wanted to believe that lie….

Mary took a sip of soup, then gave Adie a pointed look. "The reverend might be hungry."

"I'm fine," he answered.

"Don't be silly," Mary said. "Please, join us."

Josh had gained weight, but he looked thin today. He'd had milk and bread for breakfast, but not a midday meal that she knew about. She feared his company, but she couldn't let him go hungry. "Mary's right. You need to eat."

"Thank you."

As she filled another bowl, she listened to Josh taking to Mary about her choice of hymns. She knew dozens, including a few Adie had liked as a little girl.

"I'll sing, but only if you're sure," she said.

"I'm positive," he replied.

Adie set the bowl in front of him. He looked up and smiled. "Thank you."

Mary ate quickly, then carried her bowl to the counter. "Thank you, Adie. I'm going back upstairs."

"Wait—"

Mary stopped. "Do you want me to take Stephen?"

"No, I just—" She didn't want to be alone with Josh but

couldn't say it. She felt foolish. She also knew Stephen would be happier in his cradle. "Yes, take him. That would be nice."

Mary lifted the basket and the baby, then shot Adie a look. "The reverend might enjoy the bread you baked."

Adie wanted Josh to finish his soup and leave, not linger over bread and butter. She frowned but went to the bread box and removed the fresh loaf. As Mary left the kitchen, Adie sliced the bread, put it on a plate and fetched the butter crock. She set everything on the table. Before she could turn, Josh caught her eye.

"I'd like to speak to you," he said quietly.

"What is it?"

"I have something to give you." He stood and indicated Mary's chair. "Please, sit down."

His Boston manners made her nervous, but she couldn't avoid him. She sat and folded her hands. Josh reached into his coat pocket and extracted a handful of coins. As they plinked on the table, she spotted two silver dollars and a golden half eagle. As she looked up with shock, Josh sat back on the chair.

"I know money's tight." He slid the pile in her direction. "You have a need and I believe God wants to meet it. This is for you. It's today's offering from church."

She desperately needed the money, but she felt dishonest taking it from Josh. His generosity would protect her secret. The irony shamed her. "I can't accept."

"Sure you can."

She looked at her lap.

Josh made his voice light. "Don't be shy, Adie. I know your secret."

Startled, she raised her head. "What secret?"

"You're as prideful as I am."

She couldn't swallow. "Is that all?"

"I don't know. Is there more?" He touched her hand.

"Whatever's in your heart, it's between you and God. When I look at you, I see an honest, hardworking woman. I'm proud to know you."

Could she feel any lower than she did right now? Adie didn't think so.

Still holding her hand, he kept his voice low. "This gift is between you and God, too. You can toss it in the air if you want, but I hope you'll use it for the mortgage."

He released her hand and picked up his spoon. Unable to speak, she watched as he finished his soup, savoring every bite as if it were worth more than the pile of coins. When he finished, he carried the bowl to the counter, lifted his hat from the hook and went to his room without another word.

Adie looked at his retreating back, then touched the coins with a single thought. Joshua Blue was the kindest, most honorable man she'd ever know. She pushed to her feet and called down the hall. "Josh?"

He stopped but didn't turn. "Yes?"

"Thank you."

As if he wasn't sure he should look, he faced her. As a cloud passed away from the sun, light shot through the window, warming her face and making her squint. Josh faded to a shadow, but she heard his voice.

"You're welcome," he said. "But it's not from me."

The door to his room closed with a soft click. Adie should have been relieved, but she wanted to run down the hall and pound on the wood. Her heart ached with the need to confess.

I had a friend named Maggie Butler. Stephen could be your nephew.

The thought choked her. She simply couldn't do it.

She wouldn't.

She swept the coins into her palm and added them to the sugar bowl. On Tuesday she'd make the payment, but using

Josh's money—or God's money—left her bitter. Her soul, already ragged, raveled to a frayed edge. Even worse, her heart ached for Josh. She wanted to ease his burden almost as much as she wanted to protect Stephen from Maggie's brother.

Shaking inside, she closed the cupboard and turned back to the soup. As she gave it a stir, steam dampened her face. She heard footsteps in the hall, looked up and saw Caroline still wearing her Sunday best. The woman said hello, then helped herself to a glass of water. "Church was wonderful."

Adie didn't want to hear it.

"Josh is the best preacher I've ever heard."

When had *Josh* invited Caroline to use his given name? Adie used it, but they'd become friends. Her conscience lurched with another half-truth. Her feelings for Josh ran far deeper than friendship. The admission made her head spin. She didn't want to love Josh or any man. She couldn't. Not with a life built on secrets, half-truths and bald-faced lies.

Caroline headed for the pantry. "Seven people came to Brick's."

Adie thought of the offering. Someone had given generously, a sign that Josh's words had mattered.

"That's nice," she replied.

"I bet more people come next week."

Adie's felt a stab of fear. He'd asked Mary to sing. Adie had heard her friend's soprano and knew she'd attract visitors. Josh's preaching had filled a Boston cathedral. What if his little church grew each week? If he stayed in Denver, Adie would be afraid forever.

Caroline opened the pantry and removed the pie she'd baked for dessert. Adie had had enough. Looking over her shoulder, she frowned. "We don't need dessert *every* night."

"Josh likes apple pie."

Get 2 Books FREE!

Steeple Hill Books,
publisher of inspirational fiction,
presents

Love Inspired
HISTORICAL
INSPIRATIONAL HISTORICAL ROMANCE

A new series of historical love stories that promise romance, adventure and faith!

FREE BOOKS!   Use the reply card inside to get two free books
by outstanding historical romance authors!

FREE GIFTS!   You'll also get two exciting surprise gifts, absolutely free!

GET 2 BOOKS

IF YOU ENJOY A HISTORICAL ROMANCE STORY that reflects solid, traditional values, then you'll like *Love Inspired® Historical* novels. These are engaging tales filled with romance, adventure and faith set in various historical periods from biblical times to World War II.

We'd like to send you two *Love Inspired Historical* novels absolutely free. Accepting them puts you under no obligation to purchase any more books.

HOW TO GET YOUR 2 FREE BOOKS AND TWO FREE GIFTS

1. Return the reply card today, and we'll send you two *Love Inspired Historical* novels, absolutely free! We'll even pay the postage!
2. Accepting free books places you under no obligation to buy anything, ever. The two books have combined cover prices of $11.00 in the U.S. and $13.00 in Canada, but they're yours to keep, free!
3. We hope that after receiving your free books you'll want to remain a subscriber, but the choice is yours–to continue or cancel, any time at all!

EXTRA BONUS

You'll also get two free mystery gifts! (worth about $10)

FREE!

If offer card is missing, write to Steeple Hill Reader Service, 3010 Walden Ave., P.O. Box 1867, Buffalo, NY 14240-1867

POSTAGE WILL BE PAID BY ADDRESSEE

BUSINESS REPLY MAIL
FIRST-CLASS MAIL   PERMIT NO. 717   BUFFALO, NY

Steeple Hill Reader Service
3010 WALDEN AVENUE
PO BOX 1867
BUFFALO NY 14240-9952

NO POSTAGE
NECESSARY
IF MAILED
IN THE
UNITED STATES

"He's being polite." Adie knew for a fact he preferred pound cake with strawberries. She thought of the squashed berry plants and felt angry all over again.

Caroline eyed her thoughtfully. "You like him, don't you?"

"Of course not!"

She'd answered too quickly. A smile curved on Caroline's lips. "That's what I thought."

"I like him," Adie admitted. "But not in that way."

"I like him, too." Caroline's eyes turned wistful. "I was married once, you know."

To a man of color in the South…Caroline had seen him lynched. Adie felt stricken. Who was she to criticize Caroline's feelings for Josh? Or his feelings for Caroline? If he'd invited her to use his given name, perhaps he had an interest in her. Why not? Caroline had wavy dark hair, green eyes and a bow-shaped mouth. Any man would find her pretty and she had a sharp mind.

Caroline set the pie on the counter. "I know I've overdone it with the baking, but it feels good to *want* to do it."

Adie stirred the soup. "I wouldn't know."

"You've never been in love?"

"No."

Caroline made a humming sound. "It's the best feeling in the world. I remember how it was with Samuel. It was dangerous, but I don't regret a minute."

Adie didn't know what to think. All her life she'd been afraid. She'd worried that her father wouldn't come home and one day he hadn't. She'd fretted over her mother's health and she'd died. She'd feared Timothy Long and Reverend Honeycutt and they'd both harmed her. She understood fear far better than love, yet with Josh she wondered… What would it be like to live with confidence? To feel safe and be free of secrets?

She put the lid on the soup. It would simmer until supper. So would her problems and there was nothing she could do. Until Josh left Denver, she'd be a nervous wreck. Seeing no escape, she went upstairs to hold her son.

Chapter Ten

As he neared Colfax Avenue Church, Josh thought about
what to say to Reverend Tobias Oliver. With the success of the
little church in Brick's Saloon, he felt compelled to pay a call
on local clergy to introduce himself. He'd preached two
Sundays and attendance had increased to twelve. Not everyone
approved of a church in a saloon, but he'd learned in his travels
that a Harvard degree silenced his critics. Like Paul, Josh
didn't mind revealing his credentials for the cause of Christ.

He also wanted to speak to the man about Pearl. Of the two
missions, the second would be the most difficult. Josh had no
business raising such a personal matter, but how could he keep
silent? If someone had taken him to task for his hypocrisy,
Emily would be safe in Boston and he'd be... Josh didn't
know where he'd be. He rued the reason for his travels, but
the past year had made him a better man. If Emily hadn't left,
he'd have missed the biggest challenges—the biggest blessings—of his life.

Those blessings included Adie. Josh had never been on
such a twisting road. He cared for her. Every day his feelings
deepened. She also exasperated him with her silence. She

hadn't spoken to him in days, but he knew her habits. She hadn't been sleeping well. At night she wandered in the flower garden behind the wounded vegetables. He prayed constantly for her. When he left Denver, it would be with the regret that he'd failed yet another woman.

Today, though, he could help Pearl. He expected to find Reverend Oliver in the church office, but before he reached the main building, he saw a house set back from the street. A wide porch surrounded a stone cottage with a gabled roof. Ivy climbed up the sides and lilacs bloomed at the base of the steps. On the porch sat a man in a black coat, sipping tea as he read a book.

Josh strode down the brick path to the porch. "Reverend Oliver?"

"That's correct."

"I'm Joshua Blue."

"Ah," he said. "The minister from Boston. I've heard of you."

"That's why I've come," Josh said. "I'd prefer to meet face-to-face than listen to talk."

"My feelings exactly."

The older man waved Josh up the steps. After they shook hands, he indicated a chair. As Josh sat, Reverend Oliver went into the cottage. He returned a few minutes later with a refreshment tray. He set it on the table, sat and lifted a flowered teapot with a gnarled hand. He looked at Josh with stark apology. "If my daughter were here, she'd serve cake. All I can manage is tea."

"Tea is fine, sir. Thank you."

In the time between Emily's departure and his own, Josh had been in this man's position. He'd fumbled with teapots and served stale baked goods. Few men appreciated a woman's touch until they had to manage on their own.

The reverend filled Josh's cup and handed it to him. "I understand you're living at Swan's Nest. How's my Pearl?"

His openness took Josh by surprise. "She's fine."

"And the baby? It's not here yet, is it?"

"No."

The man sipped his tea. "It's a tragedy."

Josh saw an opening and took it. "It depends, sir."

He frowned. "On what?"

"What Pearl does next."

Reverend Oliver set down his cup and crossed his arms. "You seem rather sure of yourself."

"I am." Josh settled back in his chair. "I didn't come to speak of Pearl, sir. I came to tell you about myself. I have a sister. About a year ago, she left Boston under circumstances similar to your daughter's situation."

The reverend huffed. "She did you a favor."

"I don't think so."

"Come now, Reverend. You know how people talk."

"I do," Josh said. "I also know that I called my sister an unspeakable name and she left in the middle of the night. She took a westbound train and never wrote. For all I know, she could be dead. The baby—" Josh sealed his lips. "I can't stand the thought of what might have become of the child. Sir, you don't want to know what that's like."

Reverend Oliver stared hard at Josh. "My daughter sinned."

"Do you know that for a fact?"

"It's obvious!"

"Not to me," Josh said quietly. "I don't know who fathered my sister's baby. I don't know if she was seduced or raped. All I know is that she needed help and I threw stones at her."

The old man's eyes narrowed. "It's no mystery what happened to Pearl. I'll be candid with you, Reverend Blue—"

"Please, call me Josh."

"Then I'm Tobias." The old man cleared his throat. "I'm not naive. I know that men and women stumble, even good

Christians like my daughter. I've sinned. You've sinned. Frank wants to make things right. I don't understand why Pearl won't let him."

Josh knew, but he couldn't break Adie's confidence. "Ask your daughter."

"I've spoken with Frank," he said confidently. "He came to me after the buggy ride that led to this mess. I blame myself for letting them go alone, but they'd been courting for months. I trusted him."

A wolf in sheep's clothing, Josh thought.

"He confessed their mistake and asked for permission to marry Pearl immediately. Of course I granted it."

"Did you speak to Pearl?"

"Her feelings were evident." Tobias frowned. "If they'd married right away, there wouldn't have been any talk at all."

Tobias wanted to spare himself the embarrassment, but Josh didn't doubt his desire to protect Pearl. Josh had been misguided about Emily in the same way. He'd honestly thought giving up the baby was for the best.

He had another question for Tobias. "Are you aware of Mr. Dean's visits to Swan's Nest?"

"Only vaguely."

"He's been forceful."

Tobias wrinkled his brow. "He loves Pearl. He's concerned for his child."

Josh tried again. "Mr. Dean has proposed marriage. Is that right?"

"It is."

"And Pearl said no." Josh lowered his voice. "Haven't you wondered why?"

Tobias said nothing.

Josh reached for his tea, took a long sip and made a decision. He couldn't break Adie's confidence, but Reverend

Oliver had to know the truth. "Sir, do you recall the story of Amnon and Tamar?"

His eyes narrowed. "Of course, it's in Second Samuel. Amnon was a son of David. He took Tamar against her will and died at Absalom's orders."

"That's right."

"What are you implying?"

Josh raised his chin. "Amnon was the son of king, a trusted member of the household. Tamar was innocent."

Reverend Oliver's cheeks flamed. "Are you saying this happened to Pearl?"

"I'm telling a Bible story."

"Don't beat around the bush, Reverend. How do you know?"

Josh prayed to do the right thing. "I can't say, sir. But you need to speak with your daughter. Don't lose her the way I lost Emily."

Tobias's face turned red. "I just assumed…Pearl's mother is gone. I couldn't speak with her about something so—so private."

Josh understood. "It's a taboo subject, but the sin is very real."

The old man shot to his feet. "He deserves to hang for what he did!"

"It's an allegation, sir. Pearl might not want to speak up."

Tobias sat back down. "I'll do anything for my daughter. She talked about leaving Denver, but I said no. My church is here. My congregation needs me."

"May I offer a suggestion?"

The old man looked as if he'd been punched. "Please."

"Speak with Pearl."

"I will."

"Let her decide what's best."

Tobias looked across the yard to the stone church. Josh followed his gaze and saw a row of stained glass windows. The first depicted a shepherd and five sheep. Josh thought of the women at Swan's Nest. The second showed Christ with children in his lap. The third displayed an empty cross and a rising sun. Red and purple made up the cross. The sun, a yellow circle, gleamed against a royal-blue sky. The fourth window showed the woman at the well. Jesus had personally told her to go in peace, that her sins were forgiven.

Pearl's father looked back at Josh. "Do you think Pearl will see me?"

"I hope so."

He raked his hand through his iron-gray hair. "I'd go tonight, but the elders are meeting. Frank's on the board. If what you're saying is true—and I believe it is—I have to address it."

Josh knew all about church politics. Women got blamed for gossiping, but men were just as prone to talk too much. He didn't miss the chatter at all. "A suggestion, sir?"

"Of course."

"Speak to Pearl first."

"I will." Looking haggard, Tobias took a drag of tea and grunted. "It's not strong enough, is it?"

"No."

He sighed. "Pearl makes perfect tea."

"Come tomorrow," Josh said.

His eyes turned shiny. "I've missed her."

Silence settled between them. Tobias finished his tea, then straightened his back and crossed his arms. "So, I hear you've started a church. Do you intend to stay in Denver?"

"Only as long as I have to," Josh answered. "Unfortunately, there's more to the story about Mr. Dean."

His eyes narrowed. "Tell me."

Josh told him about the garden and Horace's visit to Brick's Saloon. "Miss Clarke believes—and I agree—that Dean wants her house."

"Why?"

"Land values are increasing almost daily. She's also giving sanctuary to Pearl. Until we know who's behind the vandalism, I intend to stay at Swan's Nest."

"A wise call."

"And necessary."

"Then what?" Tobias gave him an assessing look.

"I'll resume searching for Emily."

"And starting churches in saloons?"

"Sure," Josh replied. "Not everyone's comfortable behind stained glass." He wasn't, not anymore.

Tobias looked hard into Josh's eyes. "You've suffered, haven't you?"

His chest felt heavy; then his body lightened with joy. He recalled Gerard Richards telling him he'd be a better preacher after he suffered. How true those words had been…. Without the struggle of the past year, he'd still be an arrogant know-it-all parading in his black robe, speaking in high-minded tones and hiding his bottle of laudanum. Gratitude washed over him. If his story would help Tobias, he had to tell it.

He looked the older man in the eye. "I failed my sister, sir. I prayed every night and memorized scripture. I claimed to love God more than myself, but when my position was on the line, I treated Emily like a leper."

"You succumbed to pride," Tobias said. "I know the temptation."

"It's ugly."

"And unavoidable. Don't despair, Josh. We worship a God of mercy."

"That we do."

Being of one mind, the men stood at the same time. Tobias held out his hand and they shook. "Come some evening for a visit. It's lonely without Pearl."

"I'll do that."

As Josh turned to leave, his gaze landed on the window showing the shepherd and five sheep. He thought of his "sheep" at Swan's Nest and felt a tug he'd never experienced before. He didn't want to leave them, especially not Adie, but he had to go. Somewhere, Emily and her child needed him. Maybe more, he needed them.

Josh walked back to Colfax Avenue and headed for the part of town where pawnbrokers ran shops. He hoped someone had heard of Emily or seen her jewelry, but more likely, he was grasping at straws. The thought filled him with despair. Instead of visiting the stores, he headed for the café where Mary worked. He needed a strong cup of tea, one that didn't remind him of Pearl and Adie, broken lives and people who threw stones.

With the mortgage receipt tucked in her reticule, Adie left the bank and headed for the café to say hello to Mary. She'd avoided Franklin Dean, but a knot had formed in her belly the instant she entered the building. A cup of tea would settle her nerves, plus she had promised Mary that she'd stop by the café.

Ever since the vandalism, Mary had been extra vigilant. She'd told Adie to ask Josh to accompany her to the bank, but Adie had refused. Josh would visit pawnbrokers and she didn't want to go with him. She'd see the hope in his eyes, then the disappointment. All the time, she'd feel guilty.

She turned on to Grant Avenue. At the sight of Franklin Dean's carriage, she paled. She would have turned around, but his driver spotted her. With a cold smile, he tipped his hat. Adie looked away without acknowledging him and found herself looking at Dean himself. He'd just come out of a fancy barbershop. Even three feet away, she smelled his cologne.

"Good afternoon, Miss Clarke."

"Mr. Dean."

He smiled. "May I offer you a ride to Swan's Nest?"

"No, thank you."

As she tried to pass, he blocked her steps. "It's not the least bit out of my way."

He'd told a flat-out lie. Swan's Nest sat on the outskirts of town. No one traveled in that direction unless they lived in the neighborhood. Taunting the banker would fan his temper, so she tried to sound pleasant. "If you'll excuse me—"

"Tea, then."

"No, thank you."

He scowled at her. "You're making this difficult, Miss Clarke. I want to know about Pearl. The baby's due in a few weeks. I have a right—"

"You have no rights!"

His eyes narrowed to snakelike slits.

Adie regretted the outburst. She had a strong will, but she couldn't outstare a man as cold-blooded as the banker. She softened her voice. "The baby's not due for a month. Pearl's doing just fine. When the time comes, Bessie will see to them both."

Adie expected a rant. Instead he reached inside his coat and lifted his wallet. He took out several bills. "Give this to Pearl."

Adie couldn't stand the thought of touching the money. Pearl would be revolted.

He shoved it closer. "It's to pay for a real doctor."

If Adie took the money, Pearl would be indebted to this man. If she didn't, Dean's temper might explode. She risked the explosion. "Thank you, but Pearl's needs are met."

She forced her way past him. Walking as fast as she could, she headed for Mary's café. Behind her she heard the rattle of the carriage, then Dean's voice coming from the backseat. "You'll regret that, Miss Clarke."

"I don't think so."

"Then think again."

He tapped the seat with his gold-tipped walking stick. The driver gave the horses free rein and they picked up their pace, stirring dust as the carriage passed her. Shaking, Adie watched him go, then hurried into the restaurant, where she saw Mary serving a man at a back table. She couldn't see his face, but she recognized the angle of Josh's shoulders. Mary waved her forward.

Common sense told Adie to leave, but her insides felt like jelly. She needed tea and safety. Being with Josh offered both, so she walked to his table. At the sight of her, he stood and gave a slight bow. His fancy manners unnerved her even more and she wished she'd left the café.

He touched her arm. "Are you all right?"

"I'm—I just—"

He pulled out a chair. "Sit."

Mary urged her into it. "I'm bringing tea."

As the waitress hurried away, Adie took a breath to steady herself. Her chest felt as if horses were galloping inside her ribs. As Josh held her hand, the gallop turned to a dead run.

"What happened?" he said.

"I saw Franklin Dean."

She told him about the money for Pearl and how she'd refused it. When she described Dean blocking her path, his mouth thinned to a line.

Mary brought the tea but couldn't stay. Adie lifted a spoon to add sugar, but her hand shook so badly that the crystals showered the table. Josh took the spoon from her fingers, put the sugar in her cup, then added a second spoonful and a dash of milk. He knew exactly how she took her tea, a sign that he'd been watching her every move.

Using both hands, she raised the cup and sipped. If she

hadn't managed on her own, Josh would have held it to her lips. All her life, she'd stayed strong for other people. Josh wanted to be strong for *her*. What would it be like to lean on this man? Adie didn't want to know. He posed a threat of his own. Shaking, she set the cup on the saucer. Frightened or not, she had to finish her story. "Dean threatened me."

"What did he say?"

"That I'd regret not taking the money for Pearl."

Josh's fingers curled into a fist. "That low-down—" He clamped his jaws.

Adie wanted to do more than call Dean names. "The broken window, the garden…I don't know what he'll do next."

"We need to see Deputy Morgan."

"I don't want to."

"Why not?"

Adie knew about Josh's visit to the sheriff's office. He'd reported the garden incident and nothing had been said about Maggie, but that could change. Besides, what if Josh *wasn't* Stephen's uncle? What if a man as evil as Maggie had described was still looking for her? She wanted as little exposure to the law as possible. She shook her head. "It'll make things worse."

"So will doing nothing."

"But …" She couldn't think of a single excuse.

"We'll go right now."

"Tomorrow." Her insides were still trembling and she couldn't think straight. If the sheriff asked questions, she had to be calm.

Josh's mouth tightened. "Tomorrow it is."

Behind Adie, a plate crashed on the tile floor. She jumped as if she'd heard gunfire.

Josh clasped her hand. The warmth of it stole her breath. It took away the terror of Dean's threats and the coldness of being alone. She raised her gaze and saw the heat of war in his eyes.

This man would fight for her. She wanted to fight for him, too. She'd fed him bread and milk. She'd seen him hurting and she'd seen him heal. If she couldn't trust Josh, whom could she trust? Surely he wouldn't pull Stephen from her arms?

He deserved the truth about Maggie and Emily. He'd become a friend, but the possibilities scared Adie to death. Josh had integrity. He'd want to give Stephen his place in Boston and the family business. Adie felt sick with fear, but her guilt weighed more. She couldn't bear it, not while peering into Josh's eyes. Color flooded her cheeks. She looked at her lap, but she couldn't hide from his presence.

He touched her cheek. "Secrets hurt, Adie."

She bit her lip.

"Did someone harm you?"

She cringed.

"Did you fight to protect yourself?" His voice dropped to a whisper. "No matter what you did, I'll help you."

No, he wouldn't. He'd take her son to Boston. He'd hate her for hiding the truth. She'd couldn't tell Josh about Maggie, but she had to say *something* to make him leave her alone. "Someday I'll tell you about it."

She'd opened the door a tiny crack, but it was enough for the truth to shine. If she confessed to Josh, she'd be free of the guilt. Even in his black coat, he was a human being, a man with a good heart.

He squeezed her hand.

She squeezed back and felt strangled. Maybe for now, she'd said enough.

They sat in silence until Mary arrived with two pieces of pie. The dessert reminded Adie of Caroline and how she'd used Josh's first name. His feelings for Caroline were none of Adie's business, but she couldn't stop herself from feeling jealous. Someday Caroline would marry and have children.

Adie never would. She had too many secrets. She lifted her fork. "It's apple."

"It's good," he said.

She forced a smile. "It's not as good as Caroline's."

He stopped with his fork midway to his mouth, then lowered it. "I've got a problem, don't I?"

Adie didn't want to jump to conclusions. "What do you mean?"

"You haven't noticed?"

For once she could tell the truth. "Actually, we all have."

"Emily used to be my buffer. She'd spread the word—" he hooked his fingers to make quote marks "—Reverend Blue isn't interested in marriage."

Adie thought Josh would be a fine husband. "Why not?"

"Lots of reasons."

She waited for details, but he took a bite of pie. It felt good to ask questions instead of answering them, so she smiled at him. "Now who's keeping secrets?"

His lips curved up, but his eyes had a tinge of sadness. "It's not a secret. My work matters to me more than anything. Getting married—having a family—takes a big piece of a man's life. Without that responsibility, I can give everything to my work."

"So you'll never marry?"

"Probably not." The sadness returned to his eyes. "It's one of the reasons I have to find Emily. Her child's an heir to a fortune."

Adie gasped.

Josh looked quizzical. "You're surprised."

Until now she'd thought only of losing Stephen, not about what he'd gain by taking the Blue family name. If Josh claimed Stephen as his nephew, her son would have the finest clothes and a good education. He wouldn't eat broth for supper or wear old shoes as Adie did. The pie in her mouth turned to dust. She sipped her tea, but it had gone cold.

Josh took another bite of his dessert. He looked pleased. "I hope I find Emily soon. I'm going to love being an uncle."

Adie forced herself to smile. "You think so?"

"Definitely. Holding Stephen was the best feeling in the world." Josh set down his fork. "I envy you, Adie. You struggle with money, but you've got a beautiful son and wonderful friends. Someday you'll fall in love. You'll get married and have more children."

Could he torment her more? She had too many burdens to consider marriage. She had jewelry to hide and a secret to keep. Sometimes she wondered about marriage, but she pushed the notion aside. She had Stephen. Being a mother was enough.

Josh broke into her thoughts. "So tell me, *Miss* Clarke, does some Denver gentleman have his eye on you?"

"Not hardly." She decided to turn the tables. "What about you, *Reverend* Blue? You must have broken a few hearts in Boston."

"I don't think so." His gaze lingered on her face. "Sometimes, though, I wonder what it would be like."

His eyes glimmered with a discord that matched her own. Was he lonely? Did he think about sharing sunsets and morning coffee? She did, more than ever since he'd come to Swan's Nest. She was thinking about such things now, but those feelings could only cause trouble. To distract herself, she took another bite of pie. It tasted sweet, but she barely noticed. The way Josh looked at her had been even sweeter.

As he'd said, sometimes she wondered.

Chapter Eleven

"Take it away, Lord. This feeling for Adie—" Josh groaned out loud.

The sun had set hours ago. After supper, he'd helped with the dishes, then gone out the back door to avoid seeing any of the women. He wanted to speak with Pearl but didn't have the heart for it. Tonight his thoughts were on Adie, and he didn't like the direction they'd taken. How could he think about staying in Denver when Emily was still missing? As for the second turn his thoughts had taken, he had no business courting Adie or any woman. He needed to be alone to pray, so he'd gone to the far end of the flower garden.

He stood there now, a man with anxious thoughts. Josh had noticed pretty women before now, but he'd never felt a stirring in his soul the way he did for Adie. When she smiled, he felt joy. When she wept, he tasted salt. Yesterday she'd been afraid and he'd wanted to murder Franklin Dean. No one—not even Emily—had ever inspired such deep feelings.

Neither had he felt a worry like the one in his gut. Adie was in trouble; he felt sure of it. Every time he mentioned going to the law, she balked. For the past hour, Josh's imagination had run amuck. Women traveled west for all sorts of reasons. Having Stephen out of wedlock explained her secrecy but not her reaction to seeing the sheriff. When it came to shame, she had nothing to hide from him. She knew he wouldn't stand in judgment. That's why he'd told her about Emily.

She had something else to hide, something with grave consequences. Had she committed a crime? Josh looked at Swan's Nest and recalled the question he'd considered when he'd first arrived. Even with a loan, how had she been able to buy a mansion? The possibilities made his belly hurt. Maybe she'd been a servant in a fine home. She could have stolen jewelry and taken a westbound train. Maybe she'd been abused and had seen the theft as her only escape. His mind went down a dark alley, a place full of violence and tears. Had she been raped? Had she killed her attacker to save herself?

She'd suffered and the pain hadn't eased. It wouldn't until she faced the past, but at what cost? The thought of Adie going to prison filled him with horror. Stephen would be ripped from his mother's arms. If Bessie or Caroline didn't take him, he'd go to a foundling home. Pearl had problems of her own. Mary had secrets.

That left Josh. He'd never expected to have a family, but he wanted one now. Adie made him feel alive. When she entered a room, his heart sped up. His eyes would find hers and his soul would settle.

"Why, Lord?" he said to the moon. "I can't stay in Denver. I have to find Emily." He kept his eyes on the stars. "After that, you've called me to preach, but where?"

Josh's thoughts ran wild. The Lord was everywhere, including Denver. His congregation at Brick's had doubled in size. The growth indicated fertile ground. He didn't care about the number for the sake of his pride, but it proved he'd planted seeds and they'd sprouted. He wanted to water those seeds and watch them grow.

God had planted another seed, one Josh couldn't deny. He'd fallen in love with Adie. Had a man ever given her flowers? He wanted to be the first. As for the other firsts in a woman's life, someone had taken her innocence and used it to hurt her. Josh cared for Adie's sake but not his own. When he looked at her, he saw virtue and perfect beauty.

Once he found Emily, he could return to Denver and court Adie properly. But when would that be? How much longer was he destined to search? Josh looked at the stars. He saw God's power in every single one and thought of Adie sitting in the café, pale and trembling because of Franklin Dean. Or was it because of *him?* Did she return his affection?

Someone gasped.

Josh looked down the path from the house and saw Adie turning back. In Boston he never met with women alone. He'd been careful to protect his reputation as well as theirs. Adie deserved the same consideration, but he couldn't let her leave. A woman didn't wander alone at midnight unless she had a troubled heart.

"Adie?"

She stopped but didn't turn.

He kept his voice light. "Can't sleep?"

"I haven't tried." She faced him then. Moonlight revealed her upturned chin. "I wanted some air. That's all."

Josh thought of the times Emily had questioned him about his "stomach medicine." He'd worn a similar look, one that mixed defiance and desperation. Emily had been intimidated by the defiance and had left him alone. He wished she'd seen the desperation and taken him to task. Adie needed help. If she'd let Josh get close, God had the power to turn ugliness to something good.

Before Josh found the words, Adie broke the silence. "About the sheriff tomorrow, I've changed my mind."

His heart plummeted. "Why?"

"He can't help me."

"We don't know that."

"I do," she said. "Now if you'll excuse me—"

"No," he said. "I won't."

The only other time he'd spoken so forcefully to a woman had been the night Emily left. He hated himself for that outburst, but he felt no remorse for being firm now. Adie needed to face the truth.

Her face tensed with outrage, then softened with a yearning Josh understood in his gut. How many times had he hoped someone would find the laudanum and free him from the lie? He suspected Adie felt the same way, but confronting her came with a risk. She could order him to leave Swan's Nest. She might never speak to him again. He found the thought intolerable, but neither could he leave her to suffer.

Honesty required courage. He needed it now. Knowing Adie might come to hate him, he spoke with authority. "Are you wanted by the law? Is that your secret?"

"It's none of your business."

He indicated Swan's Nest with a sweep of his arm. "This house...where did you get the money? Even with a loan—"

"What are you saying?" Her voice trembled.

"I'm afraid for you."

"Don't be."

"Dean could do real harm." He gestured at the vegetable garden. "He's evil, but I'm even more worried about what you're not telling me."

Adie pulled a thin shawl around her shoulders. "There's nothing you can do."

"I can listen."

She sealed her lips.

"If you need an attorney, I'll hire one."

Her mouth gaped.

"Whatever you did, it can be forgiven. I'll help you through it, Adie. If you stole—"

"I didn't." Her voice dropped low. "At least not money."

Her confession confused him. "What *did* you steal?"

She'd stolen the truth. She had it hidden in the trunk. No matter what she'd promised Maggie, Josh had a right to know if Maggie and Emily were the same woman. Adie had robbed him of that opportunity. She'd come to the garden to avoid him and had stumbled into a trap of her own making. Lies led to more lies. She couldn't bear to look at him, but neither could she flee. If she didn't answer his questions now—at least in part—he'd keep asking.

Yesterday Bessie had urged her to tell Josh the truth. Later Mary had cornered her in the laundry room. Caroline hadn't mentioned Stephen's birth, but Adie had seen her looking closely at the baby, then at Josh. No one had told him she'd adopted the child, but the truth could slip. She could lose everything.

"Talk to me, Adie."

He took a slow step in her direction, then a second and a third. She smelled roses, then the starch of his shirt. She tried to put him in the same camp as Reverend Honeycutt but couldn't. Without knowing her mistake, he'd offered to help her. She could have committed murder and he'd look at her with the same understanding.

Adie weighed her choices. She could tell the truth and hope for the best. She could spin a tale about a rich uncle or make up a dead fiancé. Or she could say nothing. The last option appealed to her, but she doubted she had the strength. She ached to be free of the guilt. Even stronger was the desire to free Josh. They stood face-to-face, breathing in the same rhythm and feeling the same confusion. When the tears spilled down her cheeks, he wiped them with his thumb. No one had ever touched her with such tenderness. Weakened, her shoulders rolled forward. She cupped her face in her hands, but a sob still burst from her throat.

With his arm around her shoulders, Josh guided her to a stone bench, where they sat side by side, hips close but not touching. Slowly, as if they were made of wet clay, they leaned against each other.

"Cry it out," he murmured.

But she couldn't. Tears wouldn't cleanse her. Only the truth could set her free and she feared it more than ever. She jerked upright.

He kept his hand on her back. "I don't care what you've done, Adie. You need to confide in someone."

"It's private."

"I'll take your secret to the grave." He touched her chin, forcing her to look into his eyes. "If you can't tell me, take it to God."

She thought of Timothy Long and Reverend Honeycutt, then Maggie dying in spite of their shared prayers. She jumped to her feet and turned on Josh. "Where was God when my mother died? I was twelve and all alone. I tried to bury her myself, but I couldn't."

"I'm sorry."

"Where was God when Timothy Long did what he did?" Her voice shook. "And when Reverend Honeycutt sent me away like trash! Where was God when—" *When Maggie died.* She choked back a cry. Just as she feared, the truth had come to a boil.

Josh stood and clasped her hands. She tried to pull away, but he tugged her closer…closer still…until he held her in his arms and she was weeping on his shirt. She wanted to stop but couldn't. Safe in his arms, she wept for the frightened girl who'd been run out of her hometown. Through choked sobs, she told him about that year in the Long house, how Timothy had abused her and how Reverend Honeycutt had sent her away.

His arms tightened around her. "No wonder you feel bad when I mention Emily. I'm sorry, Adie. You deserved better."

So did Josh. He deserved the truth.

He tucked her head against his shoulder. "Timothy Long… Is he Stephen's father?"

She thought of Maggie bleeding out and her deathbed promise. What mattered more? Josh's peace of mind or Adie's word to Maggie? Josh had a good heart. That goodness could compel him to take his nephew home.

She wiped her nose. "Stephen's my son. That's all you need to know."

As she broke from his arms, she noticed the smell of roses for the second time. The fragrance reminded her of Maggie's burial. Across the hedge she saw the remaining vegetables. The single cornstalk had the jangled look of a skeleton. The tomato plants hung in a lifeless tangle, a reminder of Franklin Dean and his assault on Swan's Nest.

Josh stepped to her side. "I know you've suffered, Adie. I know it doesn't make sense."

She sniffed. "No, it doesn't."

"Honeycutt failed you."

Her eyes burned with the memory of boarding the train out of Liddy's Grove. The Honeycutts had arranged for her to work for relatives of theirs in Nebraska. Traveling alone, she'd gotten looks from strangers and had been afraid. The cousins had been decent folk, but Adie had been a servant when she longed to be a daughter, a sister. After a year, she'd left. She'd gone to Topeka where she'd struggled to find work. In the end, she'd been reduced to sweeping saloons and eating scraps.

Everything had changed when she'd seen Maggie Butler, obviously with child, walk proudly into the Topeka Hotel. On a whim, Adie had approached her and asked if she needed a maid.

"No," she'd said. "But I desperately need a friend."

The memory made Adie sniff. She turned to look at Swan's Nest. She hoped Maggie would be proud.

Adie felt Josh standing behind her, gazing at the mansion rising tall and dark against the purple sky. Not a single light burned in the windows, but nothing could hide the house's grandeur. The mansion brought them back to the questions of money and stealing.

He clasped her shoulders, then turned her to face him. His voice, low and strong, filled her ears. "You *know* I'm not like Honeycutt. You can trust me, Adie."

"I can't trust anyone," she insisted. "But I'm telling the truth. I didn't steal the money for Swan's Nest. And I'm not wanted by the law."

"Then Stephen's father—"

"No."

He tightened his grip. "Talk to me, Adie. I care about you."

His confession sent tremors to his hands. Josh looked startled, but his eyes held no regret. Instead he broke a rose off the hedge and handed it to her. "If it weren't for Emily, I'd stay in Denver. I'd bring you flowers like this one."

Adie pinched the stem, raised the petals to her nose and sniffed. She could love this man…except he was a minister and she'd been living a lie. Neither did she share his love of God. She lowered the rose and looked up. Josh clasped her shoulders. His eyes drifted shut as if he were in pain, then he bowed his head and kissed her forehead. She felt cherished, even blessed, until guilt flooded through her.

Angry at herself for the lies and at God for the pain, she stepped back. "You're very kind, Josh. But there's no place for you in Denver." *Or in my life.*

He lowered his voice. "I'm not so sure."

"I am."

"When I find Emily, I'm coming back."

You'll never find her.

Adie pivoted and strode down the path. What she saw filled her heart with terror. Flames were licking the back wall of Swan's Nest.

Chapter Twelve

She had to get to Stephen and wake her friends. Hiking up her skirt, she raced by the vegetable patch, coughing as the air turned into orange smoke. When she passed the carriage house, she saw fingers of flame shooting up the back wall of Swan's Nest. Someone had lit the woodpile on fire. The house itself hadn't caught, but the wood siding and shingled roof made it a tinderbox. Adie ran for the back door, but the heat intensified, forcing her to race to the front of the house.

As she rounded the corner, the door opened and her boarders came out in wrappers and white night rails. They looked like a flock of frightened swans. She searched and found Stephen in Mary's arms.

Pearl cried out. "There's Adie!"

Bessie ran forward and hugged her. "You scared us to death. We couldn't find you!"

"And Josh," Caroline cried. "He's not in his room!"

"I'm right here."

Adie turned and met his gaze. Behind him she saw billows of smoke. A roar filled the night. Had the fire spread to the house? The jewelry… The journal… She had to get them. She needed Maggie's jewelry to survive. Even more important, the trunk held answers for Josh. She broke from Bessie's grip and ran through the front door.

"Adie!"

The cry came from Josh. She heard the pounding of his boots as he ran up behind her. He grabbed her arm, but she broke loose and sped up the stairs. Smoke filled her nose and eyes. An orange glow pushed into the hallway, but she didn't see flames. Her bedroom was at the front of the house, far from the fire but still vulnerable if the roof caught.

She ran into her room and headed for the bureau where she kept the key. She grabbed it, spun around and came face-to-face with Josh.

"Get out!" he shouted. "*Nothing* is worth your life."

"This is."

She crouched in front of the trunk and inserted the key. Clanging bells signaled the arrival of the fire wagon. As she worked the lock, shouts from the street followed the smoke through the window. She heard Pearl sobbing and Mary yelling for her to get out. Josh stared at her in disbelief.

She opened the lid and tossed the contents on the floor. A swatch of fabric she'd used for curtains fluttered into a heap. Leftover yarn landed in a tangle. At last she grasped the velvet bag holding Maggie's jewels, her picture and the journal. She felt Josh's eyes on her hands, watching as she lifted the bag.

The instant she stood, he tugged her out the door and into the hallway. Smoke choked her as they hurried down the stairs. If the roof caught, she'd lose the house. The thought terrified her, but not as much as losing Stephen or even the journal. Without it, Josh would never know the truth about Emily.

When they reached the street, she risked a glance at Josh and saw questions in his eyes. The noise of the crowd, the smoke and the roar of the flames made it impossible to speak, but she knew the night wouldn't end without him hearing the truth.

Lots of women had red velvet bags…or did they? Josh couldn't block the picture of Adie on her knees, risking her life for the sake of a bag that looked like the one Emily had used to hide her jewelry. He'd seen the bag only on occasion, but he recalled the gold drawstrings.

"All able-bodied men! We need help!"

The call had come from the fire chief. Josh wanted to grab the bag and look inside, but the fire took priority. He gave Adie a firm look. "We'll speak later."

Before she could argue, he hurried to the back of the house where the woodpile was engulfed in flames. The chief directed him to the bucket brigade. Other men followed. A few women, too, including Mary and Caroline. Gallon by gallon, they hauled water from the well, passed it down the line and threw it on the fire. As the flames died, the night returned like a dark blanket falling from the sky.

When the fire chief approached with a lantern, Josh accompanied him to inspect the dying embers. Satisfied the fire wouldn't reignite, the chief looked at the back wall of Swan's Nest. Smoke had stained the white paint, but the siding hadn't caught fire. Whoever set the blaze had inflicted more fear than damage. It struck Josh as the kind of tactic Dean would use.

Deputy Morgan joined them. "It's arson."

"You're certain?" Josh asked.

He held up a kerosene bottle. "I found this in the street."

The chief took the bottle and sniffed. "It's kerosene, all right. Even without the bottle, I'd know this fire was deliberate."

Josh had known it, too. "It started fast."

The chief grunted. "Woodpiles don't catch on fire by themselves. Someone gave it a hand."

"Did you see anyone?" Morgan said to Josh.

He flashed on the moments before the blaze. He'd been about to kiss to Adie. She'd been in his arms and he'd felt a rush of love that couldn't be denied. He'd been overwhelmed and hadn't seen anything except Adie turning her back.

"I didn't notice a thing," he said to Morgan.

"I did."

The men turned and saw Pearl with Mary and Bessie flanking her sides. A wrapper covered her night rail, but nothing could disguise her belly. The men looked discreetly at her face.

"What did you see?" Morgan asked.

Pearl, always pale, looked fragile in the moonlight. "I couldn't sleep, so I went to the window for air. I saw a man hurrying down the street. A few minutes later, I smelled smoke."

The deputy frowned. "What did he look like?"

"Short and stocky." Pearl took a breath. "Do you know Horace Jones?"

The deputy raised a brow. "He's Franklin Dean's driver."

"It could have been him."

"But you're not sure?" he asked.

"It was too dark."

The fire chief traded a look with Morgan. Both men knew the repercussions of accusing Franklin Dean.

Pearl looked at Josh. "We could have died tonight. If I hadn't been up and the roof had caught—"

"It didn't," Mary said. "We're fine."

"It's still my fault."

Josh made his voice gruff. "Don't you dare blame yourself. *You* didn't light the fire."

"That's right," Bessie added.

Pearl nodded but only slightly. She looked close to giving birth in the street. Josh turned to the fire chief. "Is it safe to go inside?"

"The fire's out, but I won't say it's safe." His expression hardened. "Whoever set the fire could come back."

The women paled at the implication. The flames had been doused, but the arsonist was running loose. Josh wondered if Adie and her friends would ever feel safe again. As Mary and Bessie led Pearl into the house, he went in search of Adie. He spotted Caroline first. Next to her stood Adie, clutching Stephen and swaying in a gentle rhythm. He searched for the velvet bag and saw it clutched in her hand, dangling below the baby's back and partially hidden.

When Caroline saw him, she whipped a hankie from her pocket and tried to wipe his face. "You're covered with soot."

He brushed her hand aside. "Not now, Caroline." He couldn't take his eyes off Adie and the bag.

Adie avoided him by looking at Caroline, who'd fallen three steps behind. "I guess we can go inside."

"Not yet." He'd waited long enough for answers. He turned back to Caroline. "I need to speak to Adie in private. Would you take Stephen?"

Adie shook her head. "It's late. Tomorrow—"

"Now," he said gently. "Please."

Caroline reached for the baby. "Go on, Adie. It must be important."

He could see the battle in her eyes, but she kissed the top of Stephen's head, then handed the baby to Caroline, who turned to Josh with a wistful smile. "Good night, Reverend."

She finally understood. "Good night, Caroline. And thank you."

As she walked away, Adie looked both terrified and calm, like a prisoner resigned to an execution.

Josh guided her up the steps and into the parlor, where he lit a lamp and turned up the wick. He wanted to see every flicker of her eyes. She flinched, but she didn't turn down the brightness. As she sat on the divan, Josh dropped on to the armchair, watching as she set the velvet bag in her lap. Looking down, she pulled the drawstrings and removed a black leather journal. She laid the book flat, laced her fingers across the binding and met his gaze. "I have a confession to make. Stephen's not my flesh-and-blood son."

His neck hairs prickled.

"His mother was my best friend. She died giving birth. She made me promise—"

"Her name," he said. *"Tell me her name."*

"Maggie Butler."

His grandmother's name had been Margaret. Butler had been her surname. His grandfather's given name was Stephen. Common sense warned him to hear the whole story before he uttered a word, but his temper was flaring bright. He wanted to shout at Adie for hiding the truth. He also saw her suffering and wanted to hold her in his arms.

Her face turned white. "Maggie had an accent like yours. And a brother. A minister… She hated him."

God, forgive me.

Her fingers clutched the velvet bag. "Her brother said vile things. She was afraid he'd take the baby, so she asked me to raise Stephen as my own. She died minutes later."

Grief collided with guilt. The guilt smothered his anger at Adie for hiding the truth. He had no right to throw stones at her. He'd started the entire mess.

With her eyes downcast, she lifted a square of cardboard from the journal and held it out to him. "This is a picture of Maggie."

As he pinched the edge, glare turned the paper white. He slanted it and the whiteness fell away like a drape, revealing a copy of the tintype he'd lost in the river crossing. He couldn't bear the sight of Emily's unblinking eyes. Pressure built in his chest. He didn't want Adie to see him cry, but the tears leaked from the corners of his eyes. Emily was dead. She'd died not knowing he'd changed. She'd never hear his apology.

"Is it—" Adie couldn't finish.

"It's Emily."

Guilt whipped through him and not just because of his sister. Adie had hidden the truth for weeks. Why? Did she think he'd take her son? He couldn't imagine wrestling a baby from its mother's arms. How could she think he'd do such a thing? The thought wounded him as deeply as he'd wounded Emily.

When he looked up from Emily's still face, he saw Adie holding a strand of pearls. "These belonged to Maggie…I mean Emily."

They'd once belonged to the real Maggie Butler.

"I have most of her jewelry," Adie said with pride. "She told me to sell it to support Stephen. That's how I bought this house."

"I see," he managed.

"I'm not a thief." She raised her chin. "The jewelry belongs to Stephen, not me. That's why I borrowed to buy Swan's Nest. I'm paying my share with hard work."

Josh didn't think he could hurt any more, but Adie's confession broke his heart. Dressed in brown, she looked like a sparrow protecting her nest. Wisps of her maple hair feathered across her temple. Her lips moved, then stopped. She tried again to speak, but her voice cracked. Like a fluttering bird, she moved from the divan to the foot of his chair, dropping to her knees and clasping her hands against her chest. "Please don't take Stephen away from me! I'll do anything. I'll be his nanny. I'll go with you to Boston."

Shaken and miserable, Josh stared as she told him she'd work as a servant, that somehow she'd pay her own way. Before he found his voice, she clutched his hand. "I'm begging you, Reverend."

Reverend? He wanted to be Josh…just Josh.

She bent her neck and sobbed. "Please, don't take my son."

Her tears scalded his soul, but he couldn't be offended. He'd made that threat to his sister. He couldn't make amends to Emily, but he could give Adie peace. She needed to know Stephen was hers. Just as profound, Josh needed *her* to know *him*.

He deepened his voice. "Look at me."

When she raised her face, he cupped her cheeks in his hands. His voice came out rough. "Adie, you *know* me."

She sniffed. "Do I?"

"Yes!" He needed her respect, her faith in his heart. "You *know* what I'm going to say."

Hope filled her eyes. It vindicated him. "That's right. You're Stephen's mother. That will *never* change."

Bowing her head, she broke into a flood of new tears, murmuring "thank you" over and over. Her gratitude embarrassed him. They were simply two human beings, both flawed, battered by life and in need of kindness. He cupped her chin in his palm. As she looked up, her tears glistened and her lips parted again. Instead of thanking him, she smiled.

He brushed her cheek with his thumb. "I should be thanking you."

"Why?"

"You gave my nephew a home. You gave Emily peace when she needed it most."

"She was my friend."

If her smile made him human in a good way, her tears reflected his limitations. He couldn't kiss them away. Only God could put a woman's tears in a bottle and throw it into the sea. Josh had to settle for giving her his handkerchief. He reached in his pocket and gave her the linen. "Here."

Adie wiped her nose, then looked chagrined. "I'll wash it for you."

He didn't give a whit about the handkerchief. He pushed to his feet and offered his hand. She took it and stood. As she tipped up her chin, Josh bent his neck. He wanted to kiss her, but he didn't have the right. Tonight in the garden he'd imagined a future with this woman. He'd expected to find his sister alive and happy and had dreamed of coming back to Denver. Instead he'd found a tintype with eyes that would never blink.

His search had ended, but Emily's death kept him in chains. She'd died of natural causes, but Josh felt as if he'd killed her. How could he think of his own happiness with her blood on his hands? On the other hand, he had a duty to care for his nephew. Just as compelling for Josh, he'd made a vow the day he'd left Boston. He'd promised to serve God far and wide. Never again would he pridefully pastor a church.

As much as he wanted to tell Adie how he felt, he couldn't speak until he made peace with God and himself. After a tiny squeeze, he released her hand.

Adie picked up the journal and handed it to him. "This belongs to Stephen, but you can read it."

He wanted to know Emily's story but dreaded her accusations. Why hadn't she written to Sarah or their cousin Elliot? Before he'd left Boston, Josh had written a letter to be sent if Emily revealed her whereabouts. If she'd taken that single step, she'd have learned how deeply he regretted his mistakes. Had he hurt her that profoundly? The truth was in the journal. As he'd told Adie, secrets caused pain. Emily's secrets were in the book and she deserved to tell them. He took the journal from Adie and slipped the picture inside the back cover.

Adie sighed. "I wish I'd told you sooner."

"When did you realize?"

"The first night on the porch, when I choked on my water." She went to the divan.

Josh dreaded going to his room, so he dropped back on the chair. They both needed clarity. "I had no idea."

"But before that night, I wasn't sure. You're nothing like Maggie described."

The compliment warmed him, but guilt doused that small flame. "I was, though."

"Not anymore."

"I wish…" He shook his head. "I'd give anything to tell her how sorry I am."

"Maybe she knew."

The journal felt like a brick in his lap. "I doubt it."

"I don't know," Adie said. "At the end, she asked for the book. She wrote something, just a line or two. I've never read it."

A dying woman's words could be anything. Maybe she'd forgiven him.

"Will you read it tonight?" Adie asked.

"I have to." *Will you read it with me?*

The question made it halfway to his tongue before he stifled it. He had to face Emily alone. The cover grew warm in his hands. If Emily had forgiven him, everything would change. He'd be free to stay in Denver. Once Adie made peace with God, he'd be free to court her with whole bouquets of roses.

Please, Lord. Let it be Your will.

Josh pushed to his feet.

So did she.

He saw a new softness around her mouth. The sparrow would sleep well tonight. Slowly, as if she were unsure of herself, she kissed his cheek. Her red hair tickled his jaw, but the kiss held only innocence. She'd offered it with the same gratitude a broken woman had shown to Jesus when she'd anointed his feet with oil. The oil had been her most precious possession. Likewise, Adie's kiss had been a gift—the best she had to offer.

Josh felt honored. For all his mistakes, he'd done one thing right. He'd given Adie a son. "Just so you know, I intend to make this adoption legal. I don't want you to ever worry about someone taking Stephen away."

She stepped back with a sheen in her eyes. "You're a good man, Josh."

His pride puffed up. He had to quell it. "I'm human, Adie. Deep down, I'm as weak-minded as anyone."

Her brow furrowed. "I don't understand."

It seemed plain to Josh. "What don't you see?"

"Mary shot you and you forgave her. Caroline's been forward, but you've been gentle. You've tried to help Pearl. And Bessie…she calls you her friend. If that's not 'good,' I don't know what is."

Her praise was a balm to his conscience. He'd been a protector and friend to the women of Swan's Nest. To Adie, he wanted to be more. He wanted to be a husband. Was there hope? Did she share his tender feelings? He had to know. "Who am I to you?"

She looked into his eyes, then touched his cheek again. Her fingers left a cool trail. "You're the best man I've ever known."

He knew then that Adie, like himself, had been wondering about a future together. The thought made him feel alive, a reaction he had to control. Until he did business with God, he had no right to encourage Adie's feelings. Never mind that he wanted to kiss her and not on the cheek. In spite of his worries, his lips curled with the pleasure of the compliment. "That's the nicest thing anyone's ever said to me."

"It's true."

She sounded defiant, as if she'd fight for him. Josh intended to do whatever fighting was necessary, especially where it concerned Adie and Franklin Dean, but he treasured having her for an ally. She'd make a fine preacher's wife…except she'd stopped talking to God.

Please, Lord. I need Your help.

Josh didn't expect an answer and he didn't get one. Instead he felt a quiet prompting to read the journal. The book held the key. If Emily had forgiven him, he'd be free to stay in Denver. He couldn't court Adie, but he could be her friend. He wanted to kiss her good-night but settled for holding her hand, raising it slightly to take the weight of it. "It's been a rough night but a good one."

Her eyes shone. "Thank you, Josh, for everything."

Before he could change his mind about that kiss on the lips, he left for his room. Everything—his future, his calling—depended on what Emily had written in her journal.

Adie watched Josh leave with the notebook in hand. She hoped Emily had forgiven him in those final words. It was possible. Adie recalled her mother's last hours. For years Thelma Clarke had resented her husband for leaving for the gold fields. In her dying moments, she'd spoken to her daughter of love.

"He hurt me, child. But I love him. I forgive him for leaving us. I hope you can forgive me for dying."

Adie had forgiven her mother easily. She'd saved her anger for God.

As Josh turned the corner, she hoped Emily had let go of her resentment. The thought rocked her to the core. What would she do if Timothy Long tracked her to Denver to apologize? Even if he begged her to forgive him, she'd want to see him pay for what he'd done to her. She felt the same way about Reverend Honeycutt. He didn't deserve to run a church.

Annoyed, she blew out the lamp and walked up the stairs. Voices came from Pearl's room, so she went to join her friends. As she stepped through the door, she saw Mary sitting on the foot of the bed, Pearl propped up on pillows and Bessie at her side. Caroline sat in a stuffed chair with Stephen in her arms. All the windows were open, but the room still reeked of smoke. Tomorrow Adie would wash curtains and use vinegar on the glass. No way would Franklin Dean scare her away from Swan's Nest. She pulled up a chair from the secretary. "How's everyone?"

"It could have been worse," Mary replied.

Adie felt the same way. "Even so, we have to protect ourselves. Any ideas?"

Pearl spoke in a near whisper. "I could leave."

"No!" said all four women.

Bessie looked at Pearl. "It's not just you Dean's after. He wants Adie's house."

Pearl looked pinched. "I think his driver set the fire."

Bessie stood up from the bed. She was the oldest and tonight she looked wise. "We have to fight, ladies."

Mary broke in. "I've got the pistol—"

Caroline grimaced. "Guns don't solve problems. They make them worse. We need to be smart."

Not everyone agreed with Caroline, but no one spoke. This wasn't the time to argue, only to decide.

Bessie started to pace. "I say we keep watch. We'll take turns at night, except for Pearl."

"But I want to help," the girl insisted. "I can't sleep anyway."

Adie held the deed to Swan's Nest, but the house belonged to each of them. She looked at her friends one at a time. "I love you all."

"We love you, too," Caroline said. "You've given us a home. We're not going to let a bully take it."

"That's right." Bessie sounded like a Confederate general. "I wish we'd fought for our home in Virginia. Instead we let the Yankees take it over and we paid. I won't play dead now."

Mary's expression hardened. "We'll have to watch both doors."

Even with everyone on guard, Adie knew they all felt vulnerable. It showed in their eyes.

Pearl spoke next. "I don't want anyone to get hurt. Maybe I should speak to Frank."

"Don't," Adie said. "He's dangerous."

"I have to do *something*." Pearl knotted her fists. "If he believes I won't marry him, maybe he'll stop."

"He'll never stop," Mary said bitterly. "I know his kind."

Pearl sighed. "What else can I do?"

"I don't know," Bessie said. "But we should speak with Reverend Blue. He might have another idea."

At the mention of Josh, Caroline turned to Adie. "He wanted to speak with you. Was it about the fire?"

"In a way." Her lies had gone up in smoke. "You all know Stephen's adopted. My friend, Maggie Butler, was really Emily Blue. Josh is Stephen's uncle."

The room went deathly still.

Pearl broke the silence. "Do you get to keep the baby?"

"Josh says he's mine forever." She told the story of the journal, the picture and the jewelry. "He's going to make the adoption legal. I can't imagine anything better."

"I can." Mary looked smug. "He should marry you."

Adie's jaw dropped.

"Why not?" Mary hugged her knees to her chest. "I've seen the way he looks at you, not to mention the way *you* look at him."

"Me, too," Pearl added.

Caroline managed a faint smile. "I'm pea green with envy, but Mary's right. Josh cares for you."

"You're all being silly," Adie replied. "He's a minister. I don't even go to church."

"You could," Pearl said.

"No."

"Why not?" Bessie asked.

"Come with us on Sunday." Mary added, "I'm going to sing."

Adie crossed her arms. "I don't like church."

"I do," Pearl murmured. "I miss it."

Adie didn't know what to think. Of all the women in the room, Pearl had the most cause to be bitter. Her own father had shunned her. No one from Colfax Avenue Church, people Pearl counted as friends, had even sent a note.

Adie wrinkled her brow. "Why do you like church?"

"I just do," she said.

Mary made a humming sound. "I like to sing."

Caroline chuckled. "It's a good thing you do! Reverend Blue can't sing a note!"

Bessie and Mary tried to stifle their laughter, but it leaked through their lips and came out in guffaws. Pearl caught the bug, but Adie didn't. She'd never heard Josh sing, but she was sure he had a fine voice.

After a joke about a donkey, she'd heard enough. "You're being mean!"

Caroline dabbed at her eyes. "I think Josh would laugh, too."

"So do I," Bessie added.

Adie had never seen Mary look more excited. "It sounds like I've got a job to do."

"Goodness, yes!" Caroline said.

Pearl sighed. "I wish I could go to Brick's, but I'm huge now."

Why would Pearl want to sit in church for two hours, even one? Reverend Honeycutt's sermons had been as flat as a washboard. The times she'd listened, she'd felt like a shirt being pounded to get out the dirt. Josh's sermons had to be different because he was a different man, but church was church.

Mary eyed her thoughtfully. "Try it, Adie. Come just once."

"No!"

"Whatever you want," Bessie said. "Aside from all that, we need to be thinking of Josh right now."

"Yes," Mary said. "He just lost his sister."

Pearl folded her hands. "We should pray."

All the women—except Adie—bowed their heads.

Pearl took the lead. *"Lord Jesus, Reverend Blue—Josh—is our friend. Tonight he's grieving his sister. Please, Lord. Give him peace. Show him Your love and renew his hope for the future. Amen."*

Adie hoped God heard Pearl's prayer, but she doubted it. She pictured Josh alone in his room, reading Emily's pain-filled words by candlelight.

When Pearl yawned, the women stood.

Adie lifted Stephen from Caroline's arms. After a chorus of "good nights," she went down the hall and put him in his cradle. A faint glow in the window caught her eye and she went to the glass. Looking down, she saw a circle of light and knew Josh was on the porch, reading the journal alone.

Sure that God wouldn't answer Pearl's prayer for comfort for Josh, Adie decided to comfort him herself.

Chapter Thirteen

Josh had considered a myriad of possibilities in his search for Emily, but not once had he imagined her speaking to him from the grave. That would happen when he opened the journal.

Earlier he'd gone to his room. He'd lit the lamp, seen a haze of smoke and coughed. The room had felt cramped, even coffinlike. He'd taken a candle from the kitchen and returned to the front porch, where he'd set it on a low table, hunched forward in a chair and angled the journal to catch the light.

Looking at the black leather, he pictured Emily sitting beside him and imagined the slide of knitting needles. How many times had she listened to him banter about his day when she'd had secrets of her own? Fool that he'd been, he'd prided himself on being a good listener. In truth, he'd been so wrapped up in himself that he hadn't heard a word she'd said.

"Forgive me, Emily."

With that prayer on his lips, he started to read.

November 1874
My dear child,
You won't be born for six months, but the day will come when you'll want to know who you are. You'll want to

know your father's name and why it's not yours. You'll want to know if you have cousins and grandparents. If you have your father's red hair, you'll ask about that, too.

This diary will answer those questions. One thing I've learned, child, is that life is unpredictable. That's why I'm writing to you. If something happens to me—a possibility as I learned from your father's passing—I want you to have your history.

That history will start with your name. If you're a girl, I'm going to call you Julia Louise after my mother. If you're a boy, your name will be Stephen Paul after my grandfather. Together we're taking Grandfather's last name of Butler. I was born Emily Constance Blue, but I no longer want that name.

In the next several paragraphs, Emily detailed her personal history. She told her child that she'd loved to read and liked to play with dolls. She described growing up in a big house with servants, going to church on Sundays to hear Grandfather Stephen and how their mother grew flowers and gave fancy parties for their father's business associates.

Josh read every word, but he could have skipped the first pages of the journal. He'd lived the same life. He'd especially shared the same love for their grandfather. Stephen Blue had given him his first Bible and mentored him through his early years as a minister. He'd died three years ago.

Josh cringed at what the old man would have thought of his last sermons, then wished fervently that he'd been alive to hear them. Grandfather would have invited him to his study for a little chat. He would have noticed Josh's glazed eyes and confronted him about the laudanum. The opiate had numbed his conscience. He wanted to be numb now, but Emily deserved his full attention.

I had a good life, my child. I never went hungry, never lacked for warmth or clean clothes. My needs were met, yet I felt a constant emptiness on behalf of others.

Memories marched through Josh's mind. Emily had fed the birds in their backyard, even starlings and crows. In some ways, he'd been one of her flock. When he needed a hostess, she stepped in. She'd accompanied him on calls and had calmed mothers with sick children.

Had she longed for babies of her own? After a month at Swan's Nest, Josh knew he'd been blind to his sister's feelings. Every time Adie picked up Stephen, she smiled. Pearl, in spite of the violence of a rape, looked radiant when she mentioned her baby. He knew now that Emily had wanted a husband and family of her own.

Josh wanted to close the journal but couldn't. Squinting in the dim light, he read the next entry.

December 1874
My dearest little one,
I'll never forget the moment I first saw your father. He was an Irishman, newly arrived from Dublin, a man with a passion for life but not much money. I saw him in front of a café near the orphanage where I volunteered. How I loved to hold the babies! I thought I'd never have one of my own. I was twenty-three years old and didn't expect to marry.

It wasn't for lack of opportunity. Men had courted me. Or, more correctly, they courted my family's money. My child, if you choose to return to Boston, you'll have a right to a fortune and the Blue family name. That choice will be yours. As for my choice—to leave with nothing but my jewelry—I have no regrets. But I digress....

The day I met your father, I'd just come from the nursery where I'd spent three blissful hours rocking babies to sleep. Someday, child, I'll hold you in my arms. When I do, I'll see Dennis's eyes, maybe his red hair.

A memory flashed like a dream. Josh had been passing by the orphanage at midday and had stopped to say hello to Emily. He'd invited her to lunch but she'd declined. As he left, he'd seen a man with red hair lingering on the corner. Always friendly, Josh had nodded a greeting. The stranger had nodded back.

Josh recalled the moment because he'd been impressed with the man's bearing. His clothes had been threadbare, but he'd worn them with dignity. The Blue family often hired hands for the stables, so Josh had stopped to talk. He hadn't asked the man's name, but he'd learned he'd worked with horses in Ireland and had offered him a job. Something—or someone—had caught the man's eye. He'd politely turned down the job and walked away. A moment later, Emily had arrived. She'd looked down the street at the stranger's back. *"I'm free for lunch after all."*

As they'd headed in the opposite direction of the man, she'd looked over her shoulder. *"Who were you talking to?"*

"An Irishman in need of a job."

"What did you think?"

He relived that minute as if it were now. *"He seems decent enough."*

"You liked him?"

He'd answered with a shrug and changed the subject to church business. How could he have been so blind? He wished now that he'd put together the clues. Emily wouldn't have asked about a stranger. She'd known the man and fairly well. Josh wasn't a snob. He'd have sanctioned a marriage between

Emily and any man worthy of her love. Josh didn't judge worth by class. He judged it by a man's heart.

The thought made him frown. Dennis Hagan had walked away. If he'd loved Emily, why hadn't he spoken up? Where was the man's courage? The thought gave Josh some redemption but not enough to free him. He refocused on the journal and Emily's first glimpse of Dennis.

I'll never forget that April day. I was walking to the café with Miss Walker, the woman who ran the orphanage, when she met a friend on the street. I went ahead to get our table. Outside the restaurant, your father stopped me and asked if I worked at the orphanage. When I said yes, he gave me a nickel for the children and left.

Nearly every day for a week, he waited outside the orphanage. Each time he gave me a few coins, and with each meeting our conversation stretched until we took to walking along the river. That's where he told me his story.

He'd left Ireland to escape starvation and the shame of poverty. His parents had both perished and so had three of his eight siblings. The others had married or moved on. He'd found employment on a rich man's estate but didn't have the stomach for a lifetime of earning pennies with no hope of his own land, his own business. Ambitious and hungry, he'd come to America.

We fell in love, child.

Josh felt a small measure of peace. Emily hadn't been attacked. She'd fallen in love and given in to the most common of temptations. After his bout with laudanum, he couldn't claim to be above her in any way.

Nor was he immune to the thoughts of a lonely man. Tonight, before the fire started, he'd kissed Adie's forehead in a kind of blessing. His motives were pure, but he felt nature's way between them. Later, when she'd touched his cheek and kissed it, he'd felt the seeds of tenderness sprouting into vines of love. A few months ago, the thought would have troubled him. He'd prided himself on being like Paul, a man who had walked through life alone. Josh's path now felt wide enough for two. When he closed his eyes, he saw Adie's face. He wanted to hear her sweet voice and feel her hand tucked in his.

"Josh?"

Had he imagined her voice? His thoughts had been vivid, but he wasn't crazy. He looked to the door, where he saw Adie peering in his direction. "I'm over here."

She moved from the darkest shadows to the fainter ones made by the lone candle. He wished he'd sat in the swing so that she'd be next to him. Instead she took the chair on the other side of the table. As she looked down at the open journal, her eyelashes fluttered as she blinked to adjust to the dim light.

"Are you still reading?" she asked.

"I'm about halfway."

"How is it?"

"About what I expected."

She waited.

"It's painful," he admitted.

He needed a respite, so he let his eyes linger on Adie. Her presence gave him comfort in a way he'd never experienced. She understood his thoughts. She felt his sorrow because she'd known Emily and had witnessed the reason for his regrets. He needed to finish the journal tonight, but his strength flagged.

Wordless, Adie reached across the table, turned the book in her direction and began to read out loud.

I didn't intend to lose my heart to Dennis Hagan. He didn't intend to take it. We were as different as boiled potatoes and lemon pie, yet we connected the instant we met.

Oh, my child! To fall in love is a taste of heaven. Even when it's fraught with sacrifice, there's a joy to giving your heart to someone who treasures it. Make no mistake, your father treasured me. Perhaps *too* much, now that I look back. He treated me as if I were a porcelain doll. Only at the end did I become fully human to him.

When you're grown and fall in love for yourself, you'll understand what I'm about to say. We didn't mean to kiss. It happened on a rainy day in the middle of a busy street. A storm struck and he pulled me inside a doorway. I'd say the kiss just happened, but that wouldn't be true. He asked with his eyes and I said yes with mine. He regretted it. I didn't. He'd said he'd tasted the sweetest fruit and could never taste it again.

That's when I told him I loved him. I was tired of being coy! Tired of hiding my feelings! In the middle of Beacon Hill, I asked your father to marry me.

He said no.

I called him a coward.

He dared me to go west with him.

I told him I'd pack my things and meet him at the train station. He must have believed me because he laughed. "All right, love. You win. We'll marry, but not until I can support you. Will you wait for that?"

Another dare. I took it, but I dared him back.

Josh had wanted the truth about Emily. Now he had it. She'd been in love and she'd been bold. Dennis Hagan had succumbed to every man's temptation. Josh wanted to punch him, but he had no right to throw stones. In different ways, he'd fallen himself. Josh didn't know if Dennis Hagan had regrets, but he knew his own.

He also knew how he felt about Adie. He loved her and wanted to marry her, but reading the journal hadn't set him free. He still felt obligated to Emily. Did that mean preaching for strangers as he'd been doing? He couldn't fulfill that duty with a wife and child. Nor did Adie share his commitment to his calling. Of all the problems, that one loomed the largest.

As Josh raked his fingers through his hair, Adie looked up from Emily's delicate writing. "That's the end of the passage, but there's more."

He needed an answer. He wanted it now. "Keep going."

February 1875
My Child,

You're kicking tonight! Such a sweet feeling… Your father would have been so proud. I'm at the point of the story that's the hardest to tell, so I welcome the sense of Dennis alive in my womb. You, child, are my only comfort as I relive the darkest moment of my life.

Your father took my dare and I took his. I didn't expect to conceive. Does any woman when she succumbs to sin? By the time I realized you were on the way, he'd left for St. Louis. I had the name of his cousin and his solemn vow to send for me as soon as they claimed land and he built a house.

I knew my brother wouldn't approve, so I asked Dennis to write to me at the orphanage and he did. One precious letter and I had to burn it to keep our secret! I wrote back. I told him you were on the way. I waited for weeks to hear from him. I know he'd have sent for us immediately. We'd sinned, but your father was an honorable man. He loved me. He would have given us his name and more.

Weeks passed. I didn't hear from him and was close to panic. My middle was thickening. I had no choice but to face my brother.

Adie stopped speaking, but her eyes skimmed the page. She bit her lip, grimaced, then covered her mouth with her fingers. "I can't read this. It's vile."

"Then it's true."

"Not anymore." She closed the book.

Josh reached across the table and took it. He opened the book to the last few pages, then looked at Adie. "Aren't you leaving?"

"No," she said. "I'll stay while you read it to yourself."

Her presence gave Josh the strength he needed to go back to that night in Boston.

To fully appreciate my dilemma, you need to know that your uncle is a famous minister. People travel miles to hear him, though I don't know why! In those final weeks—when I knew you were on the way—I'd listen to him spout about righteousness and obedience and wonder if he had a drop of warm blood in his body. Josh, you see, is perfect.

At least *he* thinks he is.

I love God, too! God loves me. Jesus died for my sins and I know it. Josh doesn't think he has any sins. Well, he's wrong. That night, he became a murderer. The Bible says he who has anger in his heart might as well have committed murder. I've never seen Josh angrier than when I told him about you. I'd mustered my courage and I'd whispered the simple fact.

"I'm with child."

He ranted at me. He paced like a lion about to eat me. He didn't ask me who or why. He ignored the tears streaming down my face. My clearest memory is of the moment he pounded the table.

"Blast it, Emily! I have a reputation to uphold."

His reputation? What about *my child?* I was lost and broken and terrified. In the weeks after Dennis left, I'd had time to weigh the consequences of our recklessness. We should have waited. We should have found another way, one that protected our child. I couldn't feed you without help. I had nowhere to go except to Josh, who turned his back on me. I didn't think I could be more wounded, but his next words filled me with a pain I'd never known.

"Leave Boston, Emily. Give the baby away."

"No!" I cried.

"I'm *ordering* you to leave."

He started blathering about a long visit with cousins in Rhode Island. When I refused, he called me a horrible name. I ran to my room and packed my things. I heard him prowling in the hall. He pounded on my door, but I didn't answer. When the house finally quieted, I crept down the stairs with a valise and my jewelry and walked two miles in the cold to the train station.

Josh looked up at Adie. "Every word is true."

"I don't care," she insisted. "You wouldn't say those things again."

"No, but I said them once."

If he'd learned anything this past year, it was one simple truth. Mistakes could be forgiven, but consequences weren't so easily erased. Stephen proved his point. So did the pain in Emily's journal. Josh had dedicated his life to preaching

God's forgiveness because he needed it so badly. He couldn't change the past, but with God's grace he could claim a better future. He wanted that new start for himself. Hoping to find it, he focused on Emily's next words.

After leaving Boston, I sent a note to my best friend. She knew about Dennis, and I didn't want her to worry. I told her my plans. I intended to find your father in St. Louis and make a new life. That night I vowed to never return home, to never speak to Josh again. Even when I stood at your father's grave, I knew I'd keep that promise. Oh, child. The sadness! I found Dennis's cousin easily. He recognized me from the picture Dennis kept by his bed. As gently as he could, he told me your father had died of influenza.

"He'd been workin' too hard, Miss Blue. He saved every penny for you. Wouldn't even see a doctor."

That foolish man and his pride! My jewelry would have supported us for years. We could have married! We could have left Boston together, but he'd made me promise to wait until he'd made his own way. I weep for him every day. You, sweet child, are my comfort, my joy. You're the reason I know God has forgiven my sins. Only a loving God, a good and kind God, would share with human beings the joy of creation. You, my baby, are a miracle.

Know that I love you and always will. Someday I hope to tell you this story in person, but I know the uncertainties of life. If something happens to me, you'll have these words, a picture of me but not your father, and whatever is left of the jewelry.

With deepest love,

Your mother

Josh looked at the bottom of the page and saw writing that wasn't so perfect. These, he realized, were his sister's final words, written on her deathbed when she was bleeding and weak.

Dear Stephen,

My son! The struggle…I'm dying. Know that I love you. Adie is my best friend. She'll be a good mother. She—

So ended the journal, cut off in midsentence just as Emily's life had been cut short by tragedy. With his eyes red rimmed and hurting, both from the fire and the strain of reading, Josh bowed his head.

Dear Lord, don't let Emily's suffering be in vain. I'll serve You wherever, however, You ask.

Sometimes the Lord spoke to Josh through scripture he'd memorized. Other times he felt a quiet certainty. Tonight his heart beat with a new sense of purpose. Startled, he looked at Adie and saw the future with a sudden clarity. She needed a husband. Stephen needed a father. He loved her and wanted to marry her, but how could he? Adie believed in God but didn't share his commitment.

He didn't know what to say or do until she spoke the words that pointed the way.

"I'm going to church on Sunday."

Adie opened her mouth before she could change her mind. As Josh read Emily's words, she'd seen him grimace. Once he'd shut his eyes and groaned as if he'd been struck. She cared for this man. She'd do anything to make him happy.

To his credit, his mouth didn't gape. "I'm glad."

She wondered if she'd lost her mind. "It might be just once."

"Whatever you want."

That was the problem. Adie didn't know what she wanted. Reverend Honeycutt had sent her away. Old Man Long had ranted about hell and judgment. Josh was different, but he worshipped the same demanding God. As the candle sent shadows across his jaw, she saw the straight line of his mouth. She didn't know what Emily had written, but Josh had taken it hard.

She hurt for him. "Emily didn't forgive you, did she?"

"Not a bit. In the end, she hated me even more." He handed her the journal. "This belongs to Stephen."

As she took it, Josh stood and so did she. As he lifted the candle, gold light pulled them into the same circle. A half smile softened his mouth. "Thank you for staying. You made this easier."

"I'm glad."

She hugged the journal because she couldn't hug Josh. The smile climbed to his eyes. He motioned for her to go into the house, then guided her with his hand on her back. When they reached the stairs, he stopped and raised the candle to illuminate the steps. Their eyes locked in the shadows, but neither of them moved. She wanted to tell him that she hurt for him. She wanted to kiss his cheek and reassure him that he wasn't an ogre. She wanted to tell him that she admired him, but she couldn't. Emily no longer stood between them, but his faith did.

He stepped back, then spoke with a hush. "Good night, Adie."

"Good night."

As she climbed the stairs, questions for Josh swirled in her mind. *You've been hurt. How can you still trust God? Where was He when my mother died?* She had to fight the urge to turn around. Josh stayed until she reached her room; then the stairwell went dark. She went to the trunk, where she put away the journal and the jewelry and closed the lid. If she'd been speaking to God, she would have prayed for Josh. She would have thanked the Almighty for Stephen's life. Instead she spoke to Maggie…Emily now.

"He's changed."

Silence.

"You'd like him, Emily. You'd love him again."

Adie knew, because she felt that love now. The admission stole her breath. She'd fallen in love with Joshua Blue. A man…a minister. She'd lost her mind. No matter what the future held, Josh would always be a man of faith. He needed a wife who shared that passion. Could she be that woman? Adie didn't know, but she was willing to find out. This Sunday, she'd go to church in Brick's Saloon. She'd be among friends and she'd listen.

Chapter Fourteen

Late the next morning, Adie heard someone knocking on the front door. Bessie, Caroline and Mary had gone to work in spite of their exhaustion. Pearl had stayed upstairs and Josh was outside, cleaning up the mess from the fire. When the visitor knocked again, she peeked through the drapes and saw a horse and buggy she didn't recognize. Her stomach dropped to her toes. She couldn't imagine who'd come calling, but she knew Franklin Dean had allies. No way would she open the door.

"It's my father!"

She turned and saw Pearl lumbering down the stairs. She was clutching the railing, but Adie worried she'd fall. "Be careful."

"It's him," she said again. "I looked out the window."

Adie was concerned about Pearl's health. They'd had a rough night and the mother-to-be didn't need the upset. "I'll tell him to leave."

"No," Pearl cried. "Let him in."

Against her better judgment, Adie opened the door. The last time she'd seen Reverend Oliver, he'd stood tall in a crisp frock coat. Today he looked haggard. So did the coat.

He took off his hat, revealing thick silver hair. "Thank you for seeing me, Miss Clarke. I heard about the fire. My daughter…is she all right?"

"She's fine."

"And the baby?"

His tone didn't change. He feared as much for his grandchild as he did for Pearl. Adie glanced over her shoulder and saw the mother-to-be coming forward to answer the question herself. Adie pushed the door wide and stepped back.

Pearl froze at the threshold. "I'm fine, Papa. Thank you for—"

Reverend Oliver strode through the door, pulled his daughter into a hug and rocked her back and forth. In a torrent of choked words, he apologized for every mistake of the past months. When Pearl started to cry, he stepped back and gripped her hands in both of his. "Can you possibly forgive me?"

Her face paled. "How much do you know?"

"Everything." He clenched his jaw. "Reverend Blue paid a call on me. I know about the buggy ride and Frank's last visit. Now the fire—" He sealed his lips. "He forced you, didn't he?"

Tears welled in Pearl's eyes. "Let's sit down."

Adie, with a lump in her throat, slipped into the kitchen. As she busied herself with a pot of tea, Josh came through the back door. His shirt, a blue chambray, would need a good scrubbing and speckles of soot darkened his face. Underneath the grime, she saw bluish circles under his eyes. He'd been up all night and it showed.

As their gazes met, she recalled the emotion of the journal and her sudden decision to go to church. After she'd gone to bed, she'd tossed all night with dreams of Liddy's Grove and Franklin Dean. She'd become so angry that she'd pummeled her pillow and cursed her enemies. Just before dawn, she'd changed her mind about going to Brick's for church. She didn't want to reveal her upset, but she had to tell Josh about her change of heart.

Looking tired but relaxed, he leaned his hips against the counter. "The mess from the woodpile's gone."

"Thank you."

"I'll get paint for the wall."

She swiped at a speck of dust. "I should pay for that."

"Let me," he said easily.

"You shouldn't. You're a guest."

She kept wiping the counter. With the lightness of a bird, Josh brought his hand down on hers and stopped the motion. "Is that what I am, Adie? A *guest?*"

She hung her head.

His voice stayed low. "I thought we were friends."

"We are."

"Then allow me to buy the paint." He raised his hand, freeing her but leaving a memory of his long fingers and a trace of soot. It was a silly quarrel, one that had nothing to do with whitewash and everything to do with Adie attending church. She didn't want to explain why, so she looked for an excuse. "About Sunday…I can't go to Brick's after all. Someone should stay with Pearl."

"I'll ask Bessie."

So much for that excuse. She hunted for another. "I'd feel bad leaving Stephen."

"You can bring him."

"What if he cries?"

Adie knew a lame excuse when she heard one and so did Josh. He looked her square in the eye. "He can bellow all he wants. I'll hold him myself."

He reached for her hand. The strength of his grip made her feel small and obvious, as if he could see right through her. She looked into his eyes, then wished she hadn't.

He kept his voice low. "You're scared, aren't you?"

"I'm not *scared,*" she insisted. "It's just that…I don't know exactly."

"You've been hurt."

"Yes."

"And you're angry."

Her eyes blazed. "I am, but I don't want to be. Not anymore."

"That fight is between you and God," Josh said. "He's everywhere, but sometimes He's easier to find when a person goes looking."

Adie didn't know, but she wondered about such things. In spite of Pearl's trouble, she had peace. Mary still kept a loaded derringer, but she'd been smiling more and her humor had lost its sarcasm. They both had as much cause as Adie to be resentful, but neither of them held grudges. Neither did Bessie or Caroline. Adie wanted that calm. She also wanted to please Josh. She cared for him. She was raising his nephew and felt obliged to honor his beliefs.

Looking glum, she said, "All right. I'll go."

His eyes twinkled. "It won't be *that* bad."

When she sighed, he laughed. "What? You think I'll bore you to death?" In a deep, droning voice, he imitated a very dull preacher.

When she laughed out loud, his eyes twinkled with pleasure. "You won't be sorry, Adie. I promise."

When she looked into his eyes, she believed him. A month ago he'd collapsed on her porch. He was still lean, but he had a strength of both body and character that inspired trust. Every man she'd known had let her down, but Josh had stayed true. She'd helped him, too. Between Buttons and Adie's cooking, he'd recovered from the ulcer. The thought pleased her. "Are you hungry? I could make you a sandwich."

"I'd like that."

As she took a fresh loaf from the bread box, she thought about the simple pleasure of bread. She didn't recall many of Reverend Honeycutt's sermons, but she remembered him calling Jesus the bread of life. Adie knew about going hungry and being filled. Sometimes, especially when she'd feared losing Stephen, she'd felt as if her life were nothing but crumbs. Now she didn't. Going to church sounded better by the minute, but only because she trusted Josh and didn't feel intimidated by Brick's Saloon. She'd worked in shabby places just like it. Reverend Honeycutt wouldn't be anywhere in sight.

As she handed Josh the sandwich, she recalled Pearl and her father in the parlor. "By the way," she said, "Reverend Oliver is here."

"I thought he'd stop by." Josh had been about to take a bite, but he lowered the sandwich. "I didn't break your confidence, Adie. But I said enough to make him think twice about Franklin Dean."

"I'm glad you did." After her experience with secrets, she never wanted to keep one again. "Pearl was happy to see him."

"Good."

"He apologized to her."

Josh's expression turned wistful. She knew he was thinking of Emily. "I'm glad."

"Me, too." The voice belonged to Pearl.

Adie turned to the doorway and saw her friend, large with child and beaming with joy. Dried tears streaked her cheeks, but nothing could dim her smile as she looked at Josh. "I can't thank you enough."

He waved off her gratitude. "You just did."

She shifted her gaze to Adie. "Would you both come into the parlor? My father and I have something to tell you."

Had she decided to report Dean to the law? Adie hoped so,

but that decision belonged to Pearl. Adie would support her no matter what she decided. She followed her friend into the parlor and sat with her on the divan. Reverend Oliver had the armchair, so Josh sat across from Adie.

The old man looked first at her. "Miss Clarke, I want to thank you for helping my daughter. When I failed her, you gave her a home. If there's ever anything I can do—"

"I was glad to help," Adie said shyly.

Pearl squeezed her hand. "You're my best friend."

Adie felt honored.

Reverend Oliver cleared his throat. "Pearl and I have come to a decision. In fact, we've come to two of them. One concerns Franklin Dean. I'll get to that one. The second concerns the future. As soon as my grandchild's strong enough to travel, the three of us will be leaving Denver."

Adie pulled her friend into a hug. "I'll miss you, but it's what you wanted."

Reverend Oliver told them that he'd sent a wire to his niece in Cheyenne and she'd already answered. She had a large empty house and would welcome their company.

"Does she know about the baby?" Adie asked.

Pearl looked troubled. "I want to explain in person."

"Of course." Adie squeezed her hand. "If you have trouble of any kind, you *know* you can come back here."

Pearl smiled. "I do."

Tobias cleared his throat. "I'm looking forward to the change, but there's a problem."

"What is it, sir?" Josh asked.

"I'm worried about my congregation here in Denver. You're young, Josh. You've got a heart for the Lord and a level head. I'm hoping you'll take my place."

Josh held up his hands, palm-out to signal a hard stop. "Don't even *think* about it."

"Why not?" asked the older man.

"I know my place, and it's not in a big church."

The tension drained from Adie's spine. She could manage a service in a saloon, but Colfax Avenue Church landed her back in Kansas with Reverend Honeycutt. If a church had stained glass, she wanted nothing to do with it.

Reverend Oliver steepled his fingers. "You sound very sure, maybe *too* sure."

"I appreciate the offer, sir. But I can't take your pulpit."

"Can't or won't?"

"They're the same," Josh answered. "I left an established church in Boston. I'll never pastor another one."

"Why not?

"It's a long story, one I'll tell you another time."

"All right," said Reverend Oliver. "But I'd like to challenge you."

"Go ahead."

"Examine your heart, Josh. Are you living to serve God or serving God to avoid living?"

Josh started to speak, but the older man held up his hand. "Don't answer yet. Read Psalm 139."

Adie recognized the psalm Josh had taught at the Bible study. Even *she* knew the substance of it. David had asked God to search his heart. He'd given the Lord his anxious thoughts.

Reverend Oliver stared hard at Josh. "Pray about it, son."

"I will."

His voice carried just a trace of longing, but Adie heard it. She flashed to the day he'd walked with her to the bank. He'd seen the church and had wanted to go inside. She saw that look now and it scared her. She could handle a church of misfits in a dusty saloon, but she couldn't tolerate the spit and polish of Colfax Avenue Church. The women all wore the latest fashions. The men carried watch fobs and gold-tipped walking sticks like Franklin Dean. Worst of all, not a single member of the congregation had called on Pearl.

Reverend Oliver's jaw tightened. "This leads us to Franklin Dean. He has to be stopped."

On that, they all agreed.

"What do you suggest?" Josh asked.

The older man aimed his chin at Pearl. "This is my daughter's decision, but I support it fully."

As Pearl straightened her back, her belly made an even bigger bulge. The baby could arrive at any time. Adie had seen Maggie die in childbirth. She didn't want to lose Pearl. With her thin bones and white-blond hair, she looked too fragile for the rigors of birth.

Frail or not, Pearl set her jaw. "In a perfect world, I'd report Frank to the authorities and he'd go to prison. But this world isn't perfect. A trial would come down to my word against his and he'd win."

She was right. They all knew it.

"He may be the most powerful man in Denver," Pearl continued. "But he's *not* the most powerful woman. I'm sending notes to the elders' wives. I'm going to tell them to keep their daughters away from him and why. It's not gossip. I *know* what he did to me. If I don't speak up, he'll hurt someone else."

"That's right," Adie said.

Tobias beamed at his daughter with pride. "It won't be easy."

Adie knew from experience that Pearl's stand would come at a cost. Some women would thank her. Others would accuse her of causing her own problems. In the days before Adie left Liddy's Grove, she'd felt the same daggers in her back.

Josh focused on Reverend Oliver. "You told me Dean's on the elder board."

"That's right."

"What do you plan to do?"

"What I should have done months ago." He hammered his fingers against the armrest. "There are some good men on that board, including Halston Smythe. I'll see him tomorrow. If I know Hal—and I do—he won't let the problem slide. I'm also trusting the women to speak to their husbands. With enough pressure, Frank will resign or face a recall."

Pearl spoke up. "I hope the men listen."

"I think they will." Reverend Oliver's eyes turned misty as he looked at his daughter. "If your mother were alive, none of this would have happened. She'd have given me the what-for six ways to Sunday."

Pearl touched her belly. "I miss her."

They sat in silence, each remembering loved ones until Pearl gripped Adie's hand. "I'm worried about you. Frank still wants Swan's Nest."

"Leave that to me," Josh said.

Adie didn't know what to think. "What are you going to do?"

"It's already done." Josh leaned back in the chair. "Even before the fire I sent a letter to a cousin of mine. Elliot's a banker and a good one. Denver's ripe with opportunity, and there's nothing Elliot likes more than being in the thick of things. He's opening a branch of Boston Merchants Bank. Franklin Dean's going to have some competition."

Reverend Oliver lifted his chin. "'Be ye wise in the ways of the world.'"

"That's right," Josh replied. "Elliot's got a gift for making money. He'll drive Dean to the dogs." With his eyes bright, he turned back to Adie. "Even before last night, I asked him to pay off your mortgage. I figured you'd want to negotiate terms, but that's off the table. As soon as Elliot can arrange it, you'll own Swan's Nest free and clear."

The news stole Adie's voice, her breath. Stephen would never go hungry. Emily's dream of a place for women would be secure. If she and Josh had been alone, she'd have hugged him. "How can I ever thank you?"

"Just love my nephew."

"I do."

Her reply reminded her of a wedding vow. Judging by the intensity of his gaze, Josh heard the echo, too. So did Pearl because she hugged Adie and whispered in her ear, "He loves you, Adie. Be brave."

Except Adie didn't feel brave. She had powerful feelings for Josh. She couldn't deny them, but neither could she imagine being a minister's wife. They both had more to say, but the talk would have to wait for a private moment. With her heart brimming, she looked at Josh and saw him speaking to Reverend Oliver. "Are you headed to the parsonage?"

"I am."

"May I ride with you? I need to send another wire to Boston."

A sad one, Adie knew. He had to tell family and friends of Emily's passing.

Tobias pushed to his feet. "I'd be glad for the company, Reverend. It'll give me a chance to talk you into taking over my church."

Adie shuddered at the thought.

As Josh stood, he gave Adie a sweet look, then followed the older man out the door.

"Oh!" cried Pearl.

Adie gripped her friend's hand. "Are you all right?"

She grimaced. "My back hurts."

In the days before Stephen's birth, Emily had made the same complaint. "We better get you to bed."

Pearl shook her head. "I'd rather walk in the garden."

"I'll go with you."

Adie stood first, gave Pearl her hand and pulled her up. Together they walked out the front door and into the sunshine.

As they neared the garden, the perfume filled Adie's nose. She wasn't on speaking terms with God, but she believed in Him. She knew He'd created the heavens and the earth, plants, animals, man and woman.

He'd created *her.*

He'd created Josh, too.

For the first time in years, she felt as if she belonged with someone. On Sunday she'd test the waters at Brick's. If she found peace, she could love Josh freely. Full of hope, she went with Pearl to smell the roses.

Chapter Fifteen

As Tobias steered the buggy down the street, Josh considered the events of the past hour. Adie had accepted ownership of Swan's Nest without a fight. In the kitchen, she'd beaten back doubts about going to church. She'd been relaxed and happy until Tobias invited him to preach. She hadn't liked the idea at all.

Josh didn't know how he felt. At first he'd rejected the thought because he'd be tempted by pride. Seconds later, his blood had rushed. He'd be preaching every Sunday. He could spend weeks on the same subject, watching as the seeds took root and grew. He knew Adie disapproved, but Josh had asked God to direct his steps. He had to be open to anything.

As they passed the piles of stone from the demolished house, Tobias glanced at him. "You belong here, Josh."

Maybe he did. "What makes you think so?"

"Experience."

"Yours or mine?"

"Mine," Tobias said. "Even this old fool can see God's hand. There's nothing better than a church of your own and a wife and family."

"Hold on," Josh said, chuckling. "You've skipped way ahead of me."

"Not really." Tobias turned the buggy down a street with busy shops. "I saw the way you looked at Miss Clarke. She's a fine woman, and I know from Pearl that she adopted your nephew."

Josh didn't mention Adie's troubled faith, but he knew her doubts stood between them. As much as he liked the idea, he couldn't court her until she made peace with God. A minister's wife worked as hard as her husband.

Tobias's voice turned wistful. "My wife and I were married for twenty-nine years."

"That's a long time."

"Not long enough," he said quietly. "Ginny and I quarreled sometimes, but we always kissed good-night. That was our rule."

"It's a good one."

"You should think about getting married, Josh. A good woman keeps a man honest."

Josh thought of his past concerns. "Paul says marriage is a distraction."

"That, too," Tobias said. "But the commotion is worth what you gain. Ginny had a way of speaking her mind. Without her, I'd have driven this church into a ditch."

"She sounds like a fine woman."

"She was, but she's gone." His eyes misted. "Now it's up to me to take care of Pearl."

"Yes, sir."

"My only concern is my congregation. On that score, you and I are in the same boat."

"How so?"

"If you leave Denver, you'll worry about Miss Clarke and that baby."

Tobias had a point. Adie did a good job of running Swan's Nest, but the big house needed constant upkeep. If Josh left, she'd be wise to hire help…or to marry. He blinked and imagined a faceless man bringing her flowers. Only a fool wouldn't see Adie's fine traits, including her pretty red hair. When the right man came along, she'd fall in love and Stephen would have a father.

Josh wanted to be that man. He wanted sole claim to Adie and to raise Stephen as his own flesh-and-blood. The plan had a certain logic, but he worried about Adie's hostility to his calling. Josh had another problem, one just as big as Adie's lack of faith. Thoughts of marriage filled him with joy, but preaching in the biggest church in Denver took him back to the worst days of his life.

Tobias turned the buggy down a narrow street. "What's the *real* reason you're being stubborn about my offer?"

The answer rolled off Josh's lips. "Pride made me a hypocrite. I destroyed my sister's life."

"So you got knocked off your high horse."

"Yes," he answered. "Leading a church like Colfax Avenue might stir up my pride."

Tobias harrumphed.

Josh frowned. "You don't believe me."

"I believe you," he answered. "I *know* you're full of pride. So am I. So what?"

Josh took offense. "I'm trying to be faithful."

"Nonsense. You're acting like a whipped dog."

"Sir?"

"Good men do battle with themselves every day. You know the scriptures."

Of course he did. He'd memorized Paul's famous words to the Romans. Like every other man, Josh sometimes did what he didn't want to do, or he didn't do what he knew to be right.

"You fell off your horse at a full gallop," Tobias said. "It's about time you climbed back on."

Josh had to admire the man's insight. Tobias had seen his deepest fear and dared him to face it. Josh had a lot of faults, but being weak-willed wasn't one of them. "I'll think about it."

"That's all I'm asking." Tobias gave a crisp nod. "Go home tonight and have supper with Miss Clarke. Hold that baby in your arms and then decide."

Josh laughed. "You argue well, sir."

As the old man steered the buggy down the street behind the church, Josh looked at the stone wall and saw another stained glass window. It depicted a stream meandering through a meadow. A willow tree hung over the banks. He recognized the first of the Psalms and a particular verse, "And he shall be like a tree planted by the rivers of water." For months he'd been like the stream, wandering through a dry and thirsty land. Now he wanted to be the tree, planted firmly in Denver.

Tobias broke into his thoughts. "I'd like to hear you preach sometime."

"Come to Brick's."

"Better yet, you come to Colfax Avenue."

"I'm not—"

"Hold on," Tobias said. "All I'm asking is one Sunday."

Josh liked the idea. He could test the waters and himself, but he worried about his little flock.

"I've got a commitment to the folks at Brick's."

"Invite them."

He couldn't see bleary-eyed cowboys mixing with society matrons, nor could he imagine the girls from Miss Elsa's in the front row. As for Adie, he doubted she'd set foot in a stone building with stained glass. In the end, though, Josh knew the choice came down to one question. On Sunday morning, where did God want him to be?

Tobias's jaw hardened. "You can preach your heart out,

Reverend. Christ drove the money changers out of the temple and he wasn't gentle about it. Franklin Dean defiled my daughter. I'd like to see him taken to task."

"You could do it yourself, sir."

"I'm too angry."

Josh understood. He'd forgiven Dennis Hagan in principle, but his fists still wanted to flatten the man.

When they reached the telegraph office, Tobias stopped the buggy. As soon as Josh climbed out, the older man shook the reins. As the rig rounded the corner, a carriage approached from the same direction. Josh recognized the matched bays that belonged to Franklin Dean. In the seat sat Horace. Josh wanted to haul him to jail with his own two hands, but he couldn't prove the man's involvement. Neither could he link Dean to the crimes. On the other hand, he could take Tobias's offer and preach a barn-burner about two-faced moneychangers.

The thought tempted him, but taking Tobias's pulpit, even for one Sunday, scared Josh as a hot stove frightened a child. He knew his weaknesses. He also knew his strengths. By faith, Peter had walked on water. He'd doubted and sunk, but Christ had lifted him up. Josh felt that same hand on his shoulder, lifting him up and pointing the way to Colfax Avenue Church.

But, Lord, what about Adie?

Even as the thought formed, Josh knew it came from doubt. If he could trust God to guide his own life, surely he could trust the Almighty to shepherd Adie. A painful calm settled on his shoulders. As soon as he sent the telegram, he'd tell Tobias he'd preach this coming Sunday. Sure of his decision, he went inside the telegraph office, where he jotted a message to the Blue family attorney who'd spread the word about Emily. He paid the clerk to send it immediately, then walked out of the shop, silently praying that Adie would still come to church.

* * *

"What is it, Horace?"

"I saw something, sir."

Frank, alone at his dining room table, looked up from the pheasant his cook had prepared. The bird was done to perfection as were the julienne potatoes, baby carrots and snow peas. Later he'd enjoy the cream puffs—both of them since Pearl wasn't here to eat hers. After dessert, he'd indulge in a bottle of wine. If the liquor didn't cure his loneliness, he'd visit Miss Elsa's Social Club. He'd noticed a new girl and had asked her name. Gretchen, blond and blue-eyed, reminded him of Pearl.

Horace was standing respectfully by the door, but his eyes were devouring the delicacies on the table. The man ate well enough back in the kitchen, so he wasn't hungry for food. As for what the food represented—wealth, privilege—Horace wasn't entitled to such things. Frank swirled his wine in the fancy goblet, took a long swallow, then savored it with his eyes on Horace. The driver dared to look peeved. Frank would have ordered him to leave, but he needed his loyalty. He set the glass aside. "What have you learned?"

"I saw Revered Blue this afternoon."

"Where?"

"At the telegraph office. He sent a wire to Boston."

Frank forgot his meal. "Go on."

"I went inside," Horace said. "The operator's a fellow named Reggie. He don't say much."

Frank drummed his fingers on the table. He wanted to tell Horace to get to the point, but sometimes even *he* had to be patient. "I suppose you had a chat?"

"Not exactly." Horace grinned. "Reggie acted like he didn't know the reverend from Adam. I waited till he left the counter. Then I looked in the trash."

"Good work."

"Yes, sir." Horace stepped forward and handed him a crumpled sheet of paper.

Frank opened it and smiled. He'd been hoping for the wording of the wire and he'd gotten it, written in Joshua Blue's own hand.

Emily is deceased stop Baby is alive stop Letter to follow re trust fund stop.

Franklin understood "trust fund," but who was Emily and where did a baby fit in the story? He looked at Horace. "This is cryptic, to say the least."

"There's more," said the driver.

"Go on."

"I've been going to his church."

Frank sneered. "A sacrifice, I'm sure."

"Not so bad, sir." Horace squared his shoulders. "Three of the ladies live at Swan's Nest. One of them talked to Miss Elsa's girls about Reverend Blue having a sister. He's been looking for her and her baby."

"I see."

"The older lady told the young one to mind her manners. No gossip, she said."

Frank lived for gossip. "Go on."

"That's all I know."

Frank weighed the hodgepodge of information. Emily had to be Joshua Blue's sister. The only woman to have a baby was Adie Clarke. The baby would be heir to a fortune, which made Miss Clarke a wealthy woman. Frank muttered a curse. If he'd guessed right, and he usually did, Miss Clarke was sitting on a goldmine. He'd never get his hands on Swan's Nest. He had to drive her out while he could.

He glared at Horace. "The fire wasn't enough."

Horace frowned. "I had to be careful, sir."

"Not anymore."

"But, sir—"

"No buts, Horace. I want Swan's Nest and I want it now."

The driver's jaw stiffened. "I can't do it. Miss Pearl—she's about to give birth. And that little baby, I heard he's sickly. He could die in the smoke alone."

Frank frowned. "Horace, are you going soft on me?"

"No, sir."

"Good." He swirled the red wine, watching as it caught the light from the candelabra. Intimidating Adie Clarke hadn't worked, not with Reverend Blue interfering. Frank needed a new plan for a new enemy. "Perhaps we should take a different approach."

"Like what?"

"Use your connection at Brick's. Find out everything you can about Joshua Blue."

"Why, sir?"

"The reverend and I are going to war." Frank didn't know precisely how he'd ruin Joshua Blue, but he intended to enjoy every minute of it.

Chapter Sixteen

"How could you?" Adie cried. "Franklin Dean goes to that church!"

She and Josh were alone in the garden. The sun had set hours ago, leaving a distant moon and a sky full of stars. Adie had never felt so foolish in her life. After this afternoon, she'd dared to wonder if they had a future together. She'd fixed a special supper, complete with candied yams because she knew Josh liked them. She'd been as obvious as Caroline, glancing at him during the meal, passing the yams before he asked. After supper, he'd asked her to meet him in the garden.

Her heart had raced. She'd thought of wedding clothes and making promises as pure as white silk. She could handle going to church in Brick's Saloon. Maybe God would find her there. After listening to Pearl's excitement over Cheyenne, Adie had dared to hope for a new beginning for herself.

"God answered my prayers," Pearl had said.

Maybe, but tonight he'd ignored Adie. She'd let her feelings for Josh run free and now it hurt to look at him. Even in the dark, his hair had a shine. She couldn't see his irises, but she knew how blue they were.

"Why?" she said again. "Why can't you just preach at Brick's?"

"I can preach anywhere," he said. "That's the point. It doesn't matter if I'm in a church or on a street corner."

"I don't understand."

Josh took a step in her direction. She turned her back but couldn't escape his voice. "I have to do what God's called me to do. I'm sorry you're hurt, Adie. I was worried you'd take it hard."

"Hard!" She felt betrayed.

"I know you're upset, but when I saw Horace, I knew I had to say yes."

He'd already told her about seeing Dean's driver. "Fine. Do what you want."

"It's not what I want," he insisted. "I have to do what's right."

This was Josh, a man who would live his convictions no matter the cost. She knew what Emily's death had done to him. It took courage to preach at a church that would remind him of Boston and who he'd been. She admired his bravery but didn't share it. She'd been hurt and had no desire to go back to those bitter days. She turned and faced him. "Maybe this is for the best."

"How so?"

She saw no point in being coy. "I care for you, Josh. But we don't have a future."

"Do you mean that?" He sounded incredulous.

She tried to nod, but her head wouldn't move. "I don't know what to think."

"I do."

Two steps brought him to her side. She saw purpose in his eyes, an intent made gentle by the most tender of feelings. He clasped her arms, then drew her closer until her eyelids fluttered shut. Their lips brushed once, twice, but not a third time. He lifted his head and looked her in the eye, leaving her to wonder about their future but only for an instant. The answer cried from her heart if not her lips. She loved this man. She wanted to feed him and kiss him and bind up his wounds, except she couldn't give him what he needed most—a woman who shared his faith.

He touched her hair. "I shouldn't have done that, but I'm not sorry. I love you, Adie."

She gasped.

"I do and God knows it. I can't lie to myself or to Him. Neither will I hide my feelings from you."

"Josh, I—"

He drew her into his arms, cupping her head and tucking her face into the crook of his neck. She felt his fingers on her hair, not in it, though she could imagine him undoing the strands as gently as he'd just undone her heart. The tension left her bones until she took a breath and smelled the starch of his collar. She tried to pull way, but his arms tightened around her back.

"I know you're scared," he murmured. "But you're not a faithless woman. You're not indifferent to the Lord. You're angry. That tells me you care. Strangers don't hurt us nearly as much as the people we love."

He had a point. She'd grown to hate Timothy Long, but he'd charmed her before he'd cornered her in the attic. As a little girl, she'd admired Reverend Honeycutt. She'd prayed every night with the faith of the child she'd been. Adie wanted to cross back over that bridge, but she couldn't stand the thought of forgiving her enemies. Neither could she endure the idea of being under the same roof as Franklin Dean. Christ died for the sins of mankind, but Adie felt no mercy.

She pushed back from Josh. "I'd have gone to Brick's. Colfax Avenue Church is out of the question."

"What's the difference?"

"You *know* the difference!"

"It's bricks and glass, that's all."

"It's Franklin Dean."

Josh's stare matched hers, but it held no malice. "Will you at least think about it?"

"I don't have to." She crossed her arms. "It wouldn't be fair to you."

"To me?"

"Yes." She loved this man. If she couldn't be a full partner to him, they were better off apart.

As he stepped closer, the scent of soap and wool filled her nose. Without touching her physically, his presence surrounded her like a tent. "You need to understand who I am, Adie. I meant what I said. I love you."

"Don't."

"You can't stop me."

"But…" Her voice faded.

His stayed strong. "But what?"

I'm bitter and angry! God doesn't care, not about me. She blinked fast to hide the tears.

Josh gripped her shoulders. "I'm going after Dean with everything I've got. You're going to own Swan's Nest, and my cousin's going to put him out of business. I have a job, too. On Sunday, I need to speak the truth. I'll do it with love, but it's going to get said."

Adie gave a harsh laugh. "I almost want to be there."

"Then come."

The thought grabbed her and wouldn't let go. Dean deserved to hang for what he'd done to Pearl. Seeing him castigated in church would be almost as good as a lynching. "All right," she said bitterly. "I'll go, but I'm sitting in the back."

"You can sit wherever you'd like."

"And I'm not speaking to anyone."

"That's fine." Josh's tone didn't change, but she saw a softening around his mouth, then the curl of a smile. "As much as I'd like to start the courting right now, I'd better save it for later."

Adie didn't know what to think. On one hand, she was furious with him. On the other, she wanted to be kissed. Her confusion must have shown, because Josh lowered his chin, bringing his lips to her ear. "When the time's right, Miss Clarke, I'm going to sweep you off your feet."

He already had…. If only God would do the same. Adie wanted peace but didn't know where to find it. A silent prayer formed in her mind. *Show me, Lord. Open my heart.*

She felt nothing, but the sound of footsteps drew her gaze to the path from the house. She saw Mary hurrying in their direction. "Adie? Josh? Are you out here?"

"What's wrong?" Adie called.

"Pearl's water broke and the baby's coming fast. Bessie says it's breech."

"Oh, no." Adie thought of Maggie. The doctor who'd finally come said the baby hadn't turned. He'd done it with his hands, but it hadn't been easy.

"I'm going for Dr. Nichols." Mary looked at Josh. "Pearl's asking for her father. Will you get him?"

"Of course."

Adie heard what hadn't been said. Pearl could die. Josh squeezed her hand, then strode down the path. Mary followed him at a fast walk, but Adie froze in place. She didn't want to be in the house. Pearl would scream and she'd hear it.

Mary whirled and faced her. "Adie, hurry up! Bessie needs rags and water. It's your job to make sure she has them."

Terrified, she ran after Mary, who gripped her hand. At the corner of the house, Mary veered to the street. Adie went through the back door and added wood to the stove. She pumped water and filled two kettles, listening all the time to the creak of a rocking chair in Pearl's room, directly over her head. It sounded like a blessedly typical night until a low moan mixed with the heat of the stove.

With a lamp in hand, Adie fled to Josh's room where she stored old linens. He'd insisted on cleaning the room himself, so she hadn't been in it since the night he'd arrived. Very little had changed. She saw his Bible on his nightstand and his clothes on hooks. The saddlebags sat in a corner, flat because he'd unpacked the contents as if he planned to stay forever. Adie needed to sort her thoughts, but she couldn't do it now. Pearl needed her. She opened a trunk, removed muslin sheets and carried them to the kitchen. The moaning had stopped, so she went to Pearl's room and knocked.

"Come in," Bessie called.

Adie opened the door and smelled life. Not perfume or the aroma of bread, but sweat and work and pain. She looked at Pearl. "How are you doing?"

She forced a smile. "Good."

Bessie patted her hand. "She's doing just fine."

Except her eyes were as round as coins and her fingers looked like bones clutching at the sheet. She stared at Adie as if she'd never see her again. "Bessie says the baby's breech."

"I heard."

"The doctor will have to turn it."

Adie fought tears.

"Don't you dare cry!" Pearl scolded.

"I'm not." Except her face cracked like a clay pot, and she started to cry. *Why, God? Why does this have to be so hard? Please help Pearl, Lord. Don't let her die. Keep her baby safe.* Adie hadn't prayed with such hope since being with Maggie. She barely recognized that she was doing it now.

Pearl started to pant. She gripped Adie's hand and squeezed the blood out of it.

Please, Lord! Spare her this pain.

The panting slid into a low moan. Gripping her belly, Pearl writhed on the bed. The sight of her sent Adie back to Maggie's bedroom in the Topeka boardinghouse. Her labor had lasted for hours, almost a full day. Adie loved babies, but she had no desire to *ever* go through this torment.

As the contraction passed, Pearl's grip loosened to a touch. Bessie patted Adie's shoulder. "I'll send Caroline down for the water."

As Adie stumbled to her feet, Pearl pulled herself higher on the pillows. "Is my father here yet?"

"Josh went for him."

Pearl swallowed hard. "I need to see him."

Last words, final goodbyes. Adie thought of Maggie's journal and the last desperate scrawl. Someday she'd read it, but not for a long time. Feeling like a coward, she went back to the kitchen and checked the water. Caroline came down ten minutes later. Adie filled two pitchers to the brim. Her friend hugged her, then carried the pitchers upstairs.

Mary and Dr. Nichols arrived next. They went straight upstairs and didn't come down. Five minutes later, Josh and Reverend Oliver came down the hall to the kitchen. Adie had just stoked the stove. Heat billowed everywhere, turning the room to a furnace.

Reverend Oliver, red-faced from the walk to Swan's Nest, mopped his brow with his sleeve. "How is she?"

"She—" Adie's voice broke. "She wants to see you."

Tobias tramped up the stairs, leaving Adie alone with Josh. With her eyes blazing, she clenched her hands into fists. She wanted to hit something but settled for shouting at him. "I'll *never* go to your church! Your God is cruel and mean and—" She burst into tears.

Josh pulled her into his arms, but she shoved him away.

"She's dying!" Adie cried. "The baby's breech and it's tearing her apart. I can't stand it. I can't—" She broke into sobs. Only minutes later did she realize he'd pulled her close and her tears were soaking his shirt.

"Cry, Adie. It's all right."

At times like this, when his emotions ran hot and God seemed a hundred miles away, Josh sometimes ranted at the sky. Deep feelings weren't a lack of faith and he didn't feel guilty for having them. God understood tears and anger. He shared them.

Adie didn't know it, but her sorrow put her in the arms of the Lord. Josh didn't try to console her with words. He couldn't. Neither did he know if Pearl would live or die. He only knew that God would see them through this long night, just as he'd seen Josh through his opium addiction and losing Emily. As a minister, he'd performed more funerals than weddings. He'd prayed with gut-shot outlaws who'd suffered for days, then cried out for mercy, died and arrived at heaven's gate. Josh didn't know why life had to be so hard, but he knew that Christ had walked this earth as a man. He'd felt every lash of the whip, the sting of the thorns.

"Let's go outside," he said to Adie.

She let him guide her to the porch, where the night air carried the scent of lilacs. As she sat in the chair farthest from the door, Josh pulled a second chair to her side. He didn't know Adie's thoughts, but he knew his own. Reaching for her hand, he silently prayed for Pearl, her baby and women everywhere who'd walked in Emily's shoes.

Several minutes passed before they heard the creak of the door and Tobias joined them. Except for a hint of moonlight, the three of them were in the dark.

"How is she?" Josh asked.

Tobias lowered his tall body on to the swing. It creaked like his old bones. "It's a hard birth."

Adie glared at him. "They're *all* hard!"

What could either man say? Nothing, though Josh added Adie's complaint to his list of questions for the Alimighty when he got to heaven. Why couldn't babies just pop out? He knew the theology of the fall from grace, he just didn't like it. From his point of view, Adam had gotten off easy with the curse of toiling in the fields. The price for Eve—the pain of childbirth—seemed a hundred times worse.

Tobias grunted. "Doc Nichols says the baby might turn on its own. We have to pray."

He bowed his head. So did Josh and Adie.

"I beg you, Lord, spare my daughter's life. Save her baby." He spoke in the solemn tone of a man who'd witnessed death but believed in heaven. Just before saying amen, he paused.

Adie's voice came out in a rasp. *"Do it, Lord. Please."*

"Amen," they said together.

As the night crawled by, Mary made occasional visits to give them news. Adie made tea and toast for the men, but Josh barely tasted it. Every few minutes, moans drifted through the open windows, coming closer together with every hour. Amazingly, Stephen slept through the cries.

As dawn lightened the sky, Pearl's moaning changed to a staccato of shrieks that turned into one long scream. Josh bowed his head. Adie wept into a hankie. A second scream followed the first, then died to silence. Long seconds passed. They heard a slap, then the cry of a very angry baby.

"My grandchild," Tobias whispered.

The screams had meant Pearl was alive. The silence meant she'd escaped the pain but how? As Adie clutched his hand, thoughts of Emily pounded at him. So did the knowledge that

Adie had watched his sister die. He squeezed her hand and prayed hard. Long minutes passed before the front door opened.

As the three of them shot to their feet, Josh saw Mary holding the tiniest human being he'd ever seen.

"Pearl's fine," she said.

Tobias collapsed on the chair and bowed his head. "Thank you, Lord."

Josh swallowed a lump, then looked again at the baby. The fruit of Pearl's labor had a smattering of dark hair and a mouth that moved like a baby bird's. "Boy or girl?"

"A boy." Mary stepped to Reverend Oliver and crouched to put the baby at eye level. "Sir, meet your grandson. This is Tobias Joshua Oliver."

Josh had never felt so honored.

Adie squeezed his hand. Side by side, they watched as Tobias touched the baby's chin, then broke into a smile. "He's going to be a fine man someday."

"Yes, sir," Josh said.

Tobias looked to Mary. "May I see my daughter?"

"Yes, but just for a minute."

As he went into the house, Mary looked at Adie. "Pearl wants to see you, too."

Josh watched her expression. Either she'd see the birth as a gift of life, or she'd be bitter about the struggle. The first reaction would signal healing. The second would leave them a world apart.

Adie wanted to visit Pearl, too. For the past several hours, she'd felt as if her own body were being ripped in two. She needed to see for herself that Pearl was alive and happy.

Only a few minutes passed before Reverend Oliver came back through the door. "She's tired but smiling," he said to them.

Mary motioned for Adie to come inside. They went

upstairs, then through the door to Pearl's room. Pale and weak, Pearl reached for the baby in Mary's arms and held him close. On the far side of the room, Bessie and Caroline were chatting with Dr. Nichols. Small talk had replaced Pearl's moans, but Adie saw a wad of soiled sheets and pinkish water in the basin where Bessie had washed the baby.

She turned back to Pearl. Tobias Joshua lay sleeping against his mother's chest, listening to the beat of her heart. Adie couldn't help but smile. "He's beautiful."

Pearl's cheeks flushed with pride. "If it had been a girl, I was going to name her Adelaide Virginia, after you and my mother."

Adie's eyes misted. "That was sweet of you."

"You're my best friend, Adie. I love you."

She clasped Pearl's hand. "I love you, too."

"I'll miss you when we leave. I'll miss everyone, but I have to do what's best for Toby, don't I?"

"Always."

Pearl stroked the baby's cheek. "He was worth it, don't you think?"

"I do."

Adie felt the same way every time she held Stephen, but the realization left her thoughts in a tangle. Adie's greatest joy—her son—had come from Maggie's death. Her greatest hope—a future with Josh—had resulted from a long list of mistakes. If Emily hadn't fallen to temptation, she'd never have become Maggie Butler. Without the loss of his sister, Josh would still be in Boston, struggling with the ulcer and all it meant. They would never have met. Her insides shook with a truth she didn't want to acknowledge. If she was going to blame God for the ugliness in her life, didn't He deserve credit for the beauty? It seemed logical, but logic didn't erase her scars. She'd been hurt and wanted justice.

Suddenly agitated, she stood up from the bed. "I better go. You need your rest."

"I *am* tired," Pearl admitted.

Adie paced to her room, where she heard Stephen cooing in his cradle. When he saw her, he raised his little arms. She picked him up and held him tight. Blinking, she recalled Reverend Oliver's first arrival at Swan's Nest and how he'd clung to his daughter. He'd hurt Pearl terribly, yet she'd forgiven him even before he'd asked. Why couldn't Adie forgive the people who'd hurt *her?*

With Stephen in her arms, she looked in the mirror. She saw a child with Josh's dark hair. Her own reddish curls had pulled loose and were wisping around her face. The colors reminded her of night and the glow of a fire. What had the psalmist written?

Darkness and light are alike to Thee.

Maybe she was closer to God than she thought. With a lump in her throat, Adie spoke to God in her mind. She told Him about the anger and the bitter memories, how she'd cried for days after leaving Liddy's Grove, and how helpless she'd felt. The words came in a torrent that picked up debris until she opened her eyes.

Her prayer didn't lessen her bitterness, but she knew what she had to do. This Sunday, she'd be attending Colfax Avenue Church.

Chapter Seventeen

Adie had come to church. The woman Josh loved had stepped into her own version of a lion's den and she'd done it for him.

Seated on the dais next to Tobias, he took in her appearance as the organist played the opening hymn. Her green dress, a gown he'd never seen, complemented her ivory complexion. A straw hat hid most of her hair but not the hardness of her chin. When she raised her hand to check her hat, he saw lace gloves covering her work-worn hands.

She'd come in her Sunday best and looked ready for a fight. Josh, too, had come to church dressed for battle. This morning he'd put on a heavily starched collar and brushed his coat until it looked new. The attention to his appearance had nothing to do with pride. He'd been putting on a uniform like a soldier going to war. For three days he'd avoided Adie by working on his sermon. As Tobias suggested, he'd chosen the text about moneychangers in the temple and he'd had Franklin Dean in mind.

The banker was seated in the third row on the aisle. A strategic spot, Josh thought. If he decided to walk out on the sermon, he'd command everyone's attention. Adie, too, had picked a strategic seat. She was in the back row, a step from the door. Instead of walking to church with Caroline and Mary, she'd come by herself and had arrived with a minute to spare. As the organist played the closing notes of a hymn, Josh scanned the crowd for people from Brick's but saw no one. He'd expected the disappointment, but it still hurt. He'd hoped at least Brick would make an appearance.

When the hymn ended, Tobias handled the church business of announcements, a scripture reading and the offering. As the ushers left with the silver plates, he stepped back to the podium. "Ladies and gentleman, we have a special guest today. I'm pleased to introduce Reverend Joshua Blue, my renowned colleague from the fine city of Boston."

Tobias droned on, telling the congregation of Josh's education and the crowds he'd gathered. At one time, Josh would have soaked in the praise like a pickle in brine. Today it soured his stomach. He didn't want Tobias blowing his horn. Hearing about the person he'd been gave him a headache. If he and Tobias had been alone, he'd have corrected him. He couldn't now, not in public.

"Ladies and gentlemen," Tobias said with a flourish. "I present the honorable and esteemed Reverend Joshua Blue."

Josh felt neither honorable nor esteemed. He was a man who'd murdered his sister, a human being in need of grace. His insides curdled. How could he preach down to Franklin Dean when he was no better than anyone in this building? No better than the thieves and prostitutes he'd met in his travels? Sure, Dean was a hard case, but Christ had died for him, too. Josh's gaze narrowed to Adie. She'd raised her chin even higher. As much as he wanted to throw verbal punches at Dean—and as much as Dean had it coming—Josh didn't have the right to preach anything but love, grace and the mercy of the cross.

The sermon he'd planned went out of his head. In came the conviction he needed to speak to himself as well as Dean, Adie and everyone else in the sanctuary. When Reverend Oliver motioned him forward, Josh stepped to the podium and opened his Bible to the story of the adulterous woman. Emily would be proud. He doubted Adie would be pleased, but he had to be true to his beliefs.

The man in the pulpit had the dark hair and piercing eyes of the stranger who'd collapsed on Adie's porch, but otherwise she barely recognized Josh. He stood as straight as a steeple, scanning the crowd as he called for prayer.

"Father God," he began, "be with us today…."

She only half listened. This was the minister who'd drawn crowds in Boston and chased Maggie out of her home. It was also Josh, the man who'd kissed her and held her and given her Stephen. Listening to his prayer, she admired his sincerity. She was also aware of the sun pressing through the massive stained glass windows. When she looked at the window depicting a stream and a willow, she felt lost. When she focused on the shepherd with his sheep, she wanted to weep. Worst of all, she could see the back of Franklin Dean's head. She wanted to stand up and tell the congregation that they had vermin in their midst.

Maybe Josh would do the job for her. As he ended the prayer, Adie looked directly at him. He acknowledged her with a nod, then faced the congregation.

"I'm honored by Reverend Oliver's introduction, but I'm compelled to set the record straight. I'm neither honorable nor worthy of esteem. I'm a sinner saved by grace, a man as flawed as anyone…everyone…in this room."

Adie bristled. She hadn't come to church to hear about her flaws. She'd come for justice. She'd been harmed by Dean and men like him. If she and Josh had been alone, she'd have taken him to task.

Josh started to pace. "There's a story in the Bible that reminds me of who I am."

A natural storyteller, he took the congregation, even Adie, back in time to Jerusalem where a group of men had dragged a woman into the temple. Caught in the act of adultery, she had nowhere to go, no way to hide what she'd done. She didn't deny the accusations. She couldn't. Her disheveled appearance was plain for all to see.

Adie knew the story. She'd always wondered why the men brought the woman and not the man who'd been with her. Josh didn't mention the man, either. Instead he described how Jesus had dropped to a crouch and written something in the sand.

Pausing, he looked from person to person, then asked a question. "What do you think Christ wrote?"

Adie had never thought about it.

"We don't know," Josh continued. "It could have been anything—the woman's name, a list of her accusers. Maybe he drew a cross as a sign of things to come. What we *do* know is what happened next. Jesus stood and said, 'Let him whose slate is clean cast the first stone.'"

He paused again, giving the congregation time to think. "Can anyone here say they have a clean slate? I can't."

Adie didn't give a hoot about having a clean slate. She saw nothing but Franklin Dean's blond head. She hated him. If she'd had a rock in her hand, she'd have thrown it as hard as she could.

Josh went back to pacing. "We've all fallen short. Christ out of love died for each of us. It doesn't matter what you've done. Jesus—through his death on the cross—gives both justice to victims and mercy to those who ask."

Adie fought to keep still. How could Josh preach mercy with Franklin Dean sitting like a toad in the third row? At the end of the dais closest to her, he stopped pacing and sought her gaze. Adie knew the next words would be for her.

"It's hard to imagine such charity. It's even harder to believe that among Christ's final words were these. 'Father, forgive them. They know not what they do.'"

He turned next to Dean. "Every day we have a choice—repent and accept that gift or continue in our old ways."

Josh went back to the podium. "Most of us know what happened to the woman in the temple. One by one, her accusers dropped the stones and left, leaving her alone with the Lord, who gave a simple command. 'Go and sin no more.' I hear that as 'Go and start fresh.'"

Josh closed the Bible. "Imagine…whatever you've done, whatever mistakes you've made, they've been forgiven. That's true for everyone in this building."

Adie couldn't stand another word. When Josh bowed his head to pray, she slipped out the door and ran down the steps. She didn't want to hear about forgiveness and second chances, not with Dean under the same roof. She hated him. She hated Timothy Long, Reverend Honeycutt and everyone else who'd hurt her over the years. If she couldn't sit through a single sermon, how could she even *think* about loving Josh?

She needed time to compose herself. Instead of going home, she headed to the heart of Denver. The shops would be closed and she expected be alone, but as she turned a corner, she saw two young women in front of a hat shop. They were well dressed and she wondered if they'd been to church. Then she noticed the frippery on their dresses and the cut of their gowns. Miss Elsa's Social Club was a block away. Adie wondered if the girls were prostitutes out for a morning walk.

She couldn't look at a soiled dove without thinking of how low she'd sunk before she'd met Maggie. She hadn't turned to such a life, but she'd lived with the threat of it. As she neared the hat shop, she heard a bit of conversation.

"I hate him!" said a girl with a German accent.

Adie slowed her pace. The other girl offered her a handkerchief. "If he's cruel, tell Miss Elsa."

"I tried, but—" She bit her lip. "She said Mr. Dean is a good customer."

Adie stifled a gasp.

The German girl wiped her eyes. "She promised me extra money. The more I save, the sooner I can go home."

Adie knew the risks of speaking with this girl. Even if she held the deed to Swan's Nest, Dean could make her life miserable. She didn't care. She stopped and pretended to admire a hat.

"Be strong, Gretchen," said the girl's companion. "Someday you can leave, but for now—"

"Excuse me." Adie touched Gretchen's elbow. "I'm Adie Clarke. I run a boardinghouse. If you're in trouble—"

Gretchen's eyes widened. "You'd help me?"

"Yes."

"But I don't have money."

"You don't need it," Adie said gently.

The girl's companion hooked her arm around her waist. "Come on, Gretchen."

The girl pulled back. "No!"

"You owe Miss Elsa," her friend hissed.

Gretchen's eyes turned into clouds ready to burst. Knowing the girl couldn't simply come with her—she had clothes and possessions, things that mattered to her—Adie stepped back. "I live at Swan's Nest on Seventeenth Street. Look for the window above the door. It's round and shows a swan."

Her eyes shimmered. "My church back home had pretty windows."

"Gretchen! Let's go." Her friend tugged her down the street, but Gretchen looked over her shoulder.

Tonight Adie would be listening for footsteps on the porch. If the girl knocked, she'd open the door wide. As she headed for home, Adie thought about Gretchen's predicament and her own. In a way, they were both trapped in lives they didn't want. What would happen if Adie ran to God in the middle of the night? Would he open the door the way she'd open it for Gretchen?

She knew the answer. The Lord had died for her. He'd welcome her with open arms. The problem, she had to admit, was the hardness of her own heart. She didn't want to forgive the people who'd harmed her. Until she could cross that bridge, she had no future with Josh, who, in her opinion, was worthy of more than respect and esteem. He was worthy of love.

Josh didn't see Adie leave the church. He'd been matching stares with members of the congregation, including Dean who'd crossed his arms over his puffed-up chest. When he turned back to Adie, he'd seen the door swing shut behind the hem of her green dress.

She'd been either deeply touched or offended. Josh suspected the latter. This morning, watching her expression, he'd been struck by an odd coincidence. Both Adie and Dean had scowled at him through the entire sermon. Until that moment, Josh had thought of her as the woman being condemned. During the sermon, he realized he'd been mistaken. Adie had a handful of rocks and wanted to throw them at Dean, Honeycutt, every other person who'd hurt her. She had cause, but she wouldn't find peace until she set them down.

Josh had planned to tell the congregation his own story, but he'd preached long enough. He gave the closing prayer, then walked down the aisle with Tobias. As the organist played a rousing hymn, he took in the vaulted ceiling and mahogany trim. Sunshine lit up the windows and made a rainbow of light. To Josh's utter joy, he felt nothing more or less than the satisfaction he'd felt while preaching at Brick's Saloon.

He'd told Adie that he could preach anywhere—a cathedral or street corner—today he'd proved it to himself. He felt as if he'd come home. He could do a good job in this church, but he still had concerns. No one from Brick's had come to the service, and Adie had walked out on him. Their future hung by a thread, but Josh knew who held the future.

He wanted to leave for Swan's Nest immediately, but he and Tobias had to greet people as they left. Side by side, they shook hands with individuals and made small talk. As Dean approached, Josh made eye contact. The banker shook Tobias's hand but withheld the courtesy from Josh.

"Interesting text, *Reverend*." He used the title with utter disdain.

Josh ignored the slight. "Thank you."

Dean walked away. Josh turned slightly and spotted Horace waiting with the carriage. The driver tipped his hat, not to Dean but to Josh.

Nodding back, Josh wondered what the gesture meant. Horace had come to Brick's three Sundays in a row. The last time he'd stayed for coffee and had asked questions. Josh turned back to the reception line where a well-dressed man was offering his hand. "Reverend Blue, it's a pleasure.

Tobias introduced Halston Smythe, the owner of the Denver Imperial Hotel and a member of the elder board. Two other men stood with him, both longtime members of Colfax Avenue Church. One had a mustache; the other wore a bowler hat.

Smythe looked at Reverend Oliver. "We hate to lose you, Tobias, but I believe we've found your replacement."

"I hope so, Hal." Tobias clapped Josh on the back. "You

won't find a better preacher west of the Mississippi, maybe in America."

Josh had to interrupt. "Sir—"

"Don't be modest, Josh," Tobias insisted. "You have a gift."

Maybe, but that gift had come from God. Josh wanted no credit for himself, but he couldn't correct Tobias without being disrespectful. Neither could he let the flattery ride. A question crossed his mind, one that would shed light on his future. He focused on Smythe. "You gentlemen need to be aware. I have a small congregation of my own."

"In Denver?" said the man in the vest.

"We meet in Brick's Saloon."

The gentleman with the mustache frowned. "We weren't aware of your, uh, connections."

Smythe gave a shrewd smile, a sign Josh had an ally. "Don't trouble yourself, Pete. I liked what I heard today."

"So did I," Tobias added.

The man in the vest said nothing.

Smythe focused on Josh. "The elders meet Thursday evening. If you're agreeable, we'll ask a few questions and take a vote."

Josh would have four days to consider the possibilities. "I'll be there."

"Good." Smythe turned to the man in the vest. "I'll speak with the elders. Would you distribute a handbill to the members? I want a big turnout."

"Of course," the man answered.

Josh didn't know what would happen on Thursday night, but he knew he had a fight on his hands. The three elders continued down the walk. When the last person exited the church, Tobias turned to him. "I'm eager to see my grandson. Shall we head to Swan's Nest?"

"Sounds good," Josh replied.

His fight with Dean was nothing compared to the battle he expected from Adie. He wanted to know what she'd thought of his sermon and intended to ask. When the church was empty, Tobias closed the door and they headed up the street. They caught up with Adie three blocks shy of Swan's Nest. Judging by when she'd left church, she hadn't gone straight home. Josh suspected she'd been walking the streets, thinking about the sermon. He knew from experience that living with a hard heart didn't shield a person from pain. It locked the pain inside.

Tobias called out to her. "Miss Clarke!"

Adie pivoted abruptly. "Good morning, gentlemen."

Tobias moved to the right. Josh stepped to her left where his body would shield her from passing carriages. As they neared a rut in the path, he fought the urge to hold her hand to steady her. He didn't have that right, not yet. Unless Adie's heart softened, he never would.

Reverend Oliver winked at Josh. "Tell me, Miss Clarke. What did you think of Josh's sermon?"

Josh wanted to know but not in front of Tobias. The older man meant well, but he didn't understand Adie's struggle.

"Don't answer." Josh tried to sound jovial. "I can't take it back now."

"Nor should you," Tobias added. "You did a fine job."

Josh hoped so, but only one opinion mattered and it belonged to the Almighty. Josh had been faithful today. He'd sleep well, except for dreams of Adie throwing rocks at Dean and Honeycutt.

Silence echoed between their footsteps. Adie stared straight ahead. "The service was very nice."

She couldn't have sounded colder.

Tobias rubbed his chin. "We have seven elders. My guess is a 4-3 split, with you being elected."

Josh frowned. "That's a bad way to start."

"It could be 5-2, maybe 6-1 if Pete's wife talks to him. You won't get Dean's vote, but that's to be expected."

Adie looked at Josh. "Would you take the position?"

She wanted an answer—yes or no—but he didn't know himself. Nor did he want to have the discussion in the middle of the street with Tobias in earshot. Josh had to make his own decision. He liked stained glass. He enjoyed the choir and the massive organ, but he missed the people at Brick's Saloon and was worried about them, particularly Gretchen who'd been quieter than usual at last Sunday's service.

Adie was waiting for an answer, so he kept his voice neutral. "I'd consider it."

Tobias scoffed. "Of course you'd take the position."

"But—"

"If God opens that door, son, don't hesitate."

"We'll see," he answered.

Adie's shoulders stayed stiff. "It was a fine sermon, Josh. I'm sure the elders will offer you the position."

"I don't know."

"I do," she said. "You fit right in." Coming from Adie, it wasn't a compliment. "If you accept, I imagine you'll move into the parsonage."

Josh hadn't thought that far.

"It's the end of the month," she continued. "And I may have found a new boarder. This would be a good time to make the change."

He couldn't believe his ears. "You want me to leave Swan's Nest?"

"Yes."

Tobias interrupted. "Miss Clarke has a point. Pearl's room is empty, and it'll give us time to plan the transition."

Josh didn't even know if there would *be* a transition. He felt as if he'd been slugged in the gut. Swan's Nest had become his home. He enjoyed seeing Adie during the day, working in the garden or rocking Stephen on the porch. On the other hand, he understood the need for distance between them. Josh gave her a target, someone to fight when she needed to wrestle with her own soul.

"It's a possibility," he said. "But what about Dean?"

Adie raised her chin. "I won't let him intimidate me."

"No, but he's still a threat. Elliot arrived a few days ago, but he's still getting settled. Until the mortgage is paid—"

"Josh?" Tobias interrupted.

He did *not* want the older man's help. "What is it?"

"Frank's going to react to your sermon. I won't be surprised if he comes after you instead of Miss Clarke."

Adie's brow furrowed. "What makes you think that?"

"I've preached a lot of years, Miss Clarke. If everybody tells me I've given a good sermon, chances are I've just tickled their ears. But when someone picks a fight, I know the truth has hit home. Frank got called a sinner today. He didn't like it."

Adie had heard the same message. Judging by her scowl, she hadn't liked it, either. When they reached the front of Swan's Nest, Josh indicated the door to Tobias. "Go see your grandson. I'd like a word with Miss Clarke."

Tobias doffed his hat to Adie and went inside. As the door swung shut, Josh faced her. "Do you really want me to leave?"

"It's for the best."

"Why?"

She raised her chin. "I respect your faith, Josh. But I'll never share it. I'll hate men like Franklin Dean until I die."

They were at the crux of their differences. Josh preached forgiveness. Adie wanted vengeance. He didn't blame her, but he knew a simple truth. Withholding mercy caused more pain than it took away. Did he answer as a minister or a man?

The minister had words for her. The man wanted to draw her into his arms.

He did neither. "Give it time."

"There's no point." She squared her shoulders. "I'm grateful for everything you've done for me. You know I care about you, but we can't be more than friends."

She had a point about their differences, but Josh believed in a powerful God. The Almighty wouldn't leave Adie hanging by her thumbs and neither would Josh. He reached for her hand. "Adie—"

She stepped back. "I'm sorry, Josh. You're a good man."

He'd heard enough. As a minister *and* a man, he had to fight for her. "I'm not 'good' and you know it."

Her brows snapped together. "I'm *sick* of your humble pie!"

"It's the truth." He had to make his point. "I'm no better or worse than anyone and neither are *you*."

Her voice rose. "What do you mean by *that?*"

"The story today... Who are you, Adie? The sinful woman or one of the hypocrites throwing rocks?"

She gasped.

"It's got to be one or the other."

"I'm neither."

"That's the problem," he said. "You think you're better than Dean and Honeycutt, but deep down, *we're all the same.* God's love is so vast, we can't take it in. We're like bugs. You might be a butterfly instead of a roach like Dean, but none of us comes within a mile of God's goodness."

Josh kept his eyes on her face. Either she'd understand his intent or she'd walk away still clutching stones.

Her hazel eyes glistened, then turned hard. "You've made your point, Reverend. I'm lower than a bug. Now go pack your things."

She'd missed the point entirely. "Adie—"

"I'm tired of your talk. You act like you've got all the answers, but you don't."

"I know that."

"And *I* know why Emily left. She got *fed up* with *you* and your know-it-all ways!"

In the past year he'd endured ulcers, a bullet wound, fevers and nearly drowning. Nothing hurt as much as that verbal stone hitting his heart.

Her lips quivered. For a moment he thought she'd apologize. Instead she turned and ran up the steps.

The sun beat on his black coat, heating the wool until he felt it on his skin. The weight pressed him down, but he knew what he had to do. Adie had ordered him to leave Swan's Nest. If he fought to stay, she'd fight back and they'd end up in a bigger tangle. Her battle wasn't with Josh. It was with God and he had to stay out of the way. Bruised and hurting, he went to pack his things.

Chapter Eighteen

Early Monday morning, Adie went to the carriage house to milk Buttons. As she carried the bucket back to the kitchen, she saw a silhouette in the window. Was it Josh? Hope shot through her before she came to her senses. She'd said terrible things to him. He'd packed his saddlebags and gone to the parsonage, leaving her to explain his absence at Sunday supper. Caroline had remained quiet, but Mary had shot her a critical look. Bessie had come to her aid, saying she felt sure things would work out for the best.

Adie didn't share that hope. She regretted speaking cruelly to Josh, but she had no desire to apologize. She'd been sharp-tongued, but being put in the same camp as Franklin Dean had wounded her. Neither did she like being compared to something as common as an insect. All her life she'd felt insignificant. Josh's high-minded attitude had turned her back into that child.

She would have welcomed a chat with Bessie or Pearl, but Adie couldn't face Mary or Caroline. When the shadow moved past the window again, she saw Mary's blond hair. Before she could turn back to the carriage house, her friend opened the door. She had Stephen on her hip, making it impossible for Adie to linger in the yard.

"This baby's hungry," Mary said.

Adie smiled at her son, but she felt morose. Stephen looked like Maggie, which meant he looked like Josh.

"I'm coming," she said.

"Good," Mary replied. "I have something to say."

Reluctantly, Adie came up the steps. Mary had already started warming a bottle, so she poured the new milk into a clean pitcher. As Stephen started to fuss, she felt the same helplessness. She wanted to leave but couldn't. Mary would follow if she made an excuse, so she took Stephen, lifted the bottle and sat to feed him.

Once he settled, she looked at Mary. "What's on your mind?"

"You."

Adie said nothing.

"Why did you ask Josh to leave?"

Adie looked down at Stephen. The milk had calmed him. She wished she could find a cure for herself. Instead she had to deal with Mary, a woman who had no patience with half-truths.

"We had words," she finally said. "I didn't like the sermon and told him so."

"You didn't?"

"He let Franklin Dean off the hook."

Mary went to the stove and poured herself tea. "If that's true, he let me off the hook, too. I never told you, but I killed a man."

Adie caught her breath.

"It's true." Mary came back to the table. She took a sip from the porcelain cup, then stared out the window. "I can't bear to talk about it, except to say I made a mistake. A judge ruled it was self-defense, but the man's brother didn't agree. Neither did the town. No one threw rocks at me that day, but more than a few wanted to lynch me. I'm still afraid of the brother. He vowed to track me down."

She shook her head as if to erase the memory, then looked at Adie. "That's why Josh's sermon touched me. I was that woman in the square, standing alone while people said terrible things. I looked around that day and do you know what I saw?"

Adie was afraid to ask.

"I *knew* those people." Mary set down the teacup with a thud. "They wanted to throw stones at me, but I wasn't the only guilty person in that square. Every one of them had a secret."

Looking at her friend, Adie understood what Josh had been trying to tell her. The only person at Swan's Nest without regrets was Stephen, and he couldn't even feed himself. Adie, too, had fallen short. She'd lied to Josh and added weeks to his anguish about Emily, yet he'd forgiven her instantly. Adie didn't know if she could forgive Dean and Honeycutt, but she no longer wanted to throw rocks at anyone, certainly not at Josh. She'd hurt him yesterday. She needed to make amends.

Her stomach churned as she looked at Mary. "I understand now."

Mary smiled. "So what are you going to do?"

"I need to apologize to Josh."

"When?"

Adie sighed. "I don't know. It'll be a hard conversation."

"You love him, don't you?"

"I do, but I can't see myself as a minister's wife."

Mary added sugar to her tea. "A month ago, I couldn't see myself singing in church. If Josh takes Reverend Oliver's place, I might join the choir."

Would Mary be welcome? Reverend Honeycutt would have slammed the door in her face.

Mary ran her finger along the rim of the teacup. "That meeting is Thursday. Only the elders vote, but anyone can attend. Caroline and I are going. Pearl might if she's up to it. How about you, Adie? It would mean the world to Josh."

"I'll have to think about it."

Mary carried her cup to the washbasin, then went upstairs to get dressed. With Stephen warm in her arms, Adie wondered what would happen at the elder meeting. If they voted for Josh—and let Mary sing in the choir—maybe she could make her peace with loving a minister. If not, she wanted nothing to do with such a place.

On Tuesday at twelve noon, Halston Smythe walked into Denver National Bank and greeted Frank with a handshake. The two men rarely saw eye-to-eye. Frank suspected today's visit would be no different. At the club this morning, he'd heard talk of Reverend Blue and the plan to offer him the pulpit.

Frank objected for two reasons. He didn't want Tobias to leave with Pearl, and he hated the thought of Joshua Blue running Colfax Avenue Church. Tobias hadn't been easy to manipulate, but Frank had managed to do it. Until Sunday, he'd thought Tobias was on his side. Now he wondered. The old man hadn't confronted him directly, but his decision to leave Denver didn't bode well. Frank had visited the parsonage, but the old man had been at Swan's Nest, a sign that he'd reconciled with Pearl.

Frank didn't like being the odd man out. He didn't like Smythe, either. This morning he'd pump the man for information and send him on his way. Hiding his annoyance, he indicated the chair across from his. "Please, have a seat."

Smythe lowered his round body on to the leather. "I'll get to the point, Frank. Tobias and Pearl are leaving Denver."

"So I've heard."

"Have you heard why?"

The entire church knew about Pearl's pregnancy and his involvement. He'd survived the scrutiny by making subtle threats to members who depended on his bank, and by wearing his broken heart on his sleeve. He played that card now.

"I admit it. Pearl and I made a mistake." Frank deliberately looked morose. "I've begged her to marry me, but she won't."

"My wife tells me the 'mistake' was yours."

"What do you mean?"

Smythe rose from the chair, planted his hands on the desk and leaned so close Frank could smell peppermint on his breath. The man's voice came out in a low whisper. "You know *exactly* what I mean."

Smythe's tone meant one thing. Pearl had been spreading lies. Frank wanted to smack her. He settled for glaring at the elder. "Come on, Hal. You know how things go."

Smythe settled back on the chair. "No, Frank, I *don't*."

"We made a mistake. I want to fix it."

Smythe remained impassive, leaving Frank to wonder what had happened to make Pearl tell lies. Then it struck him. She'd had the baby and no one had told him. He didn't know if she'd given birth to a boy or a girl. He wanted to go directly to Swan's Nest but couldn't. Thanks to Smythe's visit, Frank had to be on his best behavior.

The elder cleared his throat. "Aside from all that, I wanted to make you aware of the change to Thursday's agenda. We'll be voting on Tobias's replacement."

Pictures of Pearl raced through Frank's mind. He could hardly think, but business came first. He had to finish with Smythe. "Tobias wants this Blue fellow, doesn't he?"

"Yes."

"Does he have support?"

"Quite a bit, including mine." For the second time, Smythe rose from the chair. This time he looked eager to leave. "That concludes church business, but I've also come concerning my account."

Tension eased from Frank's muscles. He knew how to handle money. "What can I do for you?"

"I'd like to make a transfer."

"Buying more land?"

"No," Smythe answered. "Boston Merchants Bank just opened. Sorry, Frank. But the new bank has better rates."

Frank leaned back in his chair. In a city as vibrant as Denver, a new bank didn't surprise him. What made him arch a brow was the mention of Boston. He also wondered why he hadn't heard talk at the supper club. The new banker had come to town in a cloak of secrecy. "Who's running it?"

"A fellow named Elliot Morse. He's a member of the Blue family."

Without the courtesy of a goodbye, Smythe walked out the door, leaving Frank to ponder the events of the past few weeks. They led him to a single conclusion. Joshua Blue was ruining his life by protecting Adie Clarke, influencing Pearl and starting a rival bank. It couldn't be tolerated.

He motioned for a clerk. As she came forward, he scowled. "Find Horace."

"Yes, sir." She set an envelope on his desk. "This came by courier."

As she left to summon Horace, Frank opened the envelope and found a letter from Boston Merchants Bank and a check for the amount of the Swan's Nest mortgage. Furious, he stared out the window, where he saw Horace walking down the boardwalk. Instead of his usual shuffling gait, the driver was striding with a sense of purpose. Frank drummed his fingers on his desk until Horace arrived.

The driver took off his hat. "You wanted me, sir?"

"Sit down."

He lowered himself onto the chair vacated by Smythe.

"I gave you a job last week," Frank said.

"Yes, sir. I recall."

"What have you found out about Reverend Blue?"

"Not much." Horace shifted in the chair. "People like the reverend. He treats everyone the same, even the girls from Miss Elsa's."

Frank's ears perked up. "He's been to Miss Elsa's?"

"Just once," Horace said quickly. "Not for what you're thinking, sir. He invited the girls to church. Two of them come regular now. The men at Brick's like him, too. I haven't heard a bad word about him, sir." Horace pursed his lips, a sign he was holding back.

"Spit it out, Horace. What else do you know?"

The driver fidgeted on the seat. "I don't like telling tales, sir."

Frank put a silver dollar on his desk. Horace eyed it but didn't move. Frank didn't like the man's reluctance. He added another silver dollar, then a third. Looking torn, Horace slid the coins across the desk and into his hand; then he met Frank's gaze. "I heard the women talking last Sunday. The reverend had a bad time in Boston."

"Go on."

"His sister got in trouble."

"I want to know about Reverend Blue, not some female."

"It's why he came west," Horace said. "He's been looking for his sister everywhere, in places a reverend don't belong."

"I see."

"There's more," Horace added. "Back in Boston, he used laudanum on the sly, too much of it if you get my drift."

So the honorable reverend was an opium addict. The more Horace spoke, the more evidence Frank had against him. Instead of dreading Thursday's meeting, he started to relish the thought of raking the esteemed Reverend Blue over the coals.

"Anything else?" he said to Horace.

"Just one thing," the driver said. "He had a talk with Brick and me and some of the fellows at the saloon the other night.

The Reverend walks like he talks, but he's still a man like you or me. He's not all high-and-mighty."

Frank laughed out loud.

Horace's mouth tightened. "I shouldn't have said anything."

"I'm glad you did." Frank slid a half eagle across the desk. "Take the afternoon off, Horace. You've earned it."

"Yes, sir." The driver turned and headed for the door.

Only after he left did Frank see the silver dollars sitting next to the gold piece. Not that it mattered…Horace had done his job and he'd done it well. On Thursday night, Reverend Blue's dirty laundry would be aired for the world to see.

"Coffee, Reverend?"

"Thanks."

As Brick filled the mug, Josh sat on the bar stool with his black coat buttoned tight and his boots freshly shined. It was Wednesday night and he'd been living at the parsonage since Sunday. He'd had all he could take of Tobias's enthusiasm for the elder meeting, so he'd gone for a walk and ended up at Brick's.

Josh liked Tobias, but he didn't share the man's confidence that he belonged at Colfax Avenue Church. The more Josh thought about it, the more he wondered if he was about to fall into a trap. In the past year, he'd learned to read men and their intentions. Halston Smythe struck him as sincere, but the two men with him had seemed weak. Dean should have been voted off the board a long time ago. The fact he remained showed a serious lack of integrity at the heart of the church's leadership.

Josh would go wherever the Lord sent him, but he'd learned a hard lesson about walking into a lion's den. If he went on his own, he'd get eaten alive. If he went with the Lord, he'd have a story to tell for years to come.

He wanted the story.

He suspected he was about to be devoured.

He sipped the coffee, then looked at Brick, who was wiping glasses with his apron. Josh felt good about the changes in the man's life. He'd taken down the tawdry picture above the bar and replaced it with a mirror. He'd written his sister, too. She might never receive the letter, but Brick had asked for forgiveness. Josh saw a new calm in his eyes.

Brick turned and wiped the counter. "I hear talk you're taking over that big church on Colfax Avenue."

"Maybe."

"Never been there myself," he said. "I'd miss Sunday mornings here."

"So go there," Josh replied.

"No, thanks." Brick kept dragging the rag in wide circles. "Tell me something, Reverend. How do you know what's best? Seems to me you can preach here or you can preach there. You've got a choice."

"That's right."

"So how do you decide?"

"I'll pray about it, maybe ask a friend for advice." Josh drummed his fingers on the warm mug. The barkeep had been in business for a while and had heard a lot of stories. "You're a smart man. Any thoughts for me?"

Brick looked pleased by the respect. "My granny had a saying. 'When you don't know what's right, do what's hard.'"

A customer called for the barkeep's attention. As Brick turned away, Josh thought about his advice. Accepting the position at Colfax Avenue Church would test him to the limits. He'd have to fight his pride every day and he'd hurt Adie's feelings more than he already had. The thought made his chest ache. He'd go wherever God led him, but he had to be sure he belonged in this particular lion's den.

As Josh sipped coffee, the perfect test came to mind. He'd take the position under one condition. The elder board had to vote unanimously to approve him. The more he considered the plan, the more he liked it. Dean would have to vote yes or resign. Either way, the banker would lose his influence over the church. Would Adie see the logic? Josh hoped so, but he couldn't let his feelings dictate his choice.

If the board didn't vote unanimously, he'd face another tough decision. He could stay in Denver and preach at Brick's, head home to Boston or go back to drifting. Josh stared at the murky dregs in his cup. Boston didn't appeal to him and neither did drifting. He wanted to stay in Denver where he could see Adie and Stephen and be a small part of their lives.

Small...

The word rankled him in the worst way. He didn't believe in a *small* God and he didn't want a *small* piece of Adie's life. He wanted to love her with everything he had to give. He'd already paid off the mortgage on Swan's Nest. Starting next month, she'd receive an allowance, one that would pay for roast beef every night.

The only loose end was Dean. Would he leave Adie alone once Pearl left? Soon Pearl and Tobias would leave for Cheyenne. Then what? Josh didn't know, but he was certain of one thing. He couldn't leave Denver until Dean no longer posed a threat to Adie. Short of death or a prison term, the banker wasn't likely to leave town.

As he swallowed the dregs of his coffee, Josh thought of the advice from Brick's grandmother.

Do what's hardest.

At tomorrow's meeting he'd stand his ground. If the elders voted unanimously to hire him, he'd accept the offer. If they didn't, he'd stay as long as Adie needed protection, loving her from afar. Both answers struck Josh as hard, but even more painful was the thought of leaving Denver for good. He didn't want to do it, but staying posed a different threat to Adie. Even if Josh kept his distance, their feelings for each other would grow. Until she made peace with God, Josh would be a distraction at best, an impediment at worst.

He set the mug on the counter, left money for Brick and left the saloon. With his thoughts in a jumble, he went back to the parsonage to pray.

Chapter Nineteen

"Tell us, Reverend Blue. What was your greatest achievement in Boston?"

The question came from Franklin Dean, but the other six elders, seated in a row at the front of the crowded meeting hall, were just as eager for Josh's answer. He'd been asked to stand at a podium placed to the side of the elders. When he looked straight ahead, he saw Dean. If he turned his head to the side, he saw a roomful of people. Mary, Bessie and Caroline had come to show their support, but he didn't know anyone else. He hadn't expected Pearl or Adie.

He'd also had a talk with Tobias. At Josh's request, the older man had refrained from repeating his achievements. He'd given a simple introduction, allowing Josh to set the tone himself. He intended to keep the focus on what he believed and why, not on who he'd been. He also wanted his personality to show. He had a dry sense of humor. If the elders didn't care for it, they deserved to know now.

Josh looked directly at Dean. "*My* greatest achievement?"

"Yes."

"Let's see." He looked at the ceiling as if he were thinking, then back at the board. "I learned to ride a pony at the age of four. I was *very* proud of myself."

Three of the elders chuckled. Three others scowled and Dean looked smug.

Josh flashed a smile. "I mean no disrespect, gentlemen. But I *do* feel strongly about the point I hope to make. There was a time when I'd have stood here and rattled off my schooling, the revivals I've preached and the size of the crowds. That day is long gone. Like the Apostle Paul, I count my achievements as dust compared to what Christ did for us on the cross."

He looked each man, even Dean, in the eye. "My greatest achievement, if there is such a thing, is remembering who I'd be without God's grace."

Smythe and another man acknowledged him with easy nods. The other five listened with a mix of boredom and disdain. Smythe started to ask a question, but Tobias, seated in the front row, stood up. "Reverend Blue is too modest to speak for himself, but his church in Boston grew in size from twenty to five hundred in just a few years."

Josh hated to contradict Tobias, but he couldn't let the remark stand. "That's true," he said to the elder board. "I took pride in filling those pews. Then a friend of mine, a shootist named Wes Daniels, said *he* could have gotten twice that number."

"How?" asked an elder.

"By giving away free drinks."

Half the crowd chuckled. Smythe looked pleased. Josh turned to the audience. "The measure of a minister's success isn't in crowded pews. It's in changed lives."

Tobias shot Josh a look, then stood again. "I agree, but it's only fair to say that you've changed more lives than most. At one revival alone, the newspaper said you spoke to—"

Josh held up his hand. "I appreciate Reverend Oliver's support, but—"

"Go on, Tobias."

The interruption came from Dean. Behind Josh, people murmured with a mix of approval and curiosity. Tobias had remained standing and was describing Josh as if he could walk on water. When he sat, Dean looked directly at Josh.

"Tell us, Reverend. With all your accomplishments, why did you leave Boston?"

At last they were on Josh's turf. "I'm glad you asked. The story starts with—"

Dean broke in. "Your sister was a woman of low moral character. Isn't that why you left?"

"What?"

The banker looked smug. "There's evidence she committed the sin of fornication—"

"Hold it right there." Josh had been ready for Dean to throw stones at him, but Emily? No way would he let his sister be dragged through the mud. He felt every eye on his face, studying the angle of his chin, the color in his cheeks, watching and waiting for his reaction. He looked at the elders one by one, reading each man's expression; then he faced the crowd. What he had to say would singe a few ears. "My sister was a fine woman. It's true she made a mistake, but the questionable character was mine. She—"

Dean interrupted. "We don't need the disgusting details."

"I think you do," Josh answered.

Three of the elders scowled. Smythe held Josh's gaze, urging him silently to continue. As Josh opened his mouth, Dean broke in. "Is it true you've suffered from a stomach ailment?"

"Yes."

"And that you used laudanum?"

"Yes."

"To excess?"

No matter how Josh answered, Dean would twist his words.

The banker didn't want truth; he wanted ammunition. Josh scrutinized the crowd. Some looked troubled, others sympathetic. No one stood to defend him. Mary, Bessie and Caroline were trading angry whispers, but this church's traditions prohibited women from speaking, a rule Josh thought was mistaken. He glanced at Tobias and saw a frown. In spite of the older man's upset, Josh could breathe easy. He'd told Tobias everything about his past.

He'd have told his story to the elder board, but he could see in their flat expressions that his fate had been decided, probably before he'd set foot in the meeting hall. Dean had poisoned the well against him and he'd done a good job. Josh wouldn't go after him personally, but a few things needed to be said.

He spoke directly to Dean. "You know my story better than I do. By all means, tell it."

Wearing a smirk masked with concern, the banker shared everything Josh had revealed to the congregation at Brick's Saloon, including failings he'd admitted to a small group of men. Horace had been in that gathering and was clearly Dean's source. Josh figured Dean would save the biggest rock for last, and he did.

The banker laced his fingers on the tabletop. "Is it true, Reverend, that you've visited Miss Elsa's Social Club?"

The congregation gasped.

"I sure have," Josh said boldly. "It paid off, too. Two young ladies come to services now." Gretchen hadn't missed a single Sunday at Brick's and had brought a friend. Josh hoped she'd leave Miss Elsa's and felt bad that he hadn't spoken to Adie about offering her a room.

"Men have their weaknesses," Dean said. "But we expect a higher standard from our minister."

Josh also knew from Brick that Dean was a frequent guest at the brothel. He crossed his arms. "Is that so?"

"Absolutely." The banker stared hard. "You live at Swan's Nest, an establishment for single women. Is that true?"

"Yes, it is."

"Some of us find that inappropriate."

Tobias shoved to his feet. He looked ready to choke the daylights out of the banker. "*You* of all people have no right to—"

"I'm pointing out facts."

"Let me help you," Josh said in a full voice. "I left Boston to search for my sister. She was with child, out of wedlock, a woman who made the mistake of falling in love and giving in to temptation. To protect my pride, I drove her out of Boston. Some of you *gentlemen*—" he looked from elder to elder "—would have applauded that decision. I see it as my biggest mistake. Instead of showing my sister the same grace Christ has shown to me, I threw stones at her."

He faced the crowd. "I was a Pharisee, a hypocrite." He told the audience about his laudanum addiction, how he'd sought praise and hidden his mistakes; then he looked back at the elders. "Mr. Dean asked what I considered my greatest accomplishment. Here it is. I learned the hard way—at the expense of my sister's life—that Christ died for all of us. That includes you *fine* gentlemen."

Josh glanced at Tobias. The man looked both stunned and pleased, as if he'd realized he should have given this speech before now.

Josh faced the elder board. "Let me ask each of you, are your lives so perfect that you can sit there and judge me?" He let a full minute pass. "Who's been to Miss Elsa's besides Frank here?"

Two of the men turned red.

"Who drinks too much?"

A third glared at him.

"How about lying?" Josh looked straight at the fifth man.

He held Josh's stare and gave a little nod. This man, Josh sensed, understood the point he hoped to make.

Josh gentled his voice. "I don't have anything else to say, only that God loves us just as we are. We're fearfully, wonderfully made. He knit each of us in our mother's womb. He counts the hairs on our heads. We can't hide from Him, ladies and gentlemen. The good news is, we don't have to."

No one said a word.

Josh turned back to the board. "If you still want me for your pastor, I'd be honored to serve, but I have a requirement of my own. Tonight's vote has to be unanimous. As it says in the Bible, a house divided against itself cannot stand. I won't be the cause of dividing this church."

Josh strode down the aisle and out the door. He'd wait outside for the vote, but he felt certain he'd never preach in this building again.

Adie had been sitting on the porch for two hours, peering down the street in search of Bessie, Caroline and Mary. She'd considered going to the meeting, even sitting outside and listening through an open window, but she'd lost her nerve. Ever since her talk with Mary, she'd felt heavy with guilt. She owed Josh amends but didn't know how to make them. Apologizing for her unkind words felt as incomplete as unrisen bread, but neither could she speak the whole truth. She loved him. She wanted to be his wife, but how could she marry a minister when she still felt bitter toward God?

She didn't know, but tonight she had hope. If the elders offered Josh the position, maybe she could see past Reverend Honeycutt and old hurts. Everything depended on tonight's vote.

Hushed voices came from the street. Adie jumped to her feet and saw her friends approaching Swan's Nest. Unable to wait, she hurried down the steps. "Did he get elected?"

"Yes and no," Bessie replied.

What did *that* mean? As the women trudged up the steps, Adie went ahead to the parlor, where she turned up the lamp. Caroline plopped onto the divan. She looked as if she'd seen a wagon accident, one where the horse broke its leg and had to be put down. Mary held her chin high, as if she were back in the town where she'd faced an angry mob. Bessie, as always, wore the placid look of a woman who'd lost everything, survived and knew others could do the same.

Mary sat in the rocking chair. Bessie took the spot next to her sister, leaving Adie to pull up a side chair. No one sat in Josh's place.

"Josh did us proud," Bessie said. "But he won't be taking the position."

"They voted him down?" Adie asked.

"Not exactly," said Mary.

Adie listened as her friends described the first half of the meeting. She could imagine Josh sparring with the elders. When Mary told about Dean's assault on Emily, Adie burned with fury. If ever a man had paid for his mistakes, it was Josh. She hated Franklin Dean more than ever. Neither did she care for the people who'd let the verbal abuse take place.

Adie's conscience spoke in a whisper. *Where were you?* She wouldn't have been allowed to speak in Josh's defense, but she could have supported him with a look, a smile at the right time. "I wish I'd gone."

"It got ugly," Caroline said.

"Did he take Dean to task?" Adie hoped so.

Mary laughed. "Josh took *everyone* to task. By the time he finished, every person in the room knew two things. No one's perfect and Jesus loves us anyway."

Caroline looked at Adie. "Josh walked out, but not before making a demand of his own. He said the vote had to be unanimous or he wouldn't take the position. He went outside to wait. That's when *everyone* started to talk. Women, too."

"Really?" Pearl walked into the parlor. "That's never happened before."

Caroline and Mary made room for her on the divan. Adie glanced at Josh's empty chair and wished she hadn't asked him to leave Swan's Nest. Crazy or not, the accusations had to have left a mark. She couldn't stand the thought of Josh enduring the ordeal alone.

"What did people say?" she asked.

Mary looked grim. "Some criticized him. Others sang his praises. Reverend Oliver and a man named Smythe took Josh's side, but two others said he was a troublemaker."

Adie's mouth gaped. "Josh is the kindest man I've ever known."

"Me, too," Mary added.

Pearl looked pinched. "Did anyone mention Frank and me?"

"Not at the meeting," Mary replied. "But lots of women asked how you are. One said to tell you her husband took his money out of Dean's bank." Mary lifted Pearl's hand and squeezed. "You won, Pearl. No matter what happens, people know not to trust Franklin Dean."

Tears welled in the girl's eyes. "I'm glad."

"Me, too," Adie said with venom. "He deserves worse."

"And someday he'll get it," Bessie answered. "Right now I'm worried about Josh."

"Me, too," Caroline said.

Adie needed to hear the rest of the story. "What was the vote?"

Bessie's lips curved up. "Four to three in Josh's favor."

Josh could have had the position, yet he'd turned it down. Had he done it for her? The thought filled her with awe. If he stayed in Denver, she'd go to the little church at Brick's. She could tell Josh she loved him without dreading the denial she'd see in his eyes. She had to speak to him tonight, so she looked at Bessie. "I need to see Josh. Would you walk with me to the parsonage?"

"I would," Bessie answered. "But he's not there."

"Where did he go?"

"I don't know," Caroline said. "But I saw him heading away from the church."

Adie felt terrible. "Maybe he went to Brick's."

"I doubt it," Mary said. "No one except us showed up. He looked disappointed."

Adie's heart broke again. Josh had faced a mob armed with lies and he'd done it alone. Now he was walking the streets of Denver in the dark. If she hadn't asked him to leave Swan's Nest, he'd be here now. She ached to go after him, but walking downtown, past saloons and brothels, would have been stupid.

Caroline looked grim. "After tonight, I won't be surprised if he leaves Denver."

"He might," Pearl said. "But he'd say goodbye. Either way, he needs us right now."

Bessie gripped Adie's left hand and Mary stretched to take her right one. Before she realized what was happening, the women had made a circle. In unison they arched their necks and bowed their heads. Pearl prayed first. She asked God to be with Josh and calm his heart. Bessie asked for safety. Mary prayed that he'd know how much he'd helped her. Caroline, her voice barely a whisper, prayed for Josh to find love and a home of his own.

Adie's throat felt tight and her fingers hurt from clutching Bessie's and Mary's hands, but she spoke from her heart. *"Bring him home, Lord. I don't understand Your ways. I don't know why—"* Her voice cracked. *"I just know Josh is hurting and he needs You. Amen."*

Adie was hurting, too. She needed to see Josh. She couldn't go to him, but she had a sudden, keen sense of Emily's journal locked in the trunk. If she read it from start to finish—including the end she'd been unable to endure— she'd be with him in spirit.

One by one, the women went in different directions. Pearl headed for the kitchen to warm milk for herself. Bessie and Caroline went upstairs to bed, and Mary walked out to the garden. Adie climbed the stairs to her room, opened the trunk and retrieved Emily's journal. Clutching it against her chest, she went to the parlor, where she dimmed the lamp to a glow. Wanting to feel close to Josh, she started reading from the beginning.

Chapter Twenty

As soon as Tobias told him about the vote, Josh shook the dust from Colfax Avenue Church off his feet. He had no regrets. He'd spoken from his heart and had honored his faith. Never mind the pain in his gut. He didn't like to fight, but some battles couldn't be avoided.

Alone on the dark street, he longed to go to Swan's Nest. He wanted to tell the story to Adie, but he couldn't go to her. He didn't want sympathy tonight. He wanted a wife, a soul mate who'd understand tonight's hullabaloo. If he went to Adie now, he'd be settling for her company when he wanted her heart. Josh had never been good at settling, so he strode in the opposite direction of Swan's Nest. If it hadn't been for Franklin Dean, he'd have left Denver to avoid the temptation of visiting her. He blinked and thought of Stephen cooing in her arms. He blinked again and pictured her in her Sunday best, seated in church with her red hair shining under the straw hat.

"Why, Lord?" he said to the dark.

Living in the shadow of Swan's Nest without courting Adie would be the hardest thing he'd ever done, but he had no choice. He had to stay in Denver until Dean no longer posed a threat. With his heart pounding, he walked to the edge of town, where he stared into the night. Darkness and light were alike to God, but Josh felt like a man in a tomb. He tried to pray, but he felt as if the heavens were brass. Neither did he want to speak with Tobias. The older man would want to rehash the meeting, something Josh had no desire to do.

As alone as he'd ever been, he walked back to the parsonage. As he turned onto Colfax Avenue, he saw the silhouette of the empty church. It rose against the sky with a majestic air, but the windows had no life. Moonlight turned the steeple into a sword, but Josh saw the dull edges.

"Good evening, Reverend."

The voice belonged to Franklin Dean. As Josh turned, the banker stepped out of the alley next to the church. Behind him came Horace, a foot shorter and the exact shape of the man who'd trampled Adie's garden. Side by side, they blocked Josh's path.

His neck hairs prickled. "What do you gentlemen want?"

Dean stepped closer. "You ruined me."

"No, I didn't."

The banker had ruined himself, but that didn't change the rage burning in his eyes. With Horace at the man's side, Josh was outnumbered two to one. He had no desire to take a beating, but he refused to run. Neither could he see Jesus swinging his fists at two thugs in an alley.

Moonlight shone on Dean's jaw. "Do you know what you did to me tonight?"

Josh resisted the urge to mouth off. "It's over, Frank. Go home."

"You humiliated me."

"No, I didn't," Josh said calmly. "I talked about second chances for everyone, myself included."

The banker slapped his walking stick against his palm. "I lost four more customers today. That's eighteen in three days."

"Change your ways," Josh said. "They'll come back."

"You stole Swan's Nest."

"I paid off the mortgage."

"You made Pearl tell lies!"

Josh had seen evil before. He'd spoken to dead-eyed men and heard vile threats. He'd had dreams twisted by opium. Never, though, had he felt the breath of violence on his face. Looking into Dean's bloodshot eyes, Josh knew the man intended grave harm. "We're done, Frank."

He tried to pass the men, but they closed ranks. Dean planted his palm on Josh's shoulder and shoved. "I'm not done with you, Blue."

Josh stumbled back. Blocked by the church on one side and the carriage on the other, he stood his ground. "Drop it, Frank. I'm done with Colfax Avenue Church. Let that be enough for you."

The banker reached inside his coat. With a jerk of his arm, he pulled a derringer and aimed it at Josh's chest. The men were just five feet apart. The gun had two shots. A single bullet would be enough to kill. Josh had nowhere to go, but neither would he raise his hands in surrender. If he died, Dean would be free to head to Swan's Nest. He had to fight but how?

Dean cocked the weapon. "You're going to die, Reverend."

Josh didn't fear death, only the thought of leaving Adie at this man's mercy. "Don't do it, Frank. You'll pay."

"Not before you do." His eyes closed to glimmering slits. "Just think, Reverend. The instant you've breathed your last, I'm going to pay a call on Swan's Nest. Horace and I are going to beat the daylights out of Adie Clarke and her friends. Then we're going to tie them up and burn the house to the ground.

That includes Pearl, except I'm going to take her baby. He's mine and I want him."

Dean meant every word. Josh had to get the gun.

Madness burned in the man's eyes. "Imagine it…Miss Clarke will scream and you won't hear it. That baby of hers—"

"Boss?" Horace stepped closer.

"What is it?" Dean demanded.

"This ain't right."

The banker jerked his head toward the driver. Josh lunged and knocked the gun from his hand. Dean cursed, then took a roundhouse swing. His knuckles slammed into Josh's jaw and sent him flying into a rosebush. As the thorns grabbed at his coat, Dean pummeled his face and ribs. With each blow, Josh sank deeper into the bush. A branch snapped and he fell to his back. Dean kicked him in the ribs, over and over, until Josh grabbed his foot and threw him off balance.

Fighting for breath, Josh pushed to his feet, hauled back and landed an uppercut on the banker's chin. As Dean fell back, Josh spotted the derringer under a second bush. He lunged for it, but Horace reached the weapon first and grabbed it. In the next instant, Josh would live or die. He'd save Adie or she'd be left to face Dean alone. He stared hard at the driver, saw the man's yellow teeth and the glint in his bleary eyes.

Without a word, Horace broke Josh's stare and took aim at Dean. "That's enough, boss. Leave the reverend alone."

Dean stared as if Horace were a stranger.

"Put your hands up," said the driver.

The banker laughed. "You little—"

"I mean it, Mr. Dean." Horace's hand stayed steady. "You've done enough harm to those ladies. You've done enough to the reverend and to me, too."

The fight could have ended there, but Dean took a step toward Horace, then another. He held out his hand. "Give me the gun."

"No, sir."

As Dean grabbed for the derringer, Horace pulled the trigger. Josh saw the muzzle flash like a shooting star. The banker looked down at his chest, then up at Horace as if he couldn't believe his eyes. With his mouth gaping, he crumpled into a heap. His legs jerked once, twice, then went still.

"God forgive me," Horace said. "But I couldn't let him hurt the babies."

"I think God will understand." Josh closed Dean's eyes, then covered the man's head and chest with his coat. Death had a way of stripping a man of all dignity. Josh had no respect for Dean, but he respected the passage of life. After a silent prayer for Dean's eternal soul, he stood and faced Horace. "You saved my life."

The driver looked down at Dean's corpse. "I couldn't let him do it, Reverend. I did enough to Miss Clarke already."

"The garden?"

"The fire, too." Horace looked disgusted with himself. "He paid me, but it ain't right to hurt women and children."

"No, it isn't."

He looked at Josh with wild eyes. "I'll tell the sheriff everything, even if it means jail. I don't ever want to smell smoke like that again. I watched the fire from across the street. I saw the ladies get out, but the baby kept coughing. It was awful."

"It was," Josh said simply.

"And tonight…" Horace looked as if he might be sick. "Mr. Dean would have killed you. I could hang for it, but I had to stop him."

"You won't hang." Josh had the bruises to prove Horace's honorable intentions. "Let's get Deputy Morgan."

They walked two blocks to the sheriff's office. The minute Morgan saw them, he jumped to his feet. They told him Dean was dead, then accompanied him to Archer's Funeral Home, where he woke up the undertaker. While Archer hitched up his hearse, Josh and Horace led Morgan to the body. As they walked, Horace told the story, including his part in the vandalism at Swan's Nest.

As he finished, Archer's wagon rattled to a stop. With the deputy's help, the undertaker lifted the body into the hearse. Horace and Josh stood in silence, watching as the black wagon rattled away.

When Archer rounded the corner, Morgan hooked his hands on his belt. "I'd say *that* problem's solved."

Horace let out a long breath. "Are you going to arrest me, Deputy?"

"Nope."

"But I killed him."

"It looks like self-defense to me. As for the problems at Swan's Nest, it's up to Miss Clarke. She can press charges or drop them."

Horace turned to Josh. "Do you think she'll talk to me?"

Josh wanted to say yes, but he didn't know what Adie would say. He also knew that Horace, yellow teeth and all, had crossed a line tonight. "I'll speak to her first—how's that?"

"Thanks, Reverend."

Morgan yawned. "That's it for tonight, gentlemen. Drop by tomorrow and I'll finish up my report."

As the deputy ambled down the street, Horace turned to Josh. "I have Mr. Dean's carriage. Do you want a ride to Swan's Nest?"

Josh ached all over, but he couldn't stand the thought of touching anything owned by Dean. "No, thanks, Horace."

"You don't look so good. Maybe you should see Doc Nichols."

The driver had a point, but Nichols would send him to bed. "I'll be all right."

Horace pursed his lips. "Can I ask you something?"

"Sure."

"Will you be staying in Denver?"

The ramifications of Dean's death struck Josh like a fresh blow. Adie no longer needed his protection. He was free to leave on the next train, but he didn't want to go. With his ribs throbbing, he wondered how she'd react to both Dean's death and the elder meeting. He also had to speak to her about dropping charges against Horace. If her heart stayed hard, Josh wouldn't be able to court her. If he stayed in Denver, he'd be tested every day. Eventually he'd fall and ask her to marry him. Adie had become laudanum to him. He resisted that temptation by avoiding its presence. If her heart stayed hard, he'd be wise to leave Denver altogether.

Horace was still waiting for an answer. Josh stifled a groan. "I haven't decided yet."

"I hope you stay, sir."

"Maybe I will."

"This Sunday," Horace said. "Will you be at Brick's? Something happened to me tonight. I want to tell about it."

Josh wouldn't miss that moment for anything. "I'll be there."

As the driver went to the carriage, Josh headed to Swan's Nest. Every step jarred his ribs, reminding him of the ulcer and the night he'd collapsed on Adie's porch. They'd come a long way, but the journey wasn't complete. It wouldn't be until he saw her reaction to Dean's passing. He didn't expect her to mourn the man. She'd be relieved just as he was, but Josh hoped she wouldn't dance on his grave.

He also worried that she'd feel vindictive toward Horace and the elders. Josh's battle with Dean had been to protect Adie from bodily harm. The next battle was for her soul. As much as he wanted to fight for her, he couldn't. The war was between Adie and God and she had to win it for herself.

* * *

A knock on the door jarred Adie to the marrow. Pearl had gone upstairs an hour ago. Mary had already come in from the garden, leaving Adie alone with the lamp turned low and Emily's journal. She'd started at the beginning and had just reread Emily's declaration of love for Dennis.

The knock came again, louder this time. Adie stepped to the window, peeked through the curtain and saw Josh. She flung the door wide, then gasped at the sight of him. Blood oozed from an abrasion on his cheek. He had a lump on his jaw and his right eye would be swollen shut by morning. Just as startling, he wasn't wearing his black coat. Dirt streaked his white linen shirt as if he'd been repeatedly kicked in the ribs.

Adie grabbed his hand and pulled him inside. "You're a wreck! What happened to you?"

He squeezed her fingers. "Dean's dead."

"Dead?"

"Horace killed him."

Adie gasped. "You were there."

"It's a long story. I'll tell you everything but—" He winced.

"You need to sit." She hooked her arm around his waist so he could lean on her. "I want to clean your cuts. Can you make it to the kitchen?"

"I'm all right."

"No, you're not." Adie didn't have the facts, but the evidence spoke for itself. Dean had accosted Josh. She didn't know if Horace was part of the beating, but she didn't care. Both men had tried for weeks to ruin her life. "I'd like to pound whoever did this to you into the ground!"

Josh stiffened. "Dean got pounded, all right."

She helped him into a chair, then filled a bowl with hot water. After taking a soft towel from a drawer, she positioned a chair across from him and went to work cleaning his cuts.

As she dabbed at the blood, he told her about the fight in front of the church, Dean's threats and how Horace had intervened. By the time he finished, Adie felt a rage so profound she couldn't contain it.

She shot to her feet. "I hate Franklin Dean. I'm glad he's dead."

"We owe that relief to Horace."

Adie scowled. "I suppose."

"He saved my life," Josh said gently. "He also confessed to the vandalism and the fire. He's afraid you'll press charges."

She huffed. "I'm not *that* hardhearted. Dean was behind it, not Horace."

"Will you speak with him? He wants to apologize."

"I guess." But her heart wouldn't be in it.

Josh said nothing.

She squeezed his hand. "Tonight's been awful for you. I heard about the meeting, how they attacked Emily and—"

"Adie, stop."

"They said terrible things about you! They—"

He cupped her face in his palms, forcing her to look into his eyes. "I don't hate them. I don't hate Dean, either. I hate what he did. There's a difference."

Adie didn't see it. "He tried to kill you!"

"Listen to me." He spoke with an urgency that made her go still. "I forgive him for what he did to me. It's harder to forgive him for what he did to you, but Christ died for those sins, too."

"I don't care!"

As soon as the words left her mouth, she realized how profoundly she meant them. She pushed to her feet and turned away, but she couldn't stop seeing Josh's bruised face. She heard the scrape of his chair, then felt his hands on her shoulders. She didn't dare turn around. He'd see bitterness in her eyes, and she'd see pity in his. She laced her arms across her chest. "I'm glad Dean's dead. I wish Honeycutt were dead, too. And Timothy Long!"

"Adie—"

She whirled to face him, tearing away from his grip. "Don't you understand? I *can't* forgive them."

"It's not a feeling," he said. "It's a choice. Believe me, I didn't feel particularly charitable while Frank was beating the stuffing out of me. But I knew deep down that he was just a damaged, stupid man."

"He's worse than that," Adie insisted. "He was a monster! I'll never believe otherwise. I don't want to!"

His voice dropped to a hush. "Why not?"

"I just don't." She didn't tell Josh, but hating men like Dean and Honeycutt made her powerful. She felt safe behind that wall, not vulnerable as Josh had been tonight. His bruises proved her point.

"I see." His tone turned brusque, like the sweep of a broom, and he sat back on the chair. "I came tonight for two reasons."

The first had been to tell her about Dean. "What's the second?"

"I'm leaving Denver."

She gasped. "You're *what?*"

"I'm going back to Boston."

"But why?"

"I think you know." He gripped her hands in both of his. "I love you, Adie. I think you care for me, too."

"I do. I love you."

The moment called for a kiss, a claiming of forever. Instead his expression turned bleak. "I can't marry you, Adie. We'd both suffer. You'd dread Sundays and church socials, even knocks on the door. You'd start to hate me. I can't ask you to share that life, and I can't give it up without hating myself."

He kissed her hands, then let her go. "I'm not strong enough to fight what feels so right. I have to leave. The sooner, the better."

She couldn't bear the thought. "But you're hurt!"

"I'll be fine."

"But Boston's so far."

"It's settled," Josh said. "I'm leaving Monday."

He'd be alone on the train. What if his ribs were broken and not just bruised? What if his ulcer flared up? Adie couldn't stand the thought.

He pushed to his feet. "I told Horace I'd be at Brick's on Sunday. I'd appreciate it if you'd tell everyone here."

His eyes held hers; then he kissed her lips, a tender brush, another, and finally a parting that felt like skin being ripped from her own body. He touched her hair one last time, looked into her eyes and stepped back. "If you need anything, see Elliot."

She didn't want to see Elliot. She wanted to marry Josh, except he was right. They couldn't walk the same path unless they served the same God.

His voice stayed strong. "I'll write to you." He kissed her one last time, then walked out the door.

Adie collapsed on a chair and wept. She couldn't bear to see Josh go, but he'd been right to leave. She loved him enough to marry him in spite of her wayward soul, but he wouldn't compromise. He wanted her heart, all of it. Silently she raged at the Almighty for leaving her adrift. Why couldn't she let go of her bitterness? Pearl had been as wounded as Adie, even more so, but she didn't hate anyone. Mary had shrugged off the chip on her shoulder. Caroline and Bessie would never forget the havoc of war, but neither did they dwell on what they'd lost.

"What's wrong with me?" Adie said out loud.

Where could she go for answers? Darkness and light were

alike to God but not to Adie. She was lost and alone in the dark. Where was God now? With her heart pounding, she wept until she felt hollow. As the tears cleared, she yearned to be filled with love. She thought of Josh and flashed to the journal she'd left on the divan. Desperate to feel close to him, she went to the parlor, turned up the lamp and opened the book to Emily's final entry, the one she'd refused to hear when Josh read it for himself.

The words were as hateful as she'd feared. *He became a murderer…a lion about to eat me.* Adie blinked and saw Josh's agony as he'd taken in the depth of Emily's feelings. Each lash of his sister's pen had marked him.

The words had once been true but not anymore. If Emily had tried to forgive him—if she'd just written home—she'd have discovered that Josh had changed. He would have moved heaven and earth for her. She and Dennis could have married. When the baby came, she would have had the finest doctors and she might have lived. If she hadn't been so bitter, she—

Adie caught her breath. How many times had she and Maggie commiserated over life's unfairness? They'd called themselves two peas in a pod. Yet tonight, reading the journal, Adie felt nothing but pity for her friend. Emily had died throwing stones at her own brother, a man who'd given up everything to search for her.

Looking at Emily's final scrawl, Adie knew she'd been making a similar mistake. She didn't know if Reverend Honeycutt had changed or if Timothy Long had been punished, but it didn't matter. Her bitterness served no purpose except to poison her own heart. In the end, these men would have to answer to God. That was enough. So was Franklin Dean's demise.

In the deepest part of her heart, Adie felt free. Just as Josh had forgiven her for hiding Stephen's identity, she could forgive the people who'd hurt her. Having been forgiven, she could forgive. She closed the journal and bowed her head. Joy welled in her chest and made her fingers tingle. She felt as spotless as snow…as light as fluffy biscuits and goose feathers and rose petals fluttering to the ground. She didn't have to walk around with rocks in her pocket a minute longer.

Speaking out loud, she forgave her father for loving gold more than he loved her. She forgave her mother for dying and Timothy Long for harming her. Next she prayed for the Honeycutts. They'd failed her, but they'd done their best. She even forgave Franklin Dean, a prayer that came easily because justice had been served. God hadn't moved swiftly, but He'd been thorough.

Last of all, she forgave herself. She'd wasted years of her life being bitter. Even worse, she'd almost lost Josh. She stood and looked out the window. Dawn was on the horizon. She wanted to run to the parsonage and tell him her news, but a thought came that made her smile. It turned into a plan that filled her with joy.

News of Dean's death spread through Denver like fire. On Friday, the six remaining elders came to Josh as a group. They asked him to reconsider his decision, but he'd made up his mind. No charges were filed against Horace. The driver hadn't shared the details with Josh, but he'd visited Adie and had made amends. When Horace said he planned to leave Denver, Josh gave the man his horse and saddle. On Saturday he purchased a train ticket for Boston and left word at Brick's that he'd be preaching one last Sunday.

Josh didn't trust himself to see Adie again, so he spent Saturday writing letters to Bessie, Mary, Caroline and Pearl. He figured at least one of them, probably Mary, would come to the service. He'd ask her to deliver the letters, then he'd pack his things. The train left early Monday and he'd be on it.

Sunday dawned like any other day. Josh put on his collar and coat, picked up his Bible and walked to Brick's Saloon. His ribs throbbed with every step, but he didn't want to stay in Denver while he recovered. Every step away from Swan's Nest took all the discipline he could muster.

As he neared the saloon, he looked for horses tied to the hitching post. He didn't see a single one. He passed the window and saw empty chairs. When he tried the door, it was locked. He'd been looking forward to seeing Gretchen and the cowboys. Horace had planned to tell his story, and Josh had wanted a final word with Brick. He didn't know the newer folks as well, but he'd hoped to leave with fond memories. Instead he felt lonelier than he'd ever been.

He also had no way to deliver his letters. He thought about dropping them at the post office, but he didn't have stamps and couldn't buy them on Sunday. Seeing Adie would rip his heart from his chest, but he couldn't leave without saying goodbye to the women who'd stuck by him through everything. As he headed for Seventeenth Street, he recalled holding Stephen and making baby talk. He thought about suppers, kitchen sounds and the laughter of women. As he passed the piles of rock from the demolished mansion, he felt a weight in his chest and wondered if it would ever go away.

When Swan's Nest came into view, he looked up at Adie's window. He listened for Stephen calling for his mother but heard nothing. The house usually felt alive as he approached. Today it looked abandoned. Confused, he climbed the porch steps, where he saw a note tacked to the front door. Stepping closer, he saw the words "Come to the garden" written in Adie's hand.

Why would she want to meet him among the roses? Anxious but hopeful, he walked down the steps and passed the plot of vegetables. As he rounded the corner, he glimpsed

Adie in her green dress, scurrying away from him. Josh picked up his pace.

As he neared the hedge, he heard a ragtag choir singing his favorite hymn, the one he'd picked that first Sunday at Brick's. He took a dozen more steps and saw a crowd. Brick greeted him with a crooked smile. Next to the barkeep stood Gretchen, the cowboys and Horace. Bessie, holding Stephen, stood between Mary and Caroline. On the other side of the path, he saw Tobias and Pearl. She had her baby in her arms and was beaming. Beau Morgan, wearing his leather vest and a string tie, stood off to the side. Josh didn't know the rest of the people by name, but he recognized faces from Colfax Avenue Church, including Halston Smythe.

A church had formed.

His church… As he searched the crowd, Adie came to stand at his side. Before he could speak, she pressed something cold and hard into his palm. He looked down and saw a rock, gray in color and smooth from years of wind and rain.

She folded his fingers over the stone, then looked into his eyes. "I'm done throwing rocks."

Josh had never heard more beautiful words. "What happened?"

She looked sheepish. "After you left, I read Emily's journal. She could have been happy. All she had to do was forgive you." She plucked the stone from his palm and let it fall to the ground. It landed with a thump.

With her hands open and empty, she looked into his eyes. "I have nothing to offer but my heart. I have a temper and I get angry. I say things I regret. I—"

"I love you just as you are." He gripped her hands and raised them to the level of his heart. "Will you marry me?"

"Yes!" Joy shone in her eyes. "Right now?"

He laughed out loud. "Nope."

"But—"

He raised her hand to his lips and kissed her knuckles. "We were standing on this very spot when I promised to sweep you off your feet."

"I remember."

"That's what I intend to do."

Josh had a good reason for not marrying Adie today. He didn't think she'd change her mind and he knew he wouldn't change his. His motives were far less dramatic. He simply wanted the fun of courting her. He wanted to bring her flowers, call her "sweetheart," buy her supper, and enjoy long walks. In the next few months, they'd share laughter and tears. They'd quarrel and make up. When their wedding day came, Adie would be wearing a beautiful dress and carrying a huge bouquet.

With God and the world watching, Josh plucked a red rose from the hedge and gave it to her. When she looked up and smiled, he smiled back. It was a sign of all the good things to come.

Epilogue

October 1875
Swan's Nest

Josh had been courting Adie for two months when Pearl announced she'd be leaving for Cheyenne in three days. Adie had enjoyed every starry-eyed minute, but she had no desire to wait until June to marry as they'd planned. She didn't need roses and a fancy dress for a wedding, but she very much needed her friends.

As soon as she heard Pearl's news, she walked to the house Josh had been renting and knocked on the door. He greeted her with a lazy smile. "Good morning, beautiful."

Adie blushed but refused to be distracted. "Pearl's leaving. I want to get married tonight."

His eyes popped wide. "But your dress—"

"I'll wear the green one."

"Flowers—"

"I don't need them."

"Are you sure?"

"I'm positive."

With that, he swept her into his arms. "What time? I'll see to everything."

They agreed on seven o'clock, and Adie ran down the street to the café. Mary threw down her apron and hurried with her to Doc Nichols's office, where they found Bessie. They fetched Caroline from the dress shop and raced to Swan's Nest.

"In the parlor," she replied.

And so the preparations began. Food arrived from people at church. Brick delivered a wedding cake. The owner of the local dress shop brought four white gowns, veils, gloves and a note from Josh telling her to pick whatever she wanted. When the clock in the hallway struck seven, Swan's Nest was full of guests and Adie was wearing white, standing in the second parlor with Bessie, Caroline and Pearl. Mary would be singing Adie's bridal march, so she was in the parlor with Reverend Oliver.

Adie had never felt more beautiful in her life. She'd chosen a dress made of satin with a scooped neckline. The high collar and tight sleeves made her feel like a real swan, and the satin rosettes holding the draped skirt reminded her of the flowers in her garden. To set off the simplicity of the dress, she'd chosen a waist-length veil made of the sheerest tulle. It covered her eyes, but she'd be able to see every detail—the candles on the hearth, the asters and greenery lining the aisle made from borrowed chairs.

Reverend Oliver knocked on the door. "Ladies? Are you ready?"

Adie had never been more ready in her life. When she nodded, he went back to the main parlor and Mary started to sing Adie's favorite hymn, a standard called "Just As I Am."

Caroline and Bessie walked down the aisle first. Pearl, Adie's maid of honor, followed and took her place next to her father. As Mary sang the final chorus, every head turned to the doorway where Adie stood alone. Halston Smythe had sent a note offering to walk her down the aisle, but she didn't feel the need. She wasn't alone today. She had her heavenly Father at her side.

She also had her friends. She wanted each of them to be as happy as she was this very minute. Soon she'd be Josh's wife. They'd speak their vows, then he'd kiss her and they'd stand together as man and wife. In a little while she'd toss her bouquet. She didn't know who'd catch it, but she had high hopes for another Swan's Nest wedding.

* * * * *

Dear Reader,

I love going to church. The music always lifts my spirits. It doesn't matter if it's a Fanny Crosby hymn or "Grace Like Rain" by Todd Agnew, the words and melody speak to my heart.

The sermons speak to my head. Over the years, my husband and I have had the privilege of hearing some of the best teachers and preachers in America, even the world. This book honors those men and women, who have opened my eyes in so many ways. Their words have given me courage. They've given me strength. I've been humbled and lifted up all at the same time.

Over the years we've gone to churches ranging in size from eight members to over eight thousand. As diverse as the settings are, these congregations all share a deep and abiding love of Jesus Christ. Thank you, pastors, for your dedication!

Best wishes,

Victoria Bylin

QUESTIONS FOR DISCUSSION

1. When the story opens, Reverend Joshua Blue is suffering from an ulcer and a guilty conscience. Do you think these afflictions are related? If so, how?

2. Adie Clarke is determined to protect her son from his birth mother's powerful family. She keeps secrets and even lies by hiding the truth. Is she at all justified in this behavior?

3. Adie has endured a difficult upbringing. She believes in God but doesn't trust in his love. Josh sees her anger. How does he counter her bitterness? How does she react?

4. In spite of mounting evidence that Josh is her son's natural uncle, Adie convinces herself that she's mistaken. Even so, she has twinges of conscience. How does she react as the facts are revealed? Does she show fear or faith?

5. In spite of Adie's reserve, Josh shows her nothing but kindness. Would he have had such compassion prior to losing his sister? How does Josh's personal suffering affect his feelings for Adie?

6. Josh teaches a Bible study on Psalm 139. The last verses are "Search me O God and know my heart, try me and know my anxious thoughts." What are Josh's anxious thoughts? What are Adie's concerns? How do they each handle their worries?

7. Emily, Josh's sister, kept a journal documenting her feelings for the father of her child. Does she have regrets?

What are the immediate and long-term consequences of her actions?

8. How does Josh react to Adie when he finally learns the truth about her son? What enables him to forgive her so quickly? Would you be able to forgive? Why or why not?

9. Josh realizes he loves Adie and wants to marry her, but he knows that she doesn't fully share his faith. Why is it important for a husband and wife to be equally yoked? What problems does Josh anticipate, and how does he propose to solve them?

10. While he's preaching at Colfax Avenue Church on the scripture about the adulterous woman, Josh sees that Adie and Franklin Dean have matching expressions. What do Adie and Dean have in common? How are they alike? Different?

11. While reading Emily's journal, Adie sees herself in her friend's bitter words. How does she react? Can you recall a moment in your own spiritual journey when God revealed something special?

12. Franklin Dean uses his driver, Horace Jones, to harass Adie and her friends. Horace, though, undergoes a major change. What factors contribute to his spiritual awakening?

13. The story begins with Adie living in fear. By the end, she's discovered a faith of her own. What factors contribute to her personal growth? What does Josh do (or not do) that helps her on her walk?

14. Having a "life verse" is a modern concept, but Josh has one. It's Psalm 139. Do you have a scripture you keep tucked in your heart? What is it? What does it mean to you?

Turn the page for a sneak peek of
RITA® Award-winner
Linda Goodnight's heartwarming story,
HOME TO CROSSROADS RANCH.
On sale in March 2009
from Steeple Hill Love Inspired®.

Chapter One

Nate Del Rio heard screams the minute he stepped out of his Ford F-150 SuperCrew and started up the flower-lined sidewalk leading to Rainy Jernagen's house. He doubled-checked the address scribbled on the back of a bill for horse feed. Sure enough, this was the place.

Adjusting his Stetson against a gust of March wind, he rang the doorbell, expecting the noise to subside. It didn't.

Somewhere inside the modest, tidy-looking brick house, at least two kids were screaming their heads off in what sounded to his experienced ears like fits of temper. A television blasted out Saturday morning cartoons—SpongeBob, he thought, though he was no expert on kids' television programs.

He punched the doorbell again. Instead of the expected *ding-dong,* a raucous alternative Christian rock band added a few more decibels to the noise level.

Nate shifted the toolbox to his opposite hand and considered running for his life while he had the chance.

Too late. The bright red door whipped open. Nate's mouth fell open with it.

When the men's ministry coordinator from Bible Fellowship had called him, he'd somehow gotten the impression that he was coming to help a little old schoolteacher. You know, the kind that only drives to school and church and has a big, fat cat.

Not so. The woman standing before him with taffy-blond hair sprouting out from a disheveled ponytail couldn't possibly be any older than his own thirty-one years. A big blotch of something purple stained the front of her white sweatshirt and she was barefooted. Plus, she had a crying baby on each hip and a little red-haired girl hanging on one leg, bawling like a sick calf. And there wasn't a cat in sight.

What had he gotten himself into?

"May I help you?" she asked over the racket. Her blue-gray eyes were a little too unfocused and bewildered for his comfort.

Raising his voice, he asked, "Are you Ms. Jernagen?"

"Yes," she said cautiously. "I'm Rainy Jernagen. And you are….?"

"Nate Del Rio."

She blinked, uncomprehending, all the while jiggling both babies up and down. One grabbed a hank of her hair. She flinched, her head angling to one side as she said, still cautiously, "Okaaay."

Nate reached out and untwined the baby's sticky fingers.

A relieved smile rewarded him. "Thanks. Is there something I can help you with?"

He hefted the red toolbox to chest level so she could see it. "From the Handy Man Ministry. Jack Martin called. Said you had a washer problem."

Understanding dawned. "Oh, my goodness. Yes. I'm so sorry. You aren't what I expected. Please forgive me."

She wasn't what he expected either. Not in the least. Young and with a houseful of kids. He suppressed a shiver. No wonder she looked like the north end of a southbound cow.

Kids, even grown ones, could drive a person to distraction. He should know. His adult sister and brother were, at this moment, making his life as miserable as possible. The worst part was they did it all the time. Only this morning his sister, Janine, had finally packed up and gone back to Sal, giving Nate a few days' reprieve.

"Come in, come in," the woman was saying. "It's been a crazy morning what with the babies showing up at three a.m. and Katie having a sick stomach. Then while I was doing the laundry, the washing machine went crazy. Water everywhere." She jerked her chin toward the inside of the house. "You're truly a godsend."

He wasn't so sure about that, but he'd signed up for his church's ministry to help single women and the elderly with those pesky little handyman chores like oil changes and leaky faucets. Most of his visits had been to older ladies who plied him with sweet tea and jars of homemade jam and talked about the good old days while he replaced a fuse or unstopped the sink. And their houses had been quiet. Real quiet.

Rainy Jernagen stepped back, motioned him in, and Nate very cautiously entered a room that should have had flashing red lights and a *danger zone* sign.

Toys littered the living room like Christmas morning. An overturned cereal bowl flowed milk onto a coffee table. Next to a playpen crowding one wall, a green package belched out disposable diapers. Similarly, baby clothes were strewn, along with a couple of kids, on the couch and floor. In a word, the place was a wreck.

"The washer is back this way behind the kitchen. Watch your step. It's slippery."

More than slippery. Nate kicked his way through the living room and the kitchen area beyond, though the kitchen actually appeared much tidier than the rest, other than the slow seepage of water coming from somewhere beyond. The shine of liquid glistening on beige tile led them straight to the utility room.

"I turned the faucets off behind the washer when this first started, but a tubful still managed to pump out onto the floor." She hoisted the babies higher on her hip and spoke to a young boy sitting in the floor. "Joshua, get out of those suds."

"But they're pretty, Miss Rainy." The brown-haired boy with bright-blue eyes grinned up at her, extending a handful of bubbles. Light reflected off each droplet. "See the rainbows? There's always a rainbow, like you said. A rainbow behind the rain."

Miss Rainy smiled at the child. "Yes, there is. But right now, Mr. Del Rio needs in here to fix the washer. It's a little crowded for all of us." She was right about that. The space was no bigger than a small bathroom. "Can I get you to take the babies to the playpen while I show him around?"

"I'll take them, Miss Rainy." An older boy with a serious face and brown plastic glasses entered the room. Treading carefully, he came forward and took both babies, holding them against his slight chest. Another child appeared behind him. This one a girl with very blond hair and eyes the exact blue of the boy's, the one she'd called Joshua. How many children did this woman have, anyway? Six?

A heavy, smothery feeling pressed against his airway. Six kids?

Before he could dwell on that disturbing thought, a scream of sonic proportions rent the soap-fragrant air. He whipped around ready to protect and defend.

The little blond girl and the redhead were going at it.

"It's mine." Blondie tugged hard on a Barbie doll.

"It's mine. Will said so." To add emphasis to her demand, the redhead screamed bloody murder. "Miss Rainy."

About that time, Joshua decided to skate across the suds,

and then slammed into the far wall next to a door that probably opened into the garage. He grabbed his big toe and set up a howl. Water sloshed as Rainy rushed forward and gathered him into her arms.

"Rainy!" Blondie screamed again.

"Rainy!" the redhead yelled.

Nate cast a glance at the garage exit and considered a fast escape.

Lord, I'm here to do a good thing. Can You help me out a little?

Rainy, her clothes now wet, somehow managed to take the doll from the fighting girls while snuggling Joshua against her side. The serious-looking boy stood in the doorway, a baby on each hip, taking in the chaos.

"Come on, Emma," the boy said to Blondie. "I'll make you some chocolate milk." So they went, slip-sliding out of the flooded room.

Four down, two to go.

Nate clunked his toolbox onto the washer and tried to ignore the chaos. Not an easy task, but one he'd learned to deal with as a boy. As an adult, he did everything possible to avoid this kind of madness. The Lord had a sense of humor sending him to this particular house.

"I apologize, Mr. Del Rio," Rainy said, shoving at the wads of hair that hung around her face like Spanish moss.

"Call me Nate. I'm not that much older than you." At thirty-one and the long-time patriarch of his family, he might feel seventy, but he wasn't.

"Okay, Nate. And I'm Rainy. Really, it's not usually this bad. I can't thank you enough for coming over. I tried to get a plumber, but being Saturday…" She shrugged, letting the obvious go unsaid. No one could get a plumber on the weekend.

"No problem." He removed his white Stetson and placed

it next to the toolbox. What was he supposed to say? That he loved wading in dirty soap suds and listening to kids scream and cry? Not likely.

Rainy stood with an arm around each of the remaining children—the rainbow boy and the redhead. Her look of embarrassment had him feeling sorry for her. All these kids and no man around to help. With this many, she'd never find another husband, he was sure of that. Who would willingly take on a boatload of kids?

After a minute, Rainy and the remaining pair left the room and he got to work. Wiggling the machine away from the wall wasn't easy. Even with all the water on the floor, a significant amount remained in the tub. This leftover liquid sloshed and gushed at regular intervals. In minutes, his boots were dark with moisture. No problem there. As a rancher, his boots were often dark with lots of things, the best of which was water.

On his haunches, he surveyed the back of the machine, where hoses and cords and metal parts twined together like a nest of water moccasins.

As he investigated each hose in turn, he once more felt a presence in the room. Pivoting on his heels, he discovered the two boys squatted beside him, attention glued to the back of the washer.

"A busted hose?" the oldest one asked, pushing up his glasses.

"Most likely."

"I coulda fixed it but Rainy wouldn't let me."

"That so?"

"Yeah. Maybe. If someone would show me."

Nate suppressed a smile. "What's your name?"

"Will. This here's my brother, Joshua." He yanked a thumb at the younger one. "He's nine. I'm eleven. You go to Miss Rainy's church?"

"I do, but it's a big church. I don't think we've met before."

"She's nice. Most of the time. She never hits us or anything, and we've been here for six months."

It occurred to Nate then that these were not Rainy's children. The kids called her Miss Rainy, not Mom, and according to Will they had not been here forever. But what was a young, single woman doing with all these kids?

* * * * *

Look for
HOME TO CROSSROADS RANCH
by Linda Goodnight,
on sale March 2009
only from Steeple Hill Love Inspired®,
available wherever books are sold.

What do you do when Mr. Right doesn't want kids? Rainy Jernagen and her houseful of foster children won't let a little thing like that get in the way of bringing handyman Nate Del Rio home to them once and for all.

Look for

Home to Crossroads Ranch

by

Linda Goodnight

Available March wherever books are sold, including most bookstores, supermarkets, drugstores and discount stores.

www.SteepleHill.com

LI87521

Love Inspired

HISTORICAL

INSPIRATIONAL HISTORICAL ROMANCE

After years of a quiet existence, young widow Jocelyn Tremayne is suddenly embroiled in a maze of deception, trickery and counterfeiting. With no one to turn to for help, Jocelyn seeks out old friend and government agent Micah Mackenzie. As they work together to uncover the truth, Micah is determined to restore Jocelyn's faith and win her trust—along with her heart.

Look for

The Widow's Secret

by

SARA MITCHELL

Available March wherever books are sold.

Steeple Hill®

NEW YORK TIMES BESTSELLING AUTHOR

ANGELA HUNT

As famine overtakes the land, Simeon leads his brothers
into Egypt to buy grain. He doesn't recognize the vengeful
ruler he must bow before: Joseph, his long-lost brother.
The very brother Simeon sold into slavery years ago.

Now it is the brash Simeon's turn to know imprisonment.
But Mandisa, the handmaid who interprets the ruler's
language, is his saving grace. The beautiful widow and her
young son see another side of Simeon—tenderness under
the tough exterior. Yet he will never be free to love them
until he unshackles the chains of his own heart.

Steeple
Hill®

Brothers

Available the first week of February, wherever books are sold!

Love Inspired

Handsome army ranger
Pierce Granger knows
he's found a friend in
Lexie Evans, the girl he
rescued from a skiing
accident. Yet as their
friendship grows,
Lexie realizes she
wants a forever love,
if Pierce is ready to be
hers for keeps.

THE McKASLIN CLAN

Look for

A Soldier
for Keeps

by

Jillian Hart

*Available March
wherever books are sold.*

www.SteepleHill.com

Steeple
Hill®

REQUEST YOUR FREE BOOKS!

2 FREE INSPIRATIONAL NOVELS
PLUS 2
FREE
MYSTERY GIFTS

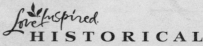

Love Inspired.
HISTORICAL
INSPIRATIONAL HISTORICAL ROMANCE

YES! Please send me 2 FREE Love Inspired® Historical novels and my 2 FREE mystery gifts (gifts are worth about $10). After receiving them, if I don't wish to receive any more books, I can return the shipping statement marked "cancel". If I don't cancel, I will receive 4 brand-new novels every other month and be billed just $4.24 per book in the U.S. or $4.74 per book in Canada, plus 25¢ shipping and handling per book and applicable taxes, if any*. That's a savings of over 20% off the cover price! I understand that accepting the 2 free books and gifts places me under no obligation to buy anything. I can always return a shipment and cancel at any time. Even if I never buy another book, the two free books and gifts are mine to keep forever.   102 IDN ERYA 302 IDN ERYM

Name	(PLEASE PRINT)

Address	Apt. #

City	State/Prov.	Zip/Postal Code

Signature (if under 18, a parent or guardian must sign)

Mail to Steeple Hill Reader Service:
IN U.S.A.: P.O. Box 1867, Buffalo, NY 14240-1867
IN CANADA: P.O. Box 609, Fort Erie, Ontario L2A 5X3

Not valid to current subscribers of Love Inspired Historical books.

Want to try two free books from another series?
Call 1-800-873-8635 or visit www.morefreebooks.com

* Terms and prices subject to change without notice. N.Y. residents add applicable sales tax. Canadian residents will be charged applicable provincial taxes and GST. Offer not valid in Quebec. This offer is limited to one order per household. All orders subject to approval. Credit or debit balances in a customer's account(s) may be offset by any other outstanding balance owed by or to the customer. Please allow 4 to 6 weeks for delivery. Offer available while quantities last.

Your Privacy: Steeple Hill Books is committed to protecting your privacy. Our Privacy Policy is available online at www.SteepleHill.com or upon request from the Reader Service. From time to time we make our lists of customers available to reputable third parties who may have a product or service of interest to you. If you would prefer we not share your name and address, please check here. ☐

LIH08R